Maxim Gorky (*Gorky* meaning *bitter*) was the pen name of Alexey Maximovich Peshkov, born in 1868 in Nizhni Novgorod on the Volga. His parents died when he was very young, and at the age of eleven, with only a few months of formal schooling, he was forced to enter the life of menial labor and impoverished vagabondage that was to provide the material for much of his future writing. In 1898 the publication of his first book of stories signaled a triumph unprecedented in Russian literature; almost overnight Gorky became, next to Tolstoy, Russia's most popular writer. Placing both his prestige and his huge earnings at the service of revolutionary movements, he was subjected to continual government harrassment. In 1906 he left Russia, not to return until 1913, settling first in the United States, where he was bitterly attacked for living with a common-law wife, and then in Capri. After the Revolution, his friendship with Bolshevik leaders allowed him to play an invaluable role in saving fellow writers from the excesses of the new regime; however, in 1921, he again left Russia for Italy, ostensibly for reasons of health. After this second exile, which like his first proved highly productive, he was persuaded to return to Russia; the nation's leading literary figure, he served as the single influential moderating force in the Soviet cultural apparatus. His death in 1936 was an occasion for national mourning.

Maxim Gorky

A SKY-BLUE LIFE
And Selected Stories

Translated and with a Foreword by
GEORGE REAVEY

A SIGNET CLASSIC
Published by THE NEW AMERICAN LIBRARY

FIRST PRINTING, JANUARY, 1964

SIGNET TRADEMARK REG. U.S. PAT. OFF. AND FOREIGN COUNTRIES
REGISTERED TRADEMARK—MARCA REGISTRADA
HECHO EN CHICAGO, U.S.A.

SIGNET CLASSICS are published by
The New American Library of World Literature, Inc.
501 Madison Avenue, New York, New York 10022

PRINTED IN THE UNITED STATES OF AMERICA

Contents

Foreword

At the turn of the century the great Russian novelists, and especially Leo Tolstoy, had almost exhausted the possibilities of analytical and psychological realism. Russian literature was being invaded by symbolism and other Western experimental trends. There was also a revival of lyrical poetry, and the "spirit of music," as Alexander Blok called it, was becoming dominant. A split was developing between the modernists and the remaining exponents of the realist tradition—a split that has persisted in Soviet literature.

Maxim Gorky was fundamentally a realist, indeed, a determined champion of realism against symbolism, mysticism, naturalism, or excessive verbal experimentation. But as he explained to Chekhov in 1896, Gorky also favored an element of romanticism, the possibility of exaggerating a trait or elevating his subject. As an enemy of pessimism, lethargy, and despair, he vehemently opposed the depressive aspects of the Russian mind and literature. Thus, while Gorky seemed to push his realism to the verge of naturalism, at the same time he rescued it from the naturalistic fact of "raw life" by imparting to it a certain romantic coloration.

Although Gorky—unlike the great Russian writers of the gentry who preceded him or such contemporaries as Chekhov, Bunin, and Leonid Andreyev—came out of the "lower depths," he was no skid-row character. The graph of his life climbed rather than descended. Nor did he write only about outcasts, prostitutes, hoboes, and the "barefoot brigade." He also wrote about artisans, workers, actresses, merchants, self-made millionaires, millionaires' sons, and intellectuals. In fact, Gorky wrote about almost every aspect of Russian life except the court circles, the gentry, and the army. No Russian writer has described such a variety of hitherto ignored humanity. Maxim Gorky had a very keen and memorable eye; his work is extremely visual, palpable, and sensual. He often picked his characters straight from the streets, as he does in his story "Chelkash." In his work, a mass of hitherto anonymous men and women acquired a face they had not seemed to possess before. Some of the characters he depicted may have been coarse, but they were at least very human and unexpectedly poetic. If many aspects of Gorky's world proved shocking (as they did to the Irishman E. J. Dillon, his first biographer, in 1902), they could no longer be kept hidden, even from polite society. But Gorky succeeded in rising above the mere naturalism of sordid fact and in endowing even some of his most hopeless characters with a measure of human dignity and romantic atmosphere. In 1900, Leo Tolstoy, at first puzzled by Gorky's contribution, commented that "Gorky . . . touches upon very important issues and answers them as the large masses of the people would." A rationalist by conviction, Gorky also set himself the task of examining the irrational aspects of Russian psychology and behavior. But in so doing he tried to find some evidence of strength of will and purpose in the national character, without having recourse to either the Dostoyevskian or the Tolstoyan solution. This in itself was symptomatic of a new age, an age of science and industry rather than of religion and rural patriarchalism.

The world Gorky described in his stories was one of uneasy fermentation, pressing change, and desperate urgency. A world of irrational fears, unsuspected energy, and hope. This world was no longer feudal Russia, a country of landowner and serf with clearly defined hierarchies, even though many vestiges of it still remained. It was, rather, a world of restless stirring and anticipation, of new pressures and emergent forces, of hierarchies reversed, and the onset of brute energies. A world of anti-intellectual and anti-cultural currents as well as of a naïve passion for learning. It was a world of almost American dynamism, but its keynote was rebellion.

Maxim Gorky's life (1868–1936)—his extremely rich, varied, and extensive biography—is the key to most of his best work. It was certainly the immediate foundation for his early stories and the new aspects of reality they revealed. As Evgeny Zamyatin, the distinguished author of *We,* has written, "Gorky could never remain a mere spectator; he always intervened in the thick of events; he wished to take action." Gorky had not gone out into the world from any established literary position; he had experienced this peculiar world at first hand and had brought it with him into literature. Instead of swallowing or disintegrating him, the "lower depths" of his experience had sharpened his vision and strengthened his will to surmount them. True, physically he was a very tall and extremely powerful man. However, his art was made possible by long and persistent application, by his insistent drive to educate himself, to learn and master the word, and by his steadily growing awareness of his struggle to surmount not only himself but his early environment.

Since Maxim Gorky's large and extraordinary life figures so prominently and so organically in his work, we must survey it, however briefly. As Zamyatin has said, "He was charged with an energy that found the pages of a book too confining: it spilled over into life. His life was a book in itself, an enthralling romance."

Maxim Gorky was born on March 28, 1868, in the city of Nizhni Novgorod on the River Volga. The city had its mediaeval relics, an annual fair, and a rapidly developing industry. In 1932 it was renamed Gorky, in honor of the writer who had been born there as Alexey Maximovich Peshkov and who assumed the nom de plume of Gorky (*Bitter*) in 1892, when he published his first story.

Gorky's father was Maxim Savvatievich Peshkov, a cabinetmaker, who died of cholera at the age of thirty-one in 1871,[1] while in charge of a steamship office in Astrakhan. Alexey, his son, was only three years of age at the time. His mother, Varvara, was the daughter of Vassily Kashirin, a former barge-hauler on the Volga, who had succeeded in starting a business of his own as a dyer of yarns in Nizhni Novgorod. After her husband's death Varvara Peshkov drifted away from the family, leaving her young son, Alexey, to be brought up by the Kashirins. As Gorky wrote later, "My mother had no influence at all on my life, for, regarding me as the cause of my father's death, she did not love me and, marrying very soon for a second time, handed me over entirely into the care of my grandfather."

---

[1] New evidence points to 1871 rather than 1872 as the date of his father's death.

The grandfather was by nature religious, despotic, and miserly. In 1913 Maxim Gorky wrote a vivid and merciless description of him in *My Childhood*. As described by Gorky, the Kashirin family might have come out of a novel by Dostoyevsky—the young Alexey suffered a great deal from the irrational and violent behavior not only of his grandfather but also of his uncles. The main consolation of his youth was his grandmother, Akulina, who not only had a heart of gold but also a gift for storytelling. This gift of hers helped to stimulate the young Alexey's imagination, his latent talents as a writer, and his own ambitions as a storyteller.

After his mother's death from consumption at the age of thirty-seven (1879), a new phase of life began for the young Alexey Peshkov; at the age of eleven he began going out into the world, trying to earn a livelihood. His first job was that of a messenger and servant boy to the owner of a shoe shop. Alexey Peshkov was not happy in his early jobs and kept changing them frequently. In 1881 he became a dishwasher on a Volga steamer, where he was befriended by the cook, Smury, who lent him books and encouraged him to read. Other jobs followed, which included work in an icon workshop, and in a theater at the Nizhni Novgorod Fair. At fourteen he was already doing some serious reading late at night. Reading had become a passion with him. He was self-educated, for all the formal education he got was six months in a parish school.

The first big break with Nizhni Novgorod came in 1884, when Alexey Peshkov traveled to Kazan in the hope of studying at Kazan University. Instead, he found himself obliged to earn a hard living as a baker's assistant, a period of his life he described in "Twenty-six Men and a Girl." Despite his many hardships and disappointments, he was able to say in 1936, ". . . Of all my 'universities' Kazan was my favorite." It was in Kazan, too, that he first came in contact with a number of provincial intellectuals who sharpened his sense of social and political problems. Nevertheless, the year 1887 ended for him in a spiritual crisis. Attempting suicide, he shot himself through the lung. This permanently affected his health. He left Kazan soon after and wandered about the lower Volga and the Caspian regions.

Tramping about as a hobo who seemed to have suspicious contacts with revolutionary-minded provincial intellectuals, Alexey Peshkov began to attract the attention of the Tsarist police. Increasingly throughout his life in Tsarist Russia, his movements were to be recorded in police dossiers. He was arrested more than once. In his story "Music" he describes a rather unusual encounter with a Gendarme officer. In April of 1889 he returned to Nizhni Novgorod where he met, among others, Olga Kaminskaya (the heroine of his story "First Love"); Lanin, a notary for whom he began working as a clerk; and V. G. Korolenko, the well-known author, who encouraged him to write. All three of them exercised an important formative influence on Alexey Peshkov as a young man in his early twenties. Falling desperately in love with Olga Kaminskaya, Alexey Peshkov lived with her for over two years (1892–94). An older, more experienced woman of superior education, who had lived in Paris, she smoothed some of the rougher edges of the erstwhile hobo, and broadened his view of the world. Lanin, on the other hand, gave him a certain security of employment and introduced him into a mixed circle of Nizhni Novgorod intellectuals and businessmen. Korolenko proved the mentor who not only gave him critical advice, but also was instrumental in placing some of his stories in the leading literary magazines.

In 1891 Alexey Peshkov took another important step, which brought him nearer to becoming Maxim Gorky. He set out on a tramping expedition to the south of Russia. It was not exactly a pleasure trip. Peshkov really tramped and lived like a hobo, picking up odd jobs on farms, in the docks of seaports, in villages and towns, and mixing with a ragged crowd of tramps, laborers, hoboes, and starving peasants. Eighteen ninety-one–ninety-two happened to be years of famine in the Volga region, and many hungry peasants had flocked south in the hope of earning a bite of bread. Like "a rolling stone," Alexey Peshkov passed through the Lower Volga region, the Don country, the Ukraine, Moldavia, the Crimea, and the Caucasus, turning back to Nizhni Novgorod at the end of September 1892. In Tiflis he had succeeded at long last in publishing his first story, "Makar Chudra." In this story of gypsy passion Maxim Gorky sounded a challenging romantic note that was almost Cyranesque. His heroes, he made it very clear, were no self-lacerating martyrs, but passionate and heroic individuals. This note, exaggerated as it may have been, struck resonantly against the backbone of a wilting *fin de siècle*. In "Makar Chudra," as in the later "Old Woman Izergil," Gorky not only stressed the courage of action but also pointed to folklore as an undying element of human renewal. In most of the stories that were to follow, such as "Chelkash," "On the Rafts," "In the Steppe," and many others, Gorky established a closer balance between romanticism and realism. And all his life he was to insist on this "blend of romanticism and realism." Both elements are certainly present in his story "A Man Is Born" (1912), which, though written in Gorky's Capri period, comes out of the same vein of experience as his earlier stories. In it he not only paints the background of the famine years, but also dramatically ennobles and colors a rather pathetic and sordid situation. Gorky's journal of hard labor and exploration certainly helped him to become a writer. His adventure into human misery and courage also provided him with a rich storehouse of memories and reminiscences, which he turned to good creative use in his later life.

It was a maturer, more bitter Peshkov-Gorky who returned to Nizhni Novgorod in October 1892. He spent the next two years and more working again as a clerk for Lanin, living the sort of life described in "First Love," and writing at night. Among other stories, he wrote "Chelkash," which Korolenko edited and placed in a leading Petersburg literary magazine, *Russkove Bogatsvo* (*Russian Treasury*). In "Chelkash" we find a clear expression of many of those elements of attitude and style which were to recur in Gorky's later work. In this story, against a background of industry and the life of a busy port, we have a study in psychological contrast between two different sorts of tramps—a wily and determined thief, who likes to mold the lives of others to his will and who is compared to a rapacious beast, and a drifting peasant lad, who personifies elemental greed. In Gorky's view, Chelkash and Gavrila are not just ordinary vagabonds and thieves, but human beings conditioned by different environments and representing two antagonistic principles—rebellious freedom

and individual greed. Gorky shows his contempt for the
peasant Gavrila's narrow proprietory instincts and approves
of Chelkash's attitude of independence and moral supe-
riority. In this context, Chelkash is portrayed as a more
emancipated man. Gorky also admires Chelkash's strength
which, in some ways, resembles that of Silan, the father
in the story "On the Rafts" (1895), and that of Foma
Gordeyev, the self-made millionaire in the novel of that
name. By contrast, Gorky has little sympathy to waste on
men of weak character—inactive talkers, such as the
dreamy, ineffective hero of his later story "A Sky-Blue
Life" (1925). But the phenomenon of this type of "superfluous man" in Russian life and literature could not help
fascinating him too.

From 1895 on, Maxim Gorky was increasingly discussed
and read in Petersburg and Moscow. But another essential
experience in the provinces awaited him before he was to
become a nationally and then an internationally famed
writer. He accepted a job (1895–96) as a journalist on
the *Samara Gazette,* a daily, for which he wrote stories,
sketches, book reviews, and commentaries, under various
pseudonyms. Here, in Samara, the present-day Kuibyshev,
he published *The Nightingale* (1894), a story of an incident on a Volga steamer, which was not included in his
Collected Works and which was only recently discovered.
He also published in a local paper the serialized version
of his first novel, *Luckless Pavel* (or *Orphan Paul*). In
May 1896 he gave up his Samara job and returned to
Nizhni Novgorod, where he contributed to a local daily
as well as to the *Odessa News.* He also married Ekaterina
Volzhin, a proofreader on the *Samara Gazette,* by whom
he had a son, Maxim. He soon had accumulated enough
stories to begin thinking of book publication. The first two
volumes of his *Tales and Sketches* came out in Petersburg
in 1898, and the third volume in the following year. They
signaled his growing popularity as an author and rebellious
spokesman.

In Petersburg and Moscow, Maxim Gorky began to meet
the prominent writers, critics, and figures of the day. In
the Crimea, he became a friend of Chekhov and an admirer
and close observer of Leo Tolstoy. Through Chekhov, who
encouraged him to write his first play, he was introduced

to the Moscow Art Theater, where his first two plays—
The Smug Citizens and the internationally famous *The
Lower Depths*—were staged. In the meantime, since 1894,
Gorky's health had begun to trouble him. In 1896 consumption developed and, till the end of his life, he periodi-
cally had to seek a warmer climate and medical care. But
this proved no obstacle to his enormous working capacity
and tremendous zest for writing, literature, politics, and
people. He always rendered great assistance to beginning
writers, hundreds of whose manuscripts he found time to
read and comment upon.

As a result of his great popularity, various political
parties tried to gain his allegiance to their cause. From
1902 he began to support, morally and financially, the
Lenin wing of the Socialist Democratic Party. In this he
was influenced by his attachment to M. F. Andreyeva, an
actress of the Moscow Art Theatre and a keen revolutionary, with whom he shared his life until 1919. As the
Revolution of 1905 approached, Gorky became more
deeply involved in politics and anti-Tsarist activities; he
was even imprisoned for a time in the Fortress of Peter
and Paul. In February 1906, he found it imperative to leave
Russia. He spent the next eight years in exile abroad—six
months in the United States, and some seven years in Italy,
where he settled in Capri. Even when he traveled, lived,
and worked abroad, Gorky kept his eyes steadily fixed on
Russia, which was always to him a constant source of hope
and wonder, puzzlement and exasperation. In the United
States, still under the impression of the Russian events of
1905–06, he wrote and published his politically oriented
"proletarian" novel *The Mother*. He also completed his play
The Enemies. In Italy he wrote several novels such as *The
Confession* and *Okurov Town,* as well as several new cycles
of stories. In his stories of the Capri period he returned
with greater mastery to the subject matter of his earlier
years. Many of them may be regarded as an offshoot from
the main literary task he had set himself after 1910—that
of writing his autobiography in several volumes. The first
of these, *My Childhood* (1913–14), was published in
Russia soon after Gorky's return there; the second, *In The
World,* followed two years later. Apart from other stories,
a play or two, and various articles in *Letopis* and *Novaya*

Zhizhn, the periodicals he edited till 1918, these autobiographical works were his main literary contributions to be published in his Russian period between 1914 and the Revolution of 1917. In his autobiographies, Gorky certainly reached one of the highest points of his achievement.

In the five years of revolution and civil war that followed, Gorky contributed only *My Recollections of Tolstoy* (1919), a short masterpiece of penetrating insight in the memoir genre. Gorky was frankly appalled at the destructive realities of the Revolution, and all his energies were employed in attempting to preserve culture and save human lives. His relations with the Bolshevik leaders became strained. In October 1921, Gorky, whose health was now in a precarious state and whose nerves had worn thin, left Russia for another lengthy period of residence abroad. It was only in 1933 that Gorky returned to live in the Soviet Union, though he had paid annual summer visits since 1928. In 1922–24, after spending a couple of years in sanitariums and elsewhere in Germany, he settled in Sorrento in Italy. From the literary point of view, his second exile proved very productive. He completed the final part of his autobiography, *My Universities* (1923), and the related autobiographical stories such as "First Love" and "The Night Watchman"; published a volume of new stories (1922–25), which included "A Sky-Blue Life," "Unrequited Love," and "The Hermit," powerful studies of human failure and isolation, and wrote a number of memoirs on Chekhov, Andreyev, Lenin, and other remarkable writers and men he had known. There followed a novel about three generations of a Volga millionaire's family—*The Artamonov Business* (1925). His final work in fiction was a four-volume cycle of novels under the general title *The Life of Klim Samgin* (1927–36). But, at his death, Gorky had not yet completed the fourth and last volume of this cycle; it was nevertheless published posthumously in 1938. These novels as a whole deal with a host of characters and forty years of Russian life up to 1918. In them Gorky fills a large canvas, but his main theme is the decline of the old Russian intelligentsia as personified in Klim Samgin. In 1932–33, two of his new plays, *Yegor Bulitchev* and *Dostigayev and Others,* were produced in Moscow.

In 1928 Maxim Gorky had begun writing many articles for the Soviet press. These articles may roughly be divided into the autobiographical, the didactic, the polemical, and the political. At the same time his works were republished in large editions. It is clear that Gorky had decided to resume his activities as a public man in his native country and that he had come to a modus vivendi with the Soviet authorities. He became increasingly involved in the problems of Soviet literature and in the organizational machinery of the Stalinist thirties, and his own literary output sharply declined. Officially he was now the writer-in-chief and the authority on literary matters. In this capacity he was able at times to exercise a moderating influence, but there are grounds for believing that he no longer relished this eminent position at the time of his death, on the eve of the Stalin purges. At his death, Maxim Gorky left some thirty thick volumes of novels, short stories, autobiographies, memoirs, plays, and articles. Of these there are six volumes of short stories and novellas. In retrospect, it may be said that Gorky had confined himself in his subject matter almost entirely to the pre-Soviet world which he knew best. Many of his short stories not only marked a new stage in Russian literature, but have become a permanent part of world literature. If it had not been for Maxim Gorky, Russia would be even more of an enigma both to itself and to the outside world.

GEORGE REAVEY

August 1963
New York City

MAKAR CHUDRA

A chill moist breeze blew from the sea, carrying over the steppes the reflective melody of the surf and the rustling of the bushes close to the beach. From time to time gusts of wind brought with them yellow, withered leaves and, dropping them into the campfire, fanned the flames. The enveloping dusk of the autumn night shuddered and, moving aside apprehensively, disclosed for an instant the boundless steppe to the left, and the endless sea to the right, and, directly opposite me, the figure of Makar Chudra, the old gypsy, who watched over the horses of the gypsy caravan camped some fifty paces from us.

Paying no attention to the cold waves of wind that, tearing open his Cossack overcoat, had bared his hairy chest and kept thrashing it mercilessly, Makar Chudra half reclined in a handsome pose, his face turned toward me, puffing methodically at his huge pipe, blowing dense puffs of smoke through his mouth and nose; and, with his eyes fixed at a point above my head in the silent gloom of the steppe, he chatted with me without pause or any attempt to shield himself from the rude whipping of the wind.

"So you're on the tramp? That's good! A fine choice that, my young falcon. That's how it should be: go on tramping, see things for yourself and, when you've seen all there is to be seen and then have had enough of it, curl up and die. That's all there is to it!

18

"Life? Other people?" he continued, after listening skeptically to my objection to his "that's how it should be!" —"H'm! And what's that to you? And are you not life yourself? Other people live and will go on living without you. Do you think anyone needs you? You're not a crust of bread or a stick. Nobody has need of you.

"To learn and teach, you say? But can you learn to make people happy? No, you can't. Talk about teaching when you've turned gray. Teach what? Everyone knows what he needs. The smarter ones take what there is; the stupider ones—get nothing; and everyone learns for himself. . . .

"They're a droll lot, the people you talk about," he continued. "They crowd in a heap and crush each other, but there's enough room on earth," and with a sweeping gesture he pointed to the steppe. "And they all labor, your people. Why? For whom? No one knows. You see a man plowing, and you think: sweating drop by drop, he will give up all his strength to the earth, and then he will lie down and rot in it. Nothing will remain of him; he can see nothing else from his own field; and he dies as he was born—a fool.

"Was he born then, I ask, just to pick at the earth and to perish without having had time even to scratch a grave for himself with his nails? Has he any notion of freedom? Does he understand the wide steppe? Does the murmur of sea waves gladden his heart? He's a slave from birth, a slave all his life, and that's all! What can he do with himself? Only choke himself if he grows any wiser.

"But I've seen so much in my fifty-eight years, don't you see, that, if it were all written down on paper, you couldn't fit it into a thousand such bags as the one you've got there. You just try and tell me where I haven't been. You wouldn't be able to. You don't even know the regions where I have been. That's how one should live: walk on and on—and that's all. Don't get stuck in any one place—for what's there? Just as day and night keep running, chasing each other around the earth, so you must run away from thinking about life lest you fall out of love with it. But if you stop to think, you will fall out of love with life. It's always like that. And it happened to me too. Aha! Yes, it did, my young falcon.

"I was sitting in prison in Galichin. 'Why am I living in this world?' I asked myself out of boredom. It's a tedious place, a prison, my young falcon, oh how tedious! And nostalgia gripped me by the heart when I saw a field through the prison window; it took hold of me and squeezed me like a pair of pincers. Who can say why he lives? No one can answer that, my young falcon! And there is no need to ask oneself that. Live, and that's all. Walk about and look around you, and tedium will never grip you then. I almost hung myself by my belt, that's how it was!

"Ha! I once had a talk with a man. An austere man, one of your Russians. 'You should live,' he told me, 'not as you want, but as it is laid down by God. Submit to God, and He will give you everything you ask for.' But he himself was dressed in holes and rags. I told him to ask God for some new clothes. He got angry and chased me away with abuse. Up to then he had been saying that one must forgive and love people. He should have forgiven me even if my speech had offended his grace. There's a teacher for you! They teach us to eat less, but they themselves eat ten times a day."

He spat into the campfire and stopped talking while he filled his pipe. The wind howled plaintively and softly; horses neighed in the dark; and from the gypsy camp a tender, passionate song drifted toward us. That was Nonka singing—a beautiful girl, Makar's daughter. I was familiar with her voice, thick and deep in timbre, a voice that always sounded somehow strange, discontented and demanding, whether she sang a song or extended a greeting. Her dull, olive complexion had the frozen look of a haughty queen, while her dark-brown eyes shone with the awareness of her irresistible beauty and with contempt for everything except herself.

Makar handed me his pipe.

"Here, take a puff! She sings well, that girl? So! You'd like a girl like that to love you? No? Good! That's how it should be—don't trust girls and keep away from them. A girl gets more pleasure from kissing than I do from smoking a pipe, but once a man has kissed a girl his heart will lose all its willpower. A girl will bind you to herself in a way you can't see, and you won't be able to break away—you just won't, and you'll give up your soul to her. It's true! Beware of girls! They always lie! 'I love you,' she'll say, 'more than anything in the world.' But prick her with a pin and she'll break your heart. I know it! Aha, how I know! Well, my falcon, would you like me to tell you about something that once happened? You should remember it; and when you do remember it, you will be a free bird for the rest of your life.

"There lived in the world a certain Zobar, a young gypsy, Loyko Zobar," he began his narrative. "The whole of Hungary, Bohemia, and Slavonia, and all the places round the seacoast, knew him—an adventurous young man he was! There wasn't a village in those parts that did not contain a half a dozen inhabitants who hadn't sworn to kill Loyko Zobar, but he went on living; and if he took a liking to a horse, even a regiment of soldiers set to guard it couldn't keep him from riding away on it! Aha! Was he afraid of anybody? If the devil himself had approached him with all his followers, and he didn't knife Satan himself, he would at least have given every devil one of them a kick apiece—he certainly would have done that.

"All the gypsy caravans knew him or had heard of him. He loved horses and nothing else, but he wouldn't ride a horse for long—he'd sell it quick, but afterwards he would be free with the money. He held nothing sacred—if you asked for his heart, he'd tear it out himself and give it to you as long as it made you feel better. That's the sort of man he was, my falcon.

"Our caravan was wandering through Bucovina at the time—that was some ten years ago. One night in spring we were sitting: I, Danilo, the soldier who had fought together with Kossuth, and old Nur, and all the others, and Radda, Danilo's daughter.

"You know my Nonka? A queenly girl! But you couldn't compare her to Radda—too great an honor for Nonka! About her, about Radda, you couldn't say anything in words. Maybe you could play the beauty of her on a fiddle, but only someone could do it who knew his fiddle like his own soul.

"She had dried up a good many young hearts, ah, very

many indeed! In Moravia a certain magnate, an elderly
man with a forelock, saw her and was dumfounded. He
sat there on his mount and stared, trembling, as though
in a fever. He was as handsome as the devil on a holiday, his coat was shot with gold, the sword at his side
flashed like lightning at the least movement his horse
made. From one end to the other his sword was set with
precious stones, and the light-blue velvet of his cap was
like a piece of sky—an important hospodar, that old man!
He stared and stared, and then said to Radda: 'Hey!
Here's a purseful if you kiss me.' But she merely turned
away, that's all. 'Forgive me if I've offended you, but do
be kinder and sweeter in your looks,' the old magnate
urged, changing his tone and throwing the purse at her
feet—a big purse, brother! But she might have pushed
him into the mud with her foot, for all the notice she
took of him.

" 'Ay, what a girl!' he sighed, hitting his horse with his
riding crop. A cloud of dust was all that could be seen.

"He reappeared the next day. 'Who's her father?' he
thundered through the caravan camp. Danilo came out.
'Sell me your daughter, take what you want!' But Danilo
said to him: 'It is only the gentry that sell everything,
their pigs as well as their conscience, but I fought with
Kossuth and am no merchant!' The other was about to
roar out and lay his hand to his sword, but one of us
thrust a brand into the horse's ear and the horse carried
off the brave fellow. We struck camp and fled. We were
on the road one day, two days, and then behold—he
caught up with us! 'Hey you,' he says, 'my conscience is
clear before God and you. Give me the girl for a wife:
I'll share all I have with you. I'm very rich!' He was
burning with passion and swayed in the saddle like clover
in the wind. We grew thoughtful.

" 'Well, daughter, speak out!' Danilo muttered in his
mustaches.

" 'If a she-eagle were to enter a raven's nest of her
own will, what would she become?' Radda asked us.

"Danilo laughed, and all of us joined in.

" 'Well spoken, daughter! Did you hear that, hospodar?
There's nothing you can do here! Better search for
little doves—they are easier to catch.' And we moved on.

"And the hospodar snatched the cap off his head and threw it to the ground, and then galloped off so that the ground shook. That's how Radda was, my falcon!

"Yes! One night as we were all sitting down we heard music in the steppe. Good music! The blood in the veins took fire from it and it kept calling us to set out somewhere. We all began to yearn for something. That is how we felt because of that music—after it there was no need to go on living. Or if we were to go on living, then we must live like lords of the earth, my falcon!

"Then out of the darkness a horse came into relief, and upon it a man sat playing as he approached us. He pulled up by the bonfire, stopped playing and, smiling, looked at us.

" 'Ah, Zobar, it is you!' Danilo cried out to him joyfully. 'It's him, Loyko Zobar!'

"His long mustaches fell on his shoulders and tangled with his curly hair; his eyes burnt like bright stars; and his smile was like the very sun, God's truth! He looked as though he had been forged from the same piece of iron as his horse. There he stood in the flame of the bonfire, all blood, smiling, his teeth sparkling. May I be damned if I didn't love him already, as much as I loved myself, before he'd even uttered a word or noticed that I too lived in this wide world.

"Yes, my falcon, there are men like that! A single glance and he'll bind your soul, and you'll feel no shame but feel proud of it. When you meet such a man, you become better yourself. There aren't many such men, friend! And it's a wonderful thing to have just a few. If there were plenty of good things in the world, you wouldn't think them so good. That's so! But listen to me further.

"Radda then said: 'You play well, Loyko! Who made your fiddle so resonant and sensitive?' And Loyko laughed: 'I made it myself! And I made it not of wood but from the breasts of a young girl whom I loved passionately, and as for the strings, I spun them out of her heart. It still lies a little, this fiddle, but I know how to hold the bow in my hands!'

"It is well known that men like us try at once to throw mist into a girl's eyes, so that she won't inflame our hearts, and then later, maybe, disappoint us. And Loyko tried that too. But he came up against the wrong girl. Radda turned away from him with a yawn and said: 'They used to say that Zobar was deft and clever—they lied!' —and she walked off.

" 'Hey, my beauty, you've got sharp teeth!' Loyko cried, his eyes flashing, as he dismounted. 'Greetings, brothers! Here I am come to visit you.'

" 'Welcome to the guest!' Danilo answered. They embraced, chatted for a while, and then retired to sleep. They slept soundly. But in the morning we noticed that Zobar's head was bandaged with a rag. What happened? Seems his horse kicked him while he slept.

"Ah, ah! We understood what sort of a horse it was and grinned in our mustaches, and Danilo grinned too. Well, wasn't Loyko good enough for Radda? No, not at all! However good she was, the girl had a small, narrow soul, and she would become no better even if you hung thirty pounds of gold around her neck. Well, enough of that!

"So we lived on and on in that same place; we weren't doing too badly then; and Zobar stayed with us. He was a fine comrade! As wise as an elder, informed about everything, and he understood both Russian and Hungarian grammar. Sometimes he would start talking—and listening to him, you wouldn't sleep a wink! And the way he played—you can kill me with a thunderbolt if anyone ever played like him! He'd draw his bow across the strings—and a shiver would go through your heart; he'd draw the bow again—and your heart would stand still, listening, but he would just play on and smile. Listening to him you'd feel like weeping and laughing at the same time. One moment someone would be moaning bitterly, asking for help and cutting at your heartstrings with a knife. The next, the steppe would be telling fairy tales to the sky, sorrowful tales. A girl would be weeping as she bade farewell to a brave young man! The young man would be calling the girl to follow him out into the steppe. And then suddenly—hey! A free, living song would thunder forth, a living song, and the sun itself would seem to be dancing in the sky to that song! That's how it was, my falcon!

"Every vein in your body understood that song, and every bit of you would become its slave. And if Loyko had shouted then: 'Fight them with knives, comrades!' we, all of us, would have attacked with knives anyone he pointed out. He could make a man do anything, and we all loved him, loved him strongly, all of us with the exception of Radda, who wouldn't even look at him; and that would not have been so bad, but she also mocked him. She had Zobar strongly by the heart, she had! He gritted his teeth, tugged at his mustaches, did Loyko, as a pair of eyes blacker than an abyss gazed at him, and at times there was such a glint in those eyes that it made him frightened for his soul. He would go off by himself at night a long way into the wastelands. And we would be lying down in the camp, puzzling what to do. We knew well enough that, when two boulders roll toward each other, one mustn't stand between them, for fear of being maimed. And that's how things continued.

"One evening we sat thus, all of us, at a gathering, discussing business. We were getting bored. Then Danilo asked Loyko: 'Sing a song for us, Zobar, give us some joy!' Zobar glanced at Radda, who was lying down nearby with face upturned, gazing at the sky, and then he struck the strings. The fiddle spoke out as if a girl's heart were talking! And Loyko began to sing:

> Hey-hey! A fire burns in my heart,
> And the steppe is so wide!
> My fast steed is swift as the wind,
> And firm is my hand!

"Radda turned her head and, rising up, smiled into the singer's eyes. He blushed like the dawn.

> Hey, hop-hey! Listen, my friend!
> Shall we gallop yonder, ahead?
> The steppe is garbed in austere dusk,
> But the dawn awaits us there!
> Hey-hey! Let's fly and meet the day.
> Ascend to the heights!
> Only don't let your horse's mane brush
> Against the lovely maiden moon!

"That how he sang! No one sings like that now! But Radda said through her teeth: 'You shouldn't fly so high, Loyko, or you'll crash down, yes—fall with your nose in a puddle and soil your mustaches. Be careful!' Loyko looked at her like a wild beast, but said nothing—he controlled himself and sang on:

> Hey-Ho! Of a sudden the day will come here,
> While you and I are asleep.
> Hey then! We shall burn then, both of us,
> In a fire of shame!

" 'That's a song!' Danilo commented. 'Never have I heard such a song. May the devil make a pipe for himself out of me if I'm lying.'

"Old Nur twitched his mustaches and shrugged his shoulders, and all of us found Zobar's bold song to our liking! Only Radda did not like it.

" 'A mosquito once droned like this, imitating an eagle's cry,' was all she said, showering us with cold snow.

" 'Is it the whip you want, Radda?' Danilo asked, making a movement toward her. But Zobar threw his cap on the ground and declared, looking as black as the earth:

" 'Hold, Danilo! A fiery horse needs a steel bit! Give me your daughter to wife!'

" 'Well spoken!' Danilo replied with a smile. 'Take her if you can.'

" 'Good!' said Loyko, and then he turned to Radda: 'Well, girl, listen to me awhile and don't stand on your pride! I've seen a lot of you womenfolk, a lot! But not one of them has touched my heart as much as you have. Ah, Radda, you've taken my soul prisoner! Well, so be it! What is fated will come to pass, and . . . no horse exists upon which you can gallop away from yourself! I'm taking you to wife before God, my honor, your father, and all these people. But beware, do not cross my will—I am a free man and shall live as I wish!' He went up to her, gritting his teeth, his eyes flashing. As we looked on, he held out his hand to her—there, we thought, Radda has bridled a wild steppe horse! But suddenly we saw him throw up his hands and hit the ground with his forehead—bang!

"What a miracle! It was as if a bullet had struck his heart. It was Radda who, with the leather thong of a whip, had entangled his legs and then given a tug. That was what caused him to fall.

"And she was lying down quietly again, a silent ironic smile on her face. We looked on, waiting to see what would happen, but Loyko sat on the ground with his hands pressed against his head as if afraid it would burst. Then he quietly got up and walked off into the steppe without a glance at anyone. Nur whispered to me: 'Keep an eye on him!' In the nocturnal dark, I crawled into the steppe after Zobar. That's the way it was, my falcon!"

Makar cleaned out his pipe and then began to fill it again. I wrapped myself tightly in my soldier's coat and, lying there, stared at his aged face, black from the sun and the wind. He muttered something to himself, shaking his head and looking severe; his gray mustaches stirred, and the wind ruffled the hair on his head. He resembled an ancient oak that had been struck by lightning but was still mighty, sturdy, and proud of its strength. As before, the sea whispered to the shore, and the wind still carried its whisper over the steppe. Nonka sang no longer, and the gathering clouds in the sky made the autumn night even darker.

"Loyko walked on, dragging his feet, his head hanging and his arms dangling like a whip, and, coming to a stream in a ravine, he sat down and sighed deeply. He gave such a sigh that my heart bled for pity of him, but I didn't approach him. You can't help grief with a word —isn't that so! That's it! Loyko sat there an hour, another, a third, without budging—just sat.

"I lay in hiding nearby. The night was clear, the moon had filled the whole steppe with silver, and you could see everything a long way.

"Suddenly I saw Radda approaching hastily from the camp.

"I felt glad! 'This is important!' I thought. 'A bold girl, this Radda.' Loyko did not hear her approach. Then she laid her hand on his shoulder; Loyko shuddered, parted his hands, and raised his head. Then he leapt up and grasped his knife! 'He'll stab the girl,' I thought, and was about to cry out to alert the camp and to run toward them when suddenly I heard Radda speak:

" 'Throw it away or I'll blow your head to pieces!' I looked, and there was Radda with a pistol in her hand, aiming at Zobar's forehead. That was a devil of a girl! 'Well,' I thought to myself, 'they're equal in strength now. What will happen now?'

" 'Listen!' Radda said, thrusting the pistol into her belt: 'I didn't come here to kill you, but to make peace. Throw the knife away!' Zobar threw down the knife and stared frowning into her eyes. It was a wonderful sight, brother! Those two human beings standing there and glaring like beasts at each other, so handsome and brave, both of them. And the bright moon gazed at them, as I did, and as did everything else.

" 'Listen to me, Loyko: I love you!' Radda declared. But he merely shrugged his shoulders as though bound hand and foot.

" 'I've seen many fine men,' she went on, 'but you're bolder and more beautiful of soul than any of them. Each of them would have shaved his mustaches off at the least wink; they'd all have fallen at my feet had I wished. But what's the sense of it? They're not really so bold, and I would have made them softer. There are very few bold gypsies left in the world, very few indeed, Loyko. I have never loved anyone else, Loyko, but I do love you. But I also love my freedom! I love freedom, Loyko, more than I love you. But you can't live without me, just as I can't live without you. So I want you to be mine, body and soul, do you hear?'

" 'I hear!' Loyko said, smiling ironically. 'It gladdens my heart to hear your speech! Speak some more!'

" 'This too, Loyko: however much you turn and twist, I'll master you. You shall be mine. So don't waste time —my kisses and caresses await you. . . . I shall kiss you passionately, Loyko! My kisses will make you forget your adventurous life . . . and your living songs that give so much pleasure to our fine gypsies will sound no more through the steppe. . . . Instead, you will sing tender love songs for me—Radda. . . . So don't waste time.

I've said it now, and that means you will submit to me tomorrow as the young do to an older comrade. You'll bow down at my feet in front of the whole camp, and you'll kiss my right hand—and then I shall be your wife.'

"That's what that devil of a girl wanted! A thing never before heard of; only with the Montenegrins was it thus in ancient days, so the old men say, but never among the gypsies! Well, my falcon, can you imagine anything more comic? You'd rack your brains for a year and never think of it!

"Loyko jumped to one side and, as though wounded in the chest, howled through the steppe. Radda gave a start, but didn't weaken.

" 'Well, farewell till tomorrow,' she said, 'but tomorrow you'll do what I command. Do you hear, Loyko?'

" 'I hear! I'll do it,' Loyko Zobar groaned, holding out his hands to her. But she didn't even look back at him; he staggered like a tree broken by the wind, and fell to the ground sobbing and laughing.

"That's how that accursed Radda worried the life out of our brave man. I was barely able to bring him round.

"Ay, who's the devil that requires people to grieve? Who is it loves to hear a human heart groan and burst with sorrow? Just puzzle that out!

"I returned to the camp and told everything to the elders. They thought it over and decided to wait and see what would come of it. This is what came of it. When we had all gathered in the evening around the campfire, along came Loyko. He looked disturbed and had grown terribly thin overnight, and his eyes were deep sunk; he lowered them and, without raising them, addressed us:

" 'This is how it is, comrades: This night I looked into my heart and found no place in it for my old carefree life. Radda alone dwells there—and that's all! And there she is, the beautiful Radda, smiling like a queen! She loves her freedom more than she does me, but I love her more than my freedom, and I've decided to bow down at Radda's feet as she commanded, so that everyone shall see how her beauty has conquered the bold Loyko Zobar, who, until she appeared, played with the girls like a gyrfalcon with the ducks. And then she will become my wife and will caress and kiss me, so that I shall not want to sing songs to you and shall have no regret for my freedom. Isn't that so, Radda?" Here he raised his eyes and looked at her quizzically. In silence she gave an austere nod of her head and pointed to her feet. We stared, not understanding. We even felt like going off somewhere to avoid witnessing Loyko Zobar fall at the feet of a girl—even though the girl was Radda. A feeling of shame, of pity and sadness, came over us.

" 'Well!' Radda cried out to Zobar.

" 'Ah, don't be in such a hurry; there's plenty of time; you'll tire of this,' he answered, laughing. And his laugh rang like steel.

" 'So that is all, comrades! What remains then? It remains to discover whether my Radda has a heart as strong as that she showed me. I'll do my best—forgive me, brothers!'

"We hadn't had time to guess what Zobar was up to when suddenly Radda lay on the ground with Zobar's curved knife up to the hilt in her bosom. We were struck numb.

"But Radda tore out the knife, threw it to one side and, stopping her wound with a tress of her black hair, exclaimed loudly and clearly, smiling the while: " 'Farewell, Loyko! I knew you would do this!' and she died there and then. . . .

"Do you understand the girl now, my falcon?" Makar Chudra asked me. "That's the sort of a devilish girl she was, may I be cursed to eternity!

" 'Ah! I will bow down at your feet, my proud queen!' Loyko shouted for all the steppe to hear and, throwing himself down on the ground, pressed his lips to the feet of the dead Radda, and lay still. We bared our heads and stood in silence.

"What have you to say about an affair like this, my falcon? That's how it was! Nur tried to say, 'We must bind him!' But no one would have raised a hand to bind Loyko Zobar, no one, and Nur knew this. With a wave of his hand, he stepped aside. But Danilo picked up the knife Radda had thrown to one side and stared at it for a long time, his gray mustaches bristling; Radda's blood had not yet dried on the knife, and it was such a sharp, curved knife. Then Danilo went up to Zobar and stuck the knife in his back just opposite his heart. He was Radda's father indeed, that old soldier Danilo.

" 'That's it!' Loyko said clearly, turning toward Danilo, and he departed to join Radda.

"We stood watching. There lay Radda, pressing a hand with a tress of her hair to her bosom; her open eyes stared at the blue sky, and at her feet sprawled the bold Loyko Zobar. His curly hair had fallen forward, hiding his face.

"We stood there pondering. Old Danilo's mustaches trembled, and his thick brows were gathered in a frown. Silently he stared at the sky, while Nur, who had gone completely white, lay down with his face to the ground and began to sob so violently that his old shoulders shook.

"There was something to cry about here, my falcon!"

"You're on the road now, so go your way and don't turn aside. Go straight on. Maybe you won't perish in vain. That's all, my falcon!"

Makar Chudra stopped talking and, putting away his pipe, pulled his coat over his chest. It was drizzling; the wind gathered force; the sea sounded dull and angry. One after another the horses walked up to the dying campfire and, having inspected us with their large, intelligent eyes, stood immobile, surrounding us in a solid ring.

"Hey-up!" Makar shouted to them affectionately and, patting with the palm of his hand the neck of his favorite raven horse, said as he turned to me: "Time to sleep!" Then he wrapped his head in his coat and, stretching out powerfully on the ground, fell silent.

I had no wish to sleep. I stared into the dark of the steppe, and in the air before my eyes floated the regally beautiful and proud figure of Radda. She had pressed a hand with a tress of black hair to the wound in her bosom and, in between her brown, slender fingers, blood dripped drop by drop, falling in fiery red little stars upon the earth.

In her footsteps floated Loyko Zobar, the bold young gypsy; thick black curls hid his face like a curtain, and from under them fell cold, large teardrops. . . .

It began to rain harder, and the sea chanted a gloomy yet triumphant hymn to a pair of proud and beautiful gypsies—Loyko Zobar and Radda, the daughter of the old soldier Danilo.

And they circled round each other, the two of them, smoothly and mutely in the dark of night and, try as he would, the handsome Loyko could never catch up with Radda.

THE NIGHTINGALE

The paddle steamer was proceeding on its way between Kazan and Kozlovka.

It was quiet and fresh on the Volga. Evening was falling. A lilac-colored mist was beginning to envelop the hilly bank of the river; the other bank, of meadowland, had been flooded and pushed far back to the horizon. In places, green islets of submerged trees rose above the water. The noise of the paddles sounded dully in the damp, thick air, heavy with the fragrance of fresh foliage. A broad band of foam stretched in the wake of the steamer, and waves were sent rolling toward both banks. The sunset was burning down ahead of the steamer, and night was catching up in the rear. Faintly, here and there, stars began to glow in the darkening sky.

A group of first-class passengers on the promenade deck was muted to a minor key by the influence of the melancholy evening, which was nascent on the river. There were four passengers seated there: an old man, tall and stooping, wearing a soft, wide-brimmed hat, the brim of which overshadowed the whole of his face, including his beard; beside him sat a young lady, wrapped closely in a gray shawl, her blue eyes staring dreamily at the hilly, wooded bank. Not far from them, on the same bench, sat another pair—a dry-looking gentleman in a gray overcoat and a buxom, shapely lady with regular features and large dark eyes. The gentleman next to her, who was nervously twisting his carefully trimmed

French beard, seemed to twitch as he leaned forward slightly. The lady, on the other hand, had settled against the back of the bench and sat there as immobile as a statue. The old man, gripping his cane with both hands and resting his chin on them, hunched himself forward and stared fixedly at the deck.

All were silent.

The steamer shuddered as it moved swiftly forward. From somewhere below could be heard the intrusive clatter of dishes, the trampling of feet and peals of laughter; and from the stern floated a subdued, almost sighing song, which was lost every now and again in all the noises that blended into one smooth, monotonous wave of abrupt and incomplete sounds.

"A bit fresh, isn't it. . . . Shouldn't we go down to our cabins, eh?" the old man suggested, raising his head.

In the meantime, floating from somewhere a good way off, came a strange, husky whistling that resembled a yearning, long-restrained sigh from some small but powerful and very passionate breast.

The passengers raised their heads.

"A nightingale!" the old man exclaimed with a laugh.

"A little early, isn't it?"

"Let's stay and listen, Papa," the young lady suggested.

"As you wish. You may stay here, and they have no objection either," he answered, rising. "But I'll be off. After all, nightingales are not my . . ." But, his sentence unfinished, the old man sat down again.

The nightingale's ringing, joyful, nerve-tingling trill rang and lilted through the air. The notes rushed so fast, so impetuously one after the other, that it seemed the songster was afraid he would have no time to say everything he wanted to say in his song. Nervously quivering roulades were suddenly interrupted by husky, sighing sounds, somehow most expressive of a deeply yearning, impassioned heart. Once more the feverish pizzicato spattered through the air, vanishing abruptly and giving place to a minor melody, interrupted in its turn by a sort of crackling sound, as if the singer were smacking his lips at his own song.

Everything on the steamer grew hushed. Every sound,

except for the monotonous thud of the paddle wheels, had vanished somewhere.

The song poured out, ruling both the river and the passengers, who listened to it in silence. The young lady smiled, entranced; the married lady's face lost something of its seriousness and strictness. The old man sighed and remarked: "There we have it, the playful and fantastic wisdom of nature! A small, useless bird is endowed with such a wealth of tone . . . but the cow, though a useful animal, is only capable of uttering a single, unpleasant mooing tone. We have become so accustomed to these peculiarities that we fail to notice them, and regard them all as in the order of things. And yet we cannot help noticing that, both in our life and in nature, we find the crude and ugly useful, whereas we find useless what is beautiful and enjoyable . . . touching to the soul."

"Don't talk, Papa. I can't hear!" the daughter exclaimed petulantly, shrugging her shoulders.

The father smiled skeptically and growled again: "Well, listen, listen . . . But you must agree that if cows sang like nightingales, it wouldn't be at all bad, eh? Or maybe we would not then appreciate the cows' singing and would be in raptures over something far cruder and much worse? As one of the Goncourt brothers has said, only the rare is beautiful. That is true, perhaps . . . But all of us humans would probably turn out to be very poor judges of the truly beautiful if its eternal ideal were revealed to us and we were able to compare it with what we now consider to be beautiful. . . . For, if we examine the matter closely, we have no eternal ideal. We ourselves have created the models . . . but we are not eternal; and our creations cannot be eternal either."

"Do stop it, Papa!" the daughter implored.

"All right . . . all right . . . I'll keep quiet! But he's stopped too . . . that rhapsodist of love . . . Have you had your fill? Well, shall we go down to the cabins?"

"Let's sit here a little longer," the married lady said in a slow, hushed voice.

The nightingale was still singing. But now his song had grown faint and dying. The sunset had burnt out. The waters of the Volga had grown dark and opaque. The

moon was climbing, and the hilly bank cast dark shadows upon the calm surface. In the hollow of a hill, a
bonfire gleamed and the crimson band of the reflected
fire sparkled and quivered on the river. It was wonderfully quiet. . . .

The nightingale's song broke off. . . .

A sailor appeared on the promenade deck.

For a while he shuffled about on one spot; then he
removed his leather cap, looked at the passengers, and
resolutely approached them.

"You wouldn't like to hear the nightingale, would
you?" he inquired rather awkwardly, for some reason.

"What's that?" the old man asked peevishly, with a
wry expression.

"The nightingale, if you wish? . . . There's a boy here
who whistles like a regular nightingale. . . . God's truth!"
the sailor explained, backing away from the old man's
piercing scrutiny.

"Bring him along," the married lady said curtly. The
man beside her began to shift nervously on the bench.

"Is it necessary, Nina?" he demanded with an acid
frown.

The young lady stared at the sailor with wide-open
eyes.

"Would you like me to bring him?" the sailor asked
again.

"Yes, of course . . . I told you so," the lady snapped
angrily.

"He'll come by himself!" the sailor clarified, and then
disappeared.

"The devil knows what this is!" the old man explained,
raising his brows. "Some sort of a boy who whistles like
a regular nightingale. . . . We've already heard him, believing he was a real nightingale and, listening to him,
one of us began philosophizing. . . . What a wild fowl!"
And he shook his head reproachfully, feeling embarrassed by this wild fowl.

A boy of about fourteen appeared on deck.

He was wearing a jacket and narrow trousers, and on
his head a new visored cap tipped slightly to one side.
His freckled face, his rolling gait, his thick, short fin-

gers and his sun-bleached yellow hair proclaimed him to be a villager. He approached the group, removed his cap, bowed, shook his head and, leaving it uncovered, silently began to fidget with the visor as if trying to straighten it. The passengers also scrutinized him in silence. There was a puzzled look in the young lady's eyes. The boy's gray eyes swept boldly over their faces.

"Would you like me to whistle?" he asked.

"Was it you whistling just now like a nightingale?" the old man inquired.

"Yes, me. The barman had asked me . . ."

"Is that all you do—whistle?"

"Exactly so. . . . I board the steamer and travel as far as Kazan. . . . Then I do the return trip from Kazan. . . ."

"Well, then let's hear you whistle, please!"

"I don't want to hear it," the young lady said in a low voice.

The boy looked at her, puzzled.

"Who taught you this?" the married lady asked the boy in a husky contralto.

"Why, I myself . . . I was a herdsboy . . . I come from hereabouts," he said, waving his hand vaguely toward the river bank, "from a village. . . . I'd mind the herd and listen all day to all sorts of birds. . . . So I began whistling to the birds myself . . . well, and so I learnt little by little . . . I can whistle like a siskin . . . a robin, too. . . . But that's not as rousing as the nightingale. And I've become such a good hand at the nightingale that even the hunters are taken in. I sit in the bushes and open up! Just like a real bird, honest!"

As he talked, the boy's face glowed with the proud awareness of his mastery and with the vanity of an artist.

"When I became such a good hand at it," he went on, "there were village folk who said: 'Just go on, Misha, don't stop. Just go on whistling. . . . You might please the gentry who travel by steamer. Maybe you'll get somewhere.' So off I went. . . . Then I started riding these steamers. . . . It's not too bad. I get on. At times they give so much money my eyes pop. Money's cheap to the gentry. . . ."

He broke off, realizing that he had said too much, and then bashfully asked:

"Would you like me to whistle now?"

A silence of several seconds ensued before the married lady uttered a curt command: "Whistle!"

The boy threw the cap at his feet, put his fingers to his mouth, and arched his throat. For some reason his face was smiling, but he took some time to begin. First, he pulled his fingers out of his mouth, wiped his lips, snorted and made all kinds of grimaces.

At last the yearning, sighing whistling resounded again. It rang out and died away. And then suddenly the full lilting trill of a nightingale's roulade rang out in the air. The young lady quivered and heaved a sorrowful sigh. . . . The married lady smiled with glum contempt; her companion hunched himself, grimacing nervously; and the old man stared with serious intentness into the boy's face. The latter had turned very red and swollen from the effort; his dilated eyes remained dull and inexpressive and did not illumine him in any way. The "nightingale" crackled, trilled, and, throbbing, stopped for an instant, then renewed its singing, calling and sighing nostalgically. The imitation was remarkably exact.

"Papa, tell him . . . to stop," the young lady said in a low voice. She suddenly rose and walked away, looking pale. There were tears in her eyes.

"Enough!" the old man said with a wave of his hand.

The "nightingale" broke off his song, wiped his lips with his hand, picked up the visored cap and held it out toward the old man's hand. There was a rustling of paper. . . .

"My humble thanks!" the boy said, and quickly disappeared, descending somewhere downstairs. The lady, following him with her eyes, smiled ironically. Her companion growled something to himself and raised the collar of his overcoat. . . . The night deepened, growing thicker and darker. The water looked black now. The banks of the river were lost in the shadow. But the stars were already gleaming in the sky and, as before, the water churned monotonously beneath the paddle wheels of the steamer.

"An artist!" the old man exclaimed, changing his po-

sition. "Another victim of the public. . . . That's how it
is—the public will swallow anything—just as it swallows
Swift and Offenbach, Heine and the glib pen of a journalist. Everything gives the public pleasure . . . the
weight-lifting of a circus strong man and a virtuoso playing the violin. And yet the public is no pig in the Gogol
manner—no, it's a more intelligent animal; all the more
intelligent because it is bigger. It is not particular about
who serves it or how, but it knows how to enjoy the
process of being served. It feels flattered when it ob-
serves that a man is ready to do anything in order to
merit its attention . . . to twist himself into any shape
for the sake of a dime and its attention. The public loves
to feel itself lord over the personality. . . ."

But apparently the others were not listening to him, for
nobody answered.

"But if that sailor had not come," he began, after a
pause, "we would have remained convinced that we had
heard a bird famed by the poets rather than a scrubby
little village boy, a pretender. H'm . . . yes! To learn the
truth is no great pleasure . . . when illusion is more
beautiful."

"Let's go," the lady suggested, rising. They all got up
to go to their cabins.

"Lena is probably weeping by now . . . she's such a
nervous girl," the old man added. "But that's all right.
. . . Gradually she must get used to the trifling, foolish
deceits of life. . . . She'll then find it easier to deal with
larger and more serious issues. . . . Why are you trembling, Nina? Is it the chill air?"

"No, it's nothing. Don't worry," the lady replied softly. Her nervous companion glanced at her with indifference through his colorless, ironically screwed-up eyes.
Then they all disappeared behind the cabin door.

The moon, ascending, cast her glimmers upon the
dark waters; and, gleaming faintly, their reflections quivered on the vacillating surface of the waves.

In the distance wavering points of light appeared.

A feeling of sadness hung over the drowsy river.

CHELKASH

The azure, dust-darkened southern sky looked blurred; and, as through a thin gray veil, the blazing sun stared down at the greenish sea. The sun was barely reflected in the water, cloven by dipping oars, ships' screws, the sharp keels of Turkish feluccas and other vessels furrowing the packed harbor in all directions. The sea waves, fettered in granite, crushed down by the enormously heavy bodies slithering over their crests, pounded against the sides of the vessels, against the shore; they pounded and growled, foaming, littered with every variety of garbage.

The clanging of anchor chains, the thudding couplings of freight cars delivering their loads, the metallic howling of sheet iron falling somewhere on the stone-paved road, the dull reverberation of wood, the rattling of carts, the hooting of steamship sirens, now penetratingly sharp, now a muffled bellow, the shouts of stevedores, sailors, and customs guards—all these sounds merged in the deafening music of a laboring day and, swaying mutinously, hovered low in the sky above the harbor. And toward them from the ground rose ever new and fresh waves of sound. Now muffled, now reverberating, their harsh impact shook everything in the vicinity; at other times, shrill or thunderous, they rent the dust-laden sultry air.

The granite, the iron, the wood, the cobblestones of

the harbor, the boats and the people—all these breathed the mighty notes of a passionate hymn to Mercury. But the voices of the men, barely audible in their midst, sounded feeble and comic. And the men themselves, who had initially given birth to all this noise, also looked feeble and comic: their figures, dusty, ragged, and agile, stooping under the weight of the goods loaded on their backs, scampered fussily here and there in clouds of dust, in a sea of heat and sound. They looked insignificant by comparison with the iron giants all around them, the mounds of freight, the rolling freight cars, and all the things they had themselves created. Their own creation had enslaved and depersonalized them.

With their steam up, the massive giant steamers whistled, hissed, sighed deeply; and in every sound they produced could be detected a note of ironic contempt for the gray, dusty figures of men crawling over their decks and heaping their deep holds with the product of their slavish labor. Pitifully comic were the long lines of stevedores shouldering tons of grain into the iron bellies of the ships in order to earn for themselves a few pounds of that very bread, to be consumed by their own stomachs. The ragged, sweating men, stupefied by exhaustion, noise, and heat, and the mighty machines these men had created, now glittering corpulently in the sun—these machines were ultimately set in motion not by steam, but by the muscles and the blood of their creators—this was contradiction containing a whole cruelly ironic poem.

The din was overpowering; the dust irritated the nostrils and blinded the eyes; the heat baked and exhausted the body; and everything in the vicinity seemed tense, out of patience, on the point of touching off some grandiose catastrophe, some explosion, in the aftermath of which it would be easier to breathe more freely in the atmosphere thus refreshed; silence would reign on earth, and this dust-laden din, so deafening and irritating, so conducive to the melancholy of insanity, would at last cease to be, so that the city and the sea and the sky might then grow calm, clear, and pleasant.

Twelve strokes of a bell, measured and sonorous, resounded. When the last clang of bronze had died away, the savage din of labor already sounded more gentle. In another minute it was transformed into a muffled murmur of discontent. The voices of men and the splashing of the sea now became more audible. It was the midday break.

1

When the stevedores stopped work and scattered in noisy groups through the docks, buying a variety of things to eat from the women vendors, and then sat down to their meal right there in shady corners on the cobblestones, Grishka Chelkash made his appearance. He was an old tracked wolf, well known on the docks, a chronic drunkard and a daring, agile thief. He was barefoot, wore a pair of old worn plush trousers, had no cap, and his dirty satin shirt with frayed collar displayed his dry angular bones sheathed in brown skin. By his disheveled black, grizzled hair and his crumpled, sharp, ravenous features, it could be seen that he had just awakened. A wisp of straw was stuck in one of his graying mustaches, while another wisp was caught in the bristles of his left cheek, and he also wore a small, freshly snapped linden twig behind one of his ears. Long-limbed, gaunt, slightly stooping, he picked his way slowly over the cobblestones and, his hooked, ravenous nose twitching from side to side, darted keen glances all around him, and his cold gray eyes gleamed as he sought out someone among the stevedores. His graying mustaches, thick and long, quivered from time to time like those of a tomcat, and his hands, thrust behind his back, rubbed against each other, while his long, crooked, grasping fingers kept nervously interlocking. Even here, among hundreds of such striking figures of hobos like him, he immediately attracted attention to himself by his resemblance to a hawk of the steppes, by his ravenous gauntness, and by that purposeful gait of his, smooth and quiet in appearance, but inwardly alert and keen as the flight of the bird of prey he so resembled.

When he drew level with one of the groups of the hobo-stevedores sitting in the shade underneath a pile of coal baskets, a short sturdy fellow stood up to meet him. He had a stupid face with purple birthmarks and a scratched neck, which suggested that he had recently been beaten up. Rising, he walked beside Chelkash, addressing him in an undertone: "The shipping people have just missed two bales of cloth. . . . They're on the prowl."

"So what?" Chelkash queried, measuring him calmly with his eyes.

"What do you mean, 'so what'? They're on the prowl, I tell you. That's all."

"Were they asking for me to help them?" Chelkash asked, with a smile, gazing in the direction of the Merchant Marine warehouse. "Go to the devil!"

The fellow turned back.

"Hey, wait! Who was it plastered you? They've sure spoiled your signpost. . . . Say, have you seen Mishka about?"

"Haven't seen him for a long while!" the other replied, going off to rejoin his group.

Chelkash walked on, greeted familiarly by everyone. But, though always cheerful and caustic, he was apparently out of sorts that day, and was short and snappy in his replies. From behind a mound of bales a customs guard materialized, all in dark green, dusty, and stiff-backed like a soldier. He barred the way to Chelkash, standing in front of him in a challenging attitude, with his left hand on his dirk and with his right attempting to grip Chelkash by the scruff of his neck.

"Stop! Where are you off to?"

Chelkash retreated a step, raised his eyes to the guard, and produced a wry smile.

The guard's good-natured yet cunning face tried to look threatening, becoming puffed out, round, and purple in the process. His eyebrows twitched, his eyes bulged. The effect was extremely comic.

"You've been told—keep out of the docks or I'll break your ribs! And you're at it again!" The guard shouted his threats.

"Good day, Semeonovitch. We haven't seen each other for a long time," Chelkash greeted him calmly, holding out his hand.

"I'd rather not see you in a century! Away with you, get out!"

But Semeonovitch, nevertheless, clasped the proffered hand.

"Tell me this," Chelkash continued, without letting Semeonovitch's hand out of his grasp and shaking it in a friendly, familiar way. "You haven't seen Mishka about, have you?"

"What Mishka's that? I don't know any Mishka! Go on with you, brother, get going! If the warehouse boss sees you, he'll . . ."

"The red-headed chap with whom I last worked on the S.S. *Kostroma*," Chelkash insisted.

"With whom you do your pilfering, you mean! He's been carted off to the hospital, your Mishka. He got his foot caught under a steel rod. Better get out of here, brother, while I'm asking you nicely, or I'll have to give it to you in the neck! . . ."

"Aha, you see! And you were saying you didn't know Mishka. . . . You do know him. What's eating you, Semeonovitch?"

"Don't be so wise now, scram!"

The guard was getting angry and, glancing around on all sides, tried to wrest his hand from Chelkash's strong grip. Chelkash stared calmly at him from under his bushy eyebrows and, not letting go of the hand, continued talking: "Don't hurry me. I'll have my fill of talking with you, and then I'll go. Well, tell me how you're getting on? Your wife and children—are they in good health?" His eyes flashing, his teeth bared in an ironic grin, he added: "I'm thinking of paying you a visit at home, but can't find the time yet— I've been drinking too much lately. . . ."

"I say, don't give me that stuff! It's no joking matter, you bony devil. I, brother, I'll really . . . Or are you about to rob houses and hold up people in the streets?"

"Why should I? There are enough goods here to last an age for the two of us. God's truth, there's quite enough, Semeonovitch! I hear you've swiped a couple of bales of cloth again. . . . Look out, Semeonovitch, keep your eyes skinned, or you'll get pinched one of these days!"

Semeonovitch shook with indignation and, showering saliva, tried to speak. Chelkash let go his hand and calmly strode back toward the harbor gates. The guard, swearing violently, followed him.

Chelkash felt more cheerful. Whistling quietly through his teeth and thrusting his hands deep into his pockets, he walked on slowly, aiming pointed quips and jokes to left and right. He was repaid in the same coin.

"I say, Grishka, the authorities look after you well!" shouted one of a crowd of stevedores who had already finished eating and were now resting on the ground.

"I'm one of the barefoot brigade, and Semeonovitch is keeping his eye on me, so I don't step on a nail," Chelkash shouted back.

They reached the gate. Two sentinels frisked Chelkash and pushed him gently into the street.

Chelkash crossed the road and sat down on a small stone curb opposite a tavern door. A caravan of loaded carts was rambling out of the harbor gateway. Toward them, at a fast trot, came a number of empty carts with the drivers bumping up and down in their seats. The harbor belched with growling thunder and biting dust. . . .

Chelkash felt at home in this crazy confusion. He saw solid gain before him, requiring little labor and much dexterity. He was convinced that he had enough dexterity and, knitting his brows, mused on the drunken bout he would embark on in the morning, when his pockets would be bulging with bills. . . . He remembered his chum, Mishka: he would come in very handy this night if he hadn't broken his leg. Chelkash swore under his breath at the thought that alone, without Mishka, he might not be able to do the job. What sort of night would it be? He glanced up at the sky and then down the street.

About six paces from him on the cobbled road near the sidewalk a young peasant sat leaning his back against a stone curb; he wore a blue homespun shirt, trousers of the same material, bast shoes, and a frayed, rusted cap. On the ground beside him lay a small sack and a scythe without a shaft wrapped in straw and neatly bound with string. The young peasant was broad-shouldered, sturdy, and flaxen-haired, with a face tanned by sun and wind and large light-blue eyes that gazed at Chelkash with good-natured trust.

Chelkash showed his teeth, stuck out his tongue and, grimacing horribly, fixed him with goggling eyes.

The boy blinked hard, taken aback at first, but then burst out laughing and cried: "Ah, you old curiosity!" Then, almost without rising, he moved awkwardly from the stone curb, closer to Chelkash, dragging his sack in the dust and bumping the heel of his scythe on the cobbles.

"Looks like you've been celebrating a bit, brother!" he ventured, turning to Chelkash and plucking him by his trousers.

"I have that, suckling babe, I certainly have!" Chelkash admitted, smiling. He'd taken an immediate liking to this robust, good-natured peasant with bright boyish eyes. "Returning from the haymaking, are you?"

"That's it! 'We scythed a mile, and earned a cent.' Things are bad! Too many people! It's not worth the labor. They knock the price down as soon as the famine-starved ones tramp in! They were paying us only sixty kopecks in the Kuban region. A real mess it is! But before that, they say, they used to pay three, four, and five rubles!"

"Before that! . . . Before that—for merely staring at a Russian laborer they paid three rubles. Some ten years ago I myself traded on that. You'd come to a cossack ranch—'I am a Russian,' you'd say! They'd look you over at once, feel you, wonder at you, and—'There's three rubles for you!' And they'd give you drink and food into the bargain! And you could stay there as long as you liked!"

Listening to Chelkash, the lad at first opened his eyes wide, his round face expressing both perplexity and wonder, but, catching on that the hobo was making it up, he smacked his lips and roared with laughter. Chelkash kept a straight face, concealing his smile in his mustaches.

"You're crazy. You seem to speak the truth, and I

listen and believe you. But, I swear, before that there . . ."

"And what was I saying? Didn't I tell you that before that . . ."

"You're talking big!" the peasant said with a wave of his hand. "Are you a cobbler or what? Or a tailor? You, I mean."

"Me, you mean," Chelkash mimicked him. Then, reflecting, he said: "A fisherman I am. . . ."

"A fish-er-man! You don't say! So you catch fish, do you?"

"Why only fish? The local fishermen here catch more than fish. Mostly drowned men, old anchors, sunken ships—everything! There are special fishing rods for that . . ."

"Lies, lies, all lies. . . . Maybe you're one of the fishermen who sing this about themselves:

> "We cast our nets
> Upon dry shores
> And barns and warehouses!"

"And have you seen any such?" asked Chelkash with an ironic twinkle.

"Where could I see any of them! But I've heard . . ."

"Do you like them?"

"Like them? Of course I do! They're a free and independent lot. . . ."

"And what's freedom to you? Do you really love freedom?"

"How otherwise? You're your own master, you go where you wish, do what you want. . . . So I'm in favor! If a man manages to keep himself in order, and has no millstones round his neck—that's the important thing! Enjoy life the way you want, only remember God. . . ."

Chelkash spat with contempt and turned away from the peasant.

"To come now to my own situation," the other went on, "my father died, the property was a small one, my mother's an old woman, the land's sucked dry—what am I to do? One has to live. But how? One doesn't know. I might join a prosperous household as a son-in-law.

All right. As long as they fix you up with a daughter! But the devil of a father-in-law isn't in such a hurry to fix you up! So I've got to break my back for him . . . for a long time. . . . For years! That's the way things go, you see! But if I was to make a hundred and fifty rubles, I'd be on my own feet and, having done the mowing, I'd put it straight to old man Antip: 'Take it or leave it,' I'd say! 'Do you wish to fix me up with Martha? No? Then I can do without her. Thank God, she's not the only girl in the village.' I'd be myself then, that is, completely free, on my own. . . . Y-yes!" The peasant sighed and went on. "But now there's nothing left to do but apprentice myself as a son-in-law. I used to think: 'Now let me go off to the Kuban, pick up a couple of hundred rubles—and that would do it! I'd be the master.' But it didn't work out that way. Well, just you try being a laborer. . . . I can't make out with my own property, not in any way! Ai-ai!"

The young peasant was very loath to work at becoming a son-in-law. Even his face looked dark and dejected. He squirmed about on the ground.

"Where do you go now?" Chelkash asked.

"How d'you mean 'where'? Home, where else?"

"Well, how was I to know that, brother! Maybe you were setting off to Turkey. . . ."

"To Turkey!" the peasant stammered. "What Orthodox Christian ever goes there? What a thing to say!"

"You're a rank fool!" Chelkash exclaimed with a sigh, turning away again from the lad sitting next to him. This robust country fellow had struck something in him.

A vague, slowly ripening feeling of concern stirred somewhere deep down and prevented him from concentrating on and planning what he aimed to do that night.

The peasant, having been put in his place, muttered something in a low voice, throwing occasional sidelong glances at the barefoot hobo. His puffed-out cheeks looked funny, his lips protruded, and his narrowed eyes, blinking too fast, produced a comic effect. But he had apparently not expected his conversation with this mustachioed down-and-out to terminate so quickly and disastrously.

The hobo paid no more attention to him. He whistled

thoughtfully as he sat on the stone curb, beating out a rhythm on it with his bare, dirty heel.

The peasant now wanted to get even with him.

"Hey you, fisherman! Do you get drunk often?" he began, but, at that moment, the "fisherman" turned his face quickly toward him, asking: "Listen, you sucker! Do you want to work with me tonight? Answer quickly!"

"Work at what?" the peasant queried suspiciously.

"Doesn't matter what! Whatever I make you do. . . . We'll go after the fish. You'll do the rowing. . . ."

"So . . . I don't mind. One can work. Only . . . one might get into trouble through you. You're hard to know, and you're a dark horse, too."

Chelkash felt a sort of burning sensation in his chest and clipped in a low, coldly angry voice: "Don't go chattering about things you don't understand. I'll give you a bang on the head, and then you'll see the light. . . ."

He jumped off the curbstone, pulled at his mustache with his left hand, clenched his hard-knotted right fist, and froze him with his glittering eyes.

The peasant took fright. He glanced rapidly about him and, blinking timidly, also jumped up. Silently, they measured each other with their eyes.

"Well?" Chelkash asked curtly. He was seething and shuddering at the insult inflicted upon him by this young milk calf, whom he had despised but now hated because of his pure, light-blue eyes, healthy sunburned face, short but powerful arms; because somewhere this young peasant had a native village, with a house of his own; and because a well-to-do peasant had invited him to become his son-in-law—because of the peasant's whole life, past and future; and, above all, because he, a child by comparison with himself, Chelkash, dared to love freedom, of which he did not know the value and which he did not need. It was always unpleasant to note that a man you consider to be worse and lower than yourself loves or hates the same thing as you do and, in this way, comes to resemble you.

The peasant stared at Chelkash and recognized a master in him.

"I'm not . . . against it. . . ." he began. "I'm looking for work. It's all the same to me with whom I work, with you or some other man. I only said what I did because you're not like a working man—you're much too ragged for that. We . . . I know, of course, this can happen to anyone. O Lord, haven't I seen a lot of drunks! Ah, plenty of them! . . . But not all of them were like you."

"Well, all right, all right! Are you agreeable?" Chelkash asked him again, more gently.

"I—then? All right, I'm willing! . . . I'll be glad! Name the price."

"My price is according to the work. The sort of work it will be. The catch we get, I mean. . . . You might land a fiver. Do you get it?"

But now that money was involved, the peasant wanted to be exact and demanded the same exactitude from his employer. His distrust and suspicion flared up again.

"That's no helping hand for me, brother!"

Chelkash began to play a role.

"Don't argue! Wait! Let's go into a tavern!"

And they went off along the street, side by side, Chelkash twirling his mustaches with the dignified look of a boss, the young peasant with an expression of ready subordination but, all the same, full of distrust and fear.

"And what's your name?" Chelkash asked.

"Gavrila!" the peasant replied.

When they entered the grimy, sooty tavern, Chelkash strode to the buffet and, in the familiar tone of a regular, ordered a bottle of vodka, some borsch, meat cutlets, and tea, and, adding up the bill, brusquely told the man behind the counter, "I'll owe you all this!" —to which the man assented with a nod. This at once filled Gavrila with great respect for his new boss who, for all his appearance of a rogue, enjoyed such fame and credit here.

"Well, let's have a bite now and talk sense. But first, sit down, and wait for me while I go out for a moment."

He went off. Gavrila looked around him. The tavern was situated in a cellar; it was damp and dark there, and the air was permeated with the stifling smell of vodka, stale tobacco smoke, tar, and something else equally pungent. At another table opposite Gavrila sat a drunken man dressed like a sailor; he had a red beard, and was covered from head to foot with coal dust and tar. He mumbled, hiccupping, some song in broken, spasmodic words, which were all either terribly sibilant or guttural. He was evidently not Russian.

Two Moldavian girls had sat down at a table behind him. They were ragged, black-haired, sunburned, and they too were grating out a song in drunken voices.

Then various other figures stepped out of the darkness, all weirdly untidy, all of them semi-intoxicated, high-pitched, and extremely restless. . . .

Gavrila felt ill at ease. He wished his master were back. The hubbub in the tavern blended into a single note: it seemed that one huge beast was growling in a hundred different voices, struggling in blind irritation to rush its way out of this stone hole, and finding no exit into the open. . . . Gavrila, apprehensively scanning the premises, sensed his body absorbing something heavy and intoxicating, which made his head whirl and his eyes grow dim.

Chelkash returned, and they started to eat and drink and talk. After his third tumbler of vodka, Gavrila began to get drunk. He felt elated and wished to say a pleasant word to his boss, who—fine fellow that he was! —had treated him so well. But the words, gushing in waves to his throat, failed for some reason to drop from his now leaden tongue.

Chelkash, observing him, said with an ironic smile: "You're loaded! Ah, you bread-and-water soup! You only had five tumblers! How are you going to work now?"

"Friend!" Gavrila mumbled. "Don't be afraid! I'll do my best! Let me kiss you! . . . eh?"

"Now, now! Here, put down another vodka!"

Gavrila continued drinking and finally reached the point where, in his eyes, everything began to sway according to an independent rhythm. This proved unpleasant and sickening. An expression of stupid rapture spread over his face. Attempting to speak, he moved his lips flabbily, mumbling. Chelkash, glancing intently at him, seemed to recall something and, twirling his mustaches, he smiled darkly.

The tavern was jumping with drunken shouts. The red-bearded sailor was dozing, his head on the table.

"Well, let's go!" said Chelkash, rising.

Gavrila tried to get up, but couldn't. Then, swearing strongly, he broke into a meaningless, besotted laugh.

"It's really got you!" Chelkash exclaimed, sitting down again opposite him.

Gavrila went on laughing, his bleary eyes fixed on his boss. The latter watched him steadily, keenly, and thoughtfully. Before him he saw a man whose life was now in the power of his own wolflike claws. He, Chelkash, was now in a position to manipulate his life this way or that. He could bend it, like a playing card, or he could also help set it up in a solid peasant framework. Feeling himself to be the other man's overlord, he reflected that this young peasant would never taste of a cup as bitter as that reserved by fate for him, Chelkash. . . . And he both envied and pitied this young life, laughed a little at it, and even grieved for it, speculating that it might once again fall into other hands such as his. . . . In the ultimate end all of Chelkash's feelings harmonized into one—a paternal, domestic feeling. The young man was to be pitied, but he was also needed. Chelkash lifted Gavrila under the arms and, shoving him lightly from behind with his knees, maneuvered him into the tavern yard, where he laid him down on the ground under the shade of a stack of logs and, sitting down beside him, lighted his pipe. After turning about for a while, Gavrila groaned a bit and then fell asleep.

2

"Well, are you ready?" Chelkash asked in a low voice of Gavrila, who was busy with the oars.

"Just a moment! A rowlock's loose. I could drive it in with an oar?"

"Don't do that! No noise! Push it down harder with your hands—that will steady it."

Quietly they busied themselves with the boat, moored to one of a whole flotilla of sailing ships laden with oak pulp, and of large Turkish feluccas filled with palm, sandalwood, and thick cypress beams.

It was a dark night. Tousled clouds moved in thick layers across the sky; the sea itself was tranquil, black and dense as petroleum. It exhaled a moist aroma of salt, and lapped with a caressing sound against the ships' sides, against the shore, causing Chelkash's boat to rock a little. For a long distance from shore the dark hulks of the vessels rose from the sea, piercing the sky with their pointed masts hung with multicolored lanterns on top. The sea, reflecting the lantern lights, was sown with a mass of yellow patches. They shimmered beautifully upon its soft, lusterless black velvet. The sea was immersed in the deep, healthy sleep of a laborer exhausted by his hard day's toil.

"Let's be off!" Gavrila exclaimed, dipping the oars in the water.

"Let's!" Chelkash agreed, and with a hefty swing of the steering oar he drove the boat into the stretch of water between the barges. The boat made swift headway through the slippery water, and the water burned with a light-blue phosphorescent glimmer under the strokes of the oars; gleaming softly, this extended ribbonlike glow wound in the wake of their boat.

"Well, and how's your head? Sore?" Chelkash inquired with solicitude.

"Couldn't be worse! It's humming like an iron rail. . . . I'll douse it now!"

"Why that? Better moisten your insides. That's a quicker remedy, maybe!" Chelkash suggested, handing Gavrila a bottle.

"Maybe I will! Oh well, God bless!"

A low gurgling sound was heard.

"Hold on! Enjoying it? That's enough for the moment!" Chelkash exclaimed, stopping him.

The boat shot forward again, maneuvering noiselessly and easily in between the ships. . . . Suddenly it burst out from the crowd of them, and the sea—the endless mighty sea—unfurled before them, stretching into the blue distance where, out of the waters, mountainous clouds rose skyward—purplish-gray clouds hemmed with puffs of yellow; greenish clouds, the color of sea water; and clouds of a dull, leaden hue that cast melancholy, ponderous shadows. Slowly the clouds crawled, now merging, now passing each other, mingling in color and form, swallowing each other and assuming new outlines again, majestic and frowning. There was something fateful about that slow movement of soulless masses. It seemed that yonder, on the edge of the sea, was an infinite multitude of them—clouds that would always continue with the same indifference to crawl higher in the sky, with the sinister intention of preventing the sky from ever glowing above the drowsy sea with a million golden eyes—stars of every color, animated and bright with reflection, stimulating high resolve in men who value their pure light.

"Good, isn't it, the sea?" asked Chelkash.

"It's all right! Only it frightens me," Gavrila answered, rowing steadily.

The water shimmered in warm, azure phosphorescence, making a barely audible resonant, lapping sound to the stroke of the long oars.

"Frightens you! You're a fool!" Chelkash growled sarcastically. Thief though he was, he loved the sea. His nervous, ebullient nature, greedy for impressions, never could have enough of contemplating this dark expanse —boundless, free, and mighty. It had hurt him to hear Gavrila's answer to his question about the beauty of what he loved. Sitting at the helm, he cut the water with his steering oar and stared calmly ahead, filled with longing to journey long and far on this smooth, velvet surface.

A warm, expansive feeling always animated him at sea—it affected the whole of his soul, cleansing it gradually of the nasty things of everyday life. He valued this experience and liked to see himself, when surrounded by air and water, a better man here, where reflections on life lost their definition and life its price.

"And where's the fishing tackle?" Gavrila suddenly asked, anxiously glancing around the boat.

Chelkash gave a start.

"Fishing tackle? I've got it here in the stern."

But it hurt him to have to lie in front of this boy,

nd he regretted those thoughts and feelings that the
easant's question had destroyed. He grew angry. The
harp, familiar sensation in his chest and throat seized
im again; he turned to Gavrila with words of harsh
dmonishment:

"Listen, you, sit quietly there in your seat! Don't poke
our nose into what doesn't concern you. You've been
ired to row, so go on rowing. But if you go on jabber-
ng, things may turn out bad. Understand?"

The boat shuddered and stopped for an instant. The
ars, trailing in the water, stirred up foam as Gavrila
dgeted uneasily in his seat.

"Row, you—"

A sharp oath shook the air. Gavrila raised the oars.
he boat, as if frightened, pressed forward in a series
f quick jerks, noisily cutting the water.

"Steady now!"

Chelkash stood up at the helm and, without letting
o the steering oar, fixed his cold eyes on Gavrila's pale
ace. Crouching forward he resembled a cat about to
pring. He could be heard gnashing his teeth, while
avrila's teeth chattered much less impressively.

"Who's that shouting?" a voice over the water de-
anded sternly.

"The devil! Go on, row! . . . Quietly . . . or I'll
ill you, you dog! Row then! One, two. . . . Just try
nd open your mouth! I'll crunch you to bits!" Chelkash
issed.

"Holy Virgin . . . Mother of . . ." Gavrila whis-
ered, trembling and almost fainting from fear and his
trenuous effort.

The boat swung around smoothly and moved in the
irection of the harbor, where the lantern lights were
rowded in a variegated group and where one could
istinguish the trunks of masts.

"Hey! Who's yelling there?" the question came again.
The voice was now further off than the first time.
helkash felt reassured.

"It's yourself yelling!" he exclaimed in answer to the
houts, and then turned to Gavrila, who was still mutter-
ng a prayer.

"Well, you're lucky this time, brother! Had those

devils come after us, it would have been the end for you! D'you sense it? I'd have thrown you at once to the fishes!"

Now that Chelkash spoke calmly and even with good humor, Gavrila, still trembling with fright, began to implore him: "Listen, let me go! For Christ's sake, let me go! Put me off somewhere! Oi-oi! I'm done for altogether! Try and remember God, and let me go! What use am I to you? I can't go through with this! . . . I've never meddled in such things. . . . The first time . . . Oh Lord! It'll be the end of me! . . . The way you've got me to work for you, brother! Ah! It's awful! . . . You're endangering my soul! . . . Ah, what a business. . . ."

"What business?" Chelkash inquired sternly. "Eh? Tell me, what business?"

The peasant's fright amused him; he was enjoying both Gavrila's fear and his own image as Chelkash the formidable man.

"It's a murky business, brother. . . . Let me go, for God's sake! . . . Why pick on me? . . . Be a good man. . . ."

"You'd better shut up! If I didn't need you, I wouldn't have taken you on. Get that? So shut up!"

"Oh Lord!" Gavrila sighed.

"Now, now! Don't blubber!" Chelkash interrupted him.

But Gavrila could no longer restrain himself and, sobbing quietly, wept, blew his nose, squirmed in his heart, but continued to row with the energy of desperation. The boat shot forward like an arrow. Once more the dark hulls of the vessels rose in their path, and their boat was soon lost among them, spinning like a top in the narrow stretches of water between the vessels.

"Hey you! Listen! If anyone asks you about anything —keep your mouth shut if you want to live! Get it?"

"Akh! . . ." Gavrila sighed hopelessly in answer to the sharp command, adding bitterly, "My wretched lot!"

"Don't whine!" Chelkash exclaimed in an imposing whisper.

This whisper made Gavrila lose all capacity for understanding and he went numb in the grip of a chilly premonition of disaster. He dipped his oars automatically, pulled at them, raised them, and dipped them again, his eyes fixed stubbornly all the time on his birch-bark shoes.

The drowsy pounding of the waves produced a sullen and terrifying roar. The harbor came in sight. . . . Now they could hear men's voices, the splash of water, song, and shrill whistles behind those walls of granite.

"Stop!" Chelkash whispered. "Stop rowing! Push against the oars. Don't make so much noise, you devil!"

Gavrila grabbed at the slippery granite and guided the boat alongside the wall. The boat glided without a sound, slithering next to the slimy stone.

"Stop! Hand over the oars! Give them to me! And where's your passport? In your knapsack? Give me your knapsack then! Hand it over. Hurry! I'll hold on to it for you, dear friend, so that you don't do a bolt! . . . Now you won't run away. You might take to your heels even without the oars, but you'd be afraid to beat it without your passport. Wait for me here! And not a squeak out of you, or I'll have to search for you at the bottom of the sea! . . ."

Then, grasping at something, Chelkash heaved himself up and vanished over the wall.

Gavrila shuddered. . . . It had all happened so swiftly. Now he began to feel the pressure and fear that he experienced in the presence of that gaunt, mustachioed thief diminish and slip away from him. . . . If only he could escape now! With a sigh of relief he glanced around him. To the left loomed a black hull without masts—a sort of enormous coffin, empty and unpeopled. Each splash of the waves against the sides of the hull produced in its depths a dull reverberant echo like a deep sigh. To the right, above the water, stretched the damp granite wall of the pier, very like a cold, heavy snake. Behind him, he could make out some black shells of buildings and, in front, in the gap between the wall and the side of that "coffin," the sea was visible, the silent, deserted sea, with black clouds overhead. The clouds, vast and massive, moved slowly, shedding terror out of their darkness, ready to crush a man under their weight. Everything was cold, black, and sinister. Gavrila became terrified. The fear he now experienced was worse than the fear Chelkash had caused him; it gripped Gavrila's chest in its strong embrace, squeezed him into a pitiful lump, and riveted him to his seat in the boat. . . .

There was silence all around. Not a sound except the sighing of the sea. The clouds crept in the sky as slowly and opaquely as before, but they rose in ever greater numbers out of the sea; and, gazing at the sky, one might have mistaken it for the sea—a turbulent inverted sea placed over another smooth and tranquil one. The clouds resembled waves that, with their gray curly crests, had swept down upon the earth, abysses from which the wind had torn these waves, and rollers that had not yet gathered momentum and that were not yet covered with the greenish foam of fury and rage.

Gavrila felt crushed by this oppressive silence and the beauty of the night, and longed for his boss to return as soon as possible. But what if Chelkash delayed coming back? . . . Time dragged, more slowly than the clouds creeping through the sky. . . . And because of the slow pace, the silence grew increasingly sinister . . . But then came a splash behind the wall of the pier, a rustling sound, and the suggestion of a whisper. Gavrila felt he might die any moment. . . .

"Hey! Are you sleeping there? Hold on to this now! . . . Carefully does it!" Chelkash's muffled voice came through.

A heavy, cubical object was lowered from the top of the wall. Gavrila took it aboard. Another such object followed. Then Chelkash's elongated figure was silhouetted against the wall, a pair of oars appeared from somewhere, Gavrila's knapsack fell at his feet, and Chelkash, breathing heavily, sat down at the steering oar.

Gavrila smiled with timid pleasure at the sight of him. "Tired?" he asked.

"One can't help being tired, you calf! Well now, start rowing! Fast! For all you're worth! . . . You've earned something already! The job's half done. Now we have to row through between their eyes, and afterwards—receive your cash and skip it to your Mashka. Do you have a Mashka, a woman of your own? Tell me that, you big baby?"

"I d-don't!" replied Gavrila, exerting all his strength, and using his chest like a bellows and his arms like steel springs. The water gurgled beneath the boat, and the azure wake was wider now. Gavrila dripped with sweat, but continued to row with all his might. Having survived a great fear twice that night he was now afraid of living through a third alarm, and so his desire was concentrated on only one thing: to finish this job as soon as possible, to step ashore, and to escape from this man before the latter either killed him or got him into prison. He decided to avoid discussion with him, not to contradict him, to do everything he commanded, and, if he succeeded in breaking away from him, to have a Mass of thanksgiving said the very next day to St. Nicholas the Miracle Worker. A passionate prayer was ready to burst from his breast. But he restrained himself, puffed like a locomotive, and held his tongue as he kept glancing at Chelkash.

The latter—wry, long-limbed, bent forward, resembling a bird about to take off—gazed into the darkness ahead with hawklike eyes and, his hooked, rapacious nose twitching, held on firmly to the steering oar with one hand while with the other he worried his mustache, which quivered each time a smile twisted his thin lips.

Chelkash was pleased with his success, with himself and this boy whom he had so intimidated and who had become his slave. He watched Gavrila straining and, taking pity, felt like encouraging him. "Hey!" he began with a smile. "You got a big fright, didn't you, eh?"

"N-no matter!" Gavrila sighed, grunting.

"You needn't pull so hard now. We've done it. There's just one more place we have to get by. . . . Take a breather."

Gavrila obediently stopped, wiped the sweat from his face with his sleeve, and then dipped the oars once again.

"Start rowing, but gently now. So that the water don't talk. We have to slip by an entrance guardpost. Gently now, gently . . . They're a watchful lot here, brother. . . . They can even joke with their rifles. They might give you such a bump on your forehead, you won't even groan."

The boat now crept through the water almost without a sound. Only azure drops fell from the oars and, where they fell into the sea, azure patches flared up for an instant. The night grew ever darker and more taciturn.

The sky no longer resembled an agitated sea—the clouds had spread and pulled a thick, even curtain over the sky—a curtain that had dropped low over the water and remained stationary there. And the sea had grown even calmer and blacker, and no longer seeming as wide as before, smelled more pungent, warm and saline.

"Ah, if only it would rain!" Chelkash whispered. "Then we'd slip through as if behind a curtain."

To left and right of their boat rose buildings or, rather, barges, immobile, gloomy, and likewise black. On one of them a light was moving—a man with a lantern. The sea, lapping the sides of the barges, sounded querulous and hollow; and they echoed back with a hollow, chilly sound as if disputing with and reluctant to yield to the sea.

"Cordons!" Chelkash whispered so you could barely hear.

Since the moment he was ordered to row more quietly, Gavrila had been once more gripped by acute and intense anxiety. He leaned forward into the darkness, and seemed to be growing bigger—his bones and veins were racked with a dull pain, his head ached with a single thought, the skin of his back quivered, and sharp cold needles pricked his feet. His eyes were strained from his concentrated scrutiny of the darkness, out of which he expected some shape to rise up suddenly and bark at them: "Stop, thief!"

At Chelkash's warning whisper of "Cordons!" Gavrila shuddered. A sharp, burning thought flashed through him, passed through him, and scraped his tightly strung nerves—he wanted to shout, call for help. . . . He had already opened his mouth and raised himself a little in his seat, pushed his chest forward, breathed in a lot of air, and was about to speak, when suddenly, in horror, as if struck by a whip, he shut his eyes and rolled off his seat.

Far ahead on the horizon a huge fiery, azure beam, like a sword lifted high, severed the darkness of the night, slipped like a sharp blade along the clouds, and came to rest in a broad azure band upon the breast of the sea. It came to rest, and into its gleaming light there floated forth out of the darkness the shapes of hitherto invisible ships, black and silent, festooned with luxuriant nocturnal gloom. They gave the impression of having rested for a long time at the bottom of the sea, drawn down there by the mighty violence of the storm, and of only now having risen thence at the command of the fiery seaborn sword—of having risen thence in order to gaze upon the sea and at everything above the water. . . . Their rigging was twined around the masts and resembled clinging seaweed risen from the bottom together with these black giants now entangled in their nets. And it was lifted high again from the sea depths, this terrifying azure sword, lifted flashing to sever the night again before coming to rest in a different direction. And where it came to rest, hulls of ships invisible until then floated up again.

Chelkash's boat stopped, rocking on the water as if in perplexity. Gavrila sprawled at the bottom of the boat, his face in his hands, while Chelkash prodded him with his foot and hissed furiously in a low voice: "You fool, that's only the Coast Guard cruiser. That's their electric searchlight! . . . Get up, you blockhead! Their light will catch us any moment! . . . You'll be the ruin of us both, you devil! Come on, now!"

Finally, when Chelkash's heel had struck Gavrila's back with more vigor, the latter jumped up with his eyes still closed in fear, took his place again and, gripping the oars by feel, got the boat moving.

"Quieter now or I'll break your neck! Quietly, I tell you! What a fool you are, the devil take you! . . . What were you frightened of? Well? You ugly mug! . . . It was a searchlight—that's all. Quieter with the oars there, you sour devil! . . . They're watching out for contraband. But they won't bother us now—they're too far away. Don't be afraid, they won't. Now we . . ." Chelkash looked round triumphantly. "It's finished, we've done it! . . . There! You can be happy now, you blockhead! . . ."

Gavrila kept his mouth shut as he rowed, breathing heavily and looking sideways in the direction where the fiery sword still rose and fell. He could not believe it was only a searchlight. The cold azure gleam, which had severed the darkness and forced the sea to glitter silver, had something inexplicable about it, and Gavrila again subsided into a hypnotically depressing fear. He rowed mechanically, hunched up as if expecting to be struck from above, and he had no desire left in him—he was emptied and dispirited. The excitements of that night had finally gnawed all human elements out of him.

Chelkash felt triumphant. His nerves, accustomed to shocks, had already calmed down. His mustaches quivered voluptuously, and a fire kindled in his eyes. He felt wonderful, whistled through his teeth, breathed deep the moist sea air, glanced in all directions, and smiled with good humor whenever his eyes rested on Gavrila.

The breeze stirred and woke the sea, suddenly agleam with a multitude of ripples. The clouds seemed to grow finer and more transparent, but they covered the whole of the sky. Though the breeze, slight as yet, moved freely over the sea, the clouds remained immobile, seemingly pondering some gray, despondent thought.

"Well, brother, pull yourself together, it's time! Funny thing—you look as if all the breath had been squeezed out of your body, leaving only a bag of bones! The end of everything, eh! . . ."

Gavrila was glad to hear a human voice, even Chelkash's.

"I hear," he replied quietly.

"Well that's it! Soft as fresh bread. . . . Come and take the rudder now. I'll take the oars. You must be tired out, you must!"

Gavrila mechanically changed his place. When Chelkash changed places with him and saw his face, and noticed him staggering about on trembling legs, he felt even more sorry for the lad. He slapped him on the back.

"There, there, don't quake! You've earned a pile. I'll reward you richly, brother. Would you like to get a twenty-five-ruble note, would you? Eh?"

"I don't need anything. I only want to get on shore. . . ."

Chelkash made a hopeless gesture, spat, and began to row, throwing the oars far back with his long arms.

The sea stirred. It shimmered with small waves, gave birth to them, fringed them with foam, made them collide with each other, and smashed them to fine spray. The foam, melting, hissed and sighed—and everything in the vicinity was alive with the music of water splashing. The darkness had somehow become more animated.

"Well, tell me," Chelkash began, "you'll go home to your village, get married, start digging the earth, sowing grain, your wife will have a swarm of children, there'll be a shortage of food; well, there you'll be crawling out of your skin all your life. . . . Well, what then? Much relish in that?"

"What relish is that!" Gavrila replied.

In places, the wind tore gaps in the clouds, revealing light-blue patches of sky with one or two stars set in them. Reflected in the shimmering sea, these tiny stars leapt about on the waves, now vanishing, now gleaming again.

"Harder to port!" Chelkash exclaimed. "We'll be there very soon. Y-yes! . . . We've finished. An important job! See how it's done? . . . Just one night, and I've picked up five hundred!"

"Five hundred?" Gavrila drawled suspiciously, but took fright immediately and, pushing the bales in the boat with his foot, quickly asked: "And what sort of a thing would this be?"

"That's an expensive thing. If one were to sell it all at its real value, it would bring in well over a thousand. Well, I'm not so demanding. . . . Smart, isn't it?"

"Y-yes," Gavrila drawled questioningly. "If I could only pull off something like that!" he sighed, remembering at once his own village, his miserable household, his mother and all those far-off things, so dear to him, for the sake of which he had gone in search of work and had worn himself out this very night. . . . A wave of memories swept over him: his village, descending toward a small river hidden in a grove of birches, willows, rowan trees, and bird-cherry . . . "Ah, it would really be something!" he sighed glumly.

"Y-yes! . . . I fancy you'd make straight home by rail. . . . And the girls at home would just love you, and how! . . . Take your pick! You'd build yourself a wooden cottage—well, for a cottage the money wouldn't stretch too far, I suppose. . . ."

"That's true. There wouldn't be enough for a cottage. Timber's expensive in our parts."

"Never mind. You'd put the old hut in order. How about a horse? Have you got one?"

"A horse? There's a horse, but it's on its last legs, the devil take it!"

"Well, you'd get another horse. A *good* horse! A cow . . . Sheep . . . Fowl of every sort . . . Eh?"

"Say no more! . . . Oh Lord! That would be a life!"

"Y-yes, brother, it wouldn't be a bad life. . . . I also understand what's what in this matter. I had my own nest once. . . . My father was one of the richest ones in our village."

Chelkash rowed slowly. The boat rolled as the waves playfully splashed against its sides; it hardly moved through the dark sea, which, in its play, grew rougher and rougher. Two men were now dreaming as they swayed upon the water and stared musingly about them. Chelkash, wishing to cheer up and reassure Gavrila a little, began to turn his thoughts back to his native village. At first he spoke, smiling into his mustaches; but then, as he talked on and reminded Gavrila of the joys of that peasant life in which he himself had long ago become disillusioned, which he had forgotten and only now remembered, he was gradually carried away and, instead of questioning the boy about the village and its affairs, he, talking to himself, began giving his own opinions:

"The main thing about peasant life—is freedom, brother! You're your own master! You have your own cottage—it may be worth very little, but it's your own. You have your own land—a handful merely—but it's yours, too! A king you are on your own land! . . . You have a face of your own. . . . You can demand respect for yourself from anyone. . . . Isn't that so?" Chelkash ended with animation.

Gavrila, growing animated himself, looked at him with curiosity. During this conversation he had forgotten with whom he was dealing, and saw before him merely another peasant like himself, stuck for ages to the soil by the sweat of many generations, tied to it by childhood memories, voluntarily separated from it and its cares, and duly punished for this separation.

"That's true, brother! Ah, how true! Now just look at yourself. What are you now without any land? The land's like a mother—you can't forget it for long."

Chelkash had second thoughts. . . . He felt the irritating, burning sensation in his chest that always manifested itself whenever his vanity—the vanity of a reckless daredevil—was rubbed the wrong way by anyone, especially by a man he considered of no value.

"Grinding away, you are!" he exclaimed fiercely. "You fancied maybe I took it all seriously. . . . You should keep your wits about you!"

"You're an odd one, really odd!" said Gavrila, timidly again. "Was it you I was talking about? There are a lot of men like you! Oh, how many unhappy people there are in the world! Homeless wanderers!"

"Take the oars now, you lout!" Chelkash barked curtly, for some reason restraining a whole torrent of violent swear words gushing to his throat.

They changed places again; and Chelkash, as he clambered over the bales toward the steering oar, restrained a keen desire to kick Gavrila into the water.

Their brief conversation ended here, but now even Gavrila's silence was, for Chelkash, redolent with the peasant countryside. . . . Reviewing the past, he forgot to steer the boat, which had now turned off course in the excitement of it all and was heading toward the open sea. The waves seemed to understand that this boat had lost direction and, tossing it higher, toyed lightly with it as they flashed azure, tender and gleaming. Scenes of the past flashed through Chelkash's mind—scenes of the remote past divided from the present by the solid wall of his eleven years as a hobo. He had time to see himself as a child, to see his village, his mother, a plump red-cheeked woman with kindly gray eyes, and his father, a red-bearded giant with a stern face; he saw himself as a bridegroom and his wife, the black-eyed Anfisa, with a long plait of hair, buxom, soft, cheerful; and then himself again as a handsome soldier in the Guards; his father again, already gray and stooped from labor, and his mother, wrinkled and bent; he saw the scene, too, of his reception by the village on his return from the army; he saw the pride his father had taken in him, his son Gregory, a sturdy, mustachioed soldier, smart and handsome. . . . Memory, the scourge of the unhappy, animates even the stones of the past and adds a few drops

of honey even to the poison imbibed once upon a
time. . . .

Chelkash felt himself bathed in a tender, reconciling
dream of his native air, which had brought with it to his
ears both the tender words of his mother and the forth-
right speeches of his fervently peasant father, as well as
a multitude of forgotten sounds and a variety of juicy
smells emanating from Mother Earth, just thawing or
plowed or only recently covered with the emerald silk
of winter crops. . . . He felt himself alone, uprooted, and
cast out forever from that order of life from which the
blood in his veins had come into being.

"Hey! Where are we going?" Gavrila suddenly asked.

Chelkash started and glanced around with the watchful look of a beast of prey.

"Look where the devil's brought us! . . . Stick the oars
in deeper. . . ."

"Been thinking?" Gavrila asked, smiling.

"I'm tired. . . ."

"So we won't get run in now because of this?" Gavrila
asked, prodding the bales with his foot.

"No . . . Be easy. I'll hand the stuff over very soon and
get the dough. . . . Y-yes!"

"Five hundred?"

"No less."

"That's quite a sum! If only the likes of me could get
that much! . . . Ah, I'd make the money sing."

"Peasantlike?"

"That's the measure! At once I'd . . ."

And Gavrila flew off on the wings of his dream. Chelkash kept silent. His mustaches drooped, his right side
was wet from the splashing waves, his eyes looked sunken
and lusterless. All that suggested the beast of prey about
him had now become soft, shaded by the humility and
thoughtfulness now apparent even in the folds of his
dirty shirt.

He swung the boat around sharply and steered it toward a black-looking shape sticking out of the water.

The sky was once more covered with clouds, and rain
began to fall, fine, warm rain, pattering merrily as it hit
the crests of the waves.

"Stop! Quietly!" Chelkash commanded.

The boat nosed up to a ship.

"Are they asleep, the devils?" Chelkash growled, seizing hold of a dangling cable with a boat-hook. "Lower the gangway! . . . Now we have the rain—couldn't it have started earlier! Hey, you sponges! . . . Hey there!"

"That iz Selkash." came a welcoming murmur from above.

"Well, lower the ladder!"

"Kalimera, Selkash!"

"Lower the ladder, you smoked devil!" Chelkash roared.

"Oh, you iz very angry today . . . Eloy!"

"Up you go, Gavrila!" Chelkash said.

In a minute they were on deck, where three dark, bearded figures, animatedly chattering in a strange sibilant language, were looking down into Chelkash's boat. The fourth, wrapped in a long loose gown, came up to him and silently gripped his hand, and then glanced suspiciously at Gavrila.

"Get the money ready for tomorrow," Chelkash told him briefly. "Now I'm off to sleep. Let's go, Gavrila! Do you want a bite?"

"I'd rather sleep," Gavrila replied, and within five minutes he was snoring, while Chelkash, sitting beside him, tried on a pair of boots, spat reflectively to one side, and whistled sadly through his teeth. Then he stretched out beside Gavrila, his hands tucked beneath his head and his mustaches bristling.

The ship swayed gently on the swell; somewhere wood creaked plaintively; the rain pattered softly on the deck; and the waves splashed against the sides. . . . It was a mournful scene and sounded like a cradle song crooned by a mother who held out no hope for the future happiness of her son. . . .

Chelkash, showing his teeth, raised his head, glanced around and, whispering something, stretched out again. . . . Spreading out his legs, he resembled a pair of large scissors.

3

Chelkash was the first to awake and, having glanced around him anxiously, felt reassured; he then gazed at the still sleeping Gavrila, who was snoring, a smiling expression on his childlike, healthy, and sunburned face. He sighed and then mounted the narrow rope ladder. A leaden lump of sky showed through the open hatch. It was light already, but autumnally dull and gray.

Chelkash reappeared in about a couple of hours. His face was red, his mustaches were twirled up. He now wore a pair of sturdy top boots, a jacket, and leather trousers. He looked like a hunter. The whole of his getup was rather worn, but still serviceable, and suited him very much, making him look broader and less gaunt, and giving him a military appearance.

"Hey, you calf, get up!" he cried, pushing Gavrila with his foot.

Gavrila jumped up and, not recognizing him in his still sleepy state, stared apprehensively at him with bleary eyes. Chelkash burst out laughing.

"So that's what you're like!" Gavrila blurted out at last, smiling broadly. "You're a gent now!"

"It doesn't take long for the likes of us! But you're a scared rabbit all right! How many times were you on the point of dying last night?"

"But judge for yourself. I'm a greenhorn at this business! My soul might have been damned forever!"

"And you'd try it again, eh?"

"Again? . . . That's—what shall I call it? And how much would it bring? . . . That's the point!"

"And what if it be a couple of 'rainbows'?"

"A couple of hundred, you mean? That's all right. . . . It's possible. . . ."

"But hold! What about the perdition of your soul?"

"Maybe there won't be any . . . perdition!" Gavrila replied with a smile.

"There won't, and you'll be a man for the rest of your

life," Chelkash said with a merry laugh. "Well, that's fine! Enough joking. Let's make for shore. . . ."

Soon they were in the boat again. Chelkash held the steering oar; Gavrila, the oars. The gray sky above them was covered with clouds, and the turbidly gray sea played with their boat, heaving it noisily on the waves, which, though still small, splashed them boisterously with bright salty spray. Far in front of the bow of the boat could be seen a yellow strip of sandy beach, while the sea astern stretched to the horizon. Many ships were visible in the distance and far to the left rose a whole forest of masts and a mass of white town houses. A muffled, reverberating roar poured over the sea from that direction and, together with the splashing of the waves, created a pleasant, compelling music. . . . And over it all was spread a thin layer of ashy mist, blotting out every object. . . .

"Ah, it will really start flowing by evening!" Chelkash exclaimed, nodding at the sea.

"A storm?" Gavrila queried, mightily harrowing the waves with powerful thrusts of his oars. He was already wet from head to foot from the sea spray cast up by the wind.

"Looks like it!" Chelkash confirmed.

Gavrila looked searchingly at him.

"Well, how much did they give you?" he asked at length, seeing that Chelkash was not inclined to talk.

"There!" said Chelkash, holding out something he took from his pocket.

Gavrila saw the notes of many different colors, and everything in his eyes assumed the bright hues of a rainbow.

"Ah! And I thought you might lie to me! . . . How much is there?"

"Five hundred and forty!"

"That's smart!" Gavrila whispered, his greedy eyes following the five hundred and forty rubles, which Chelkash now tucked away once more into a pocket. "Ah, yes! . . . With that money! . . ." And he sighed despondently.

"We'll make a splash of it in town, lad!" Chelkash cried with enthusiasm. "Yes, we'll hit the town. . . . You mustn't fancy I'll give you—— Forty is all I'll give you! Ah? Will that satisfy you? I'll hand it to you now if you wish."

"If it's no trouble—why, I'll take it!"

Gavrila quivered all over, with prickly expectation sucking at his heart.

"Ah, you devil's spawn! 'I'll take it!' Take it, brother, please take it! I implore you, take it! I don't know where to stuff such a pile of money! Relieve me of it. Here, take it! . . ."

Chelkash held out several notes. Gavrila seized them with a trembling hand, let go the oars, and began to stuff them under his shirt, his eyes squinting greedily and his lips noisily sucking in the air as if he were drinking something very hot. Chelkash kept glancing at him with an ironic smile. . . .

Gavrila grabbed the oars and, with eyes lowered, began rowing fast and furiously, as if frightened. His shoulders and ears quivered.

"Ah, you're a greedy guts! . . . That's not good. . . . However, what does it matter? . . . A peasant . . ." Chelkash thought.

"The things one could do with the money!" Gavrila exclaimed, flaring up suddenly in passionate excitement. And he began to talk fast and spasmodically, as if trying to catch up with his own thoughts and to seize words in flight, speaking of life in his village with and without money. Money brought respect, plenty, enjoyment!

Chelkash heard him attentively, a serious expression on his face, and his eyes seemed concentrated on a thought. At times he smiled a smile of satisfaction.

"We've arrived!" he interrupted Gavrila.

A wave picked up the boat and shoved it neatly into the sand.

"Well, brother, it's over now. We'll pull the boat in as far as we can, so it's not washed away. They'll fetch it. But it's good-by for the two of us! . . . It's about five miles to town. What are you going to do? Go back to town, eh?"

A good-natured, cunning smile lighted Chelkash's face, and he looked, every inch of him, like a man who held something very pleasant for himself and something unexpected for Gavrila. Thrusting a hand into his pocket, he made a rustling sound with the notes.

"No . . . I . . . won't go . . . I . . ." Gavrila replied, breathing hard and choking.

Chelkash stared at him.

"What's gnawing at you?" he asked.

"It's just . . ." But Gavrila, his face turning now red, now gray, shuffled on one spot as if he either wished to throw himself upon Chelkash or was torn by another wish hard to carry out.

The sight of the lad's extreme agitation made Chelkash feel strange. He waited for the agitation to burst out.

Gavrila began to laugh in a queer way that sounded like sobbing. He held his head lowered; Chelkash could not see the expression of his face, but noticed his vaguely outlined ears turning now red, now pale.

"The devil take you!" exclaimed Chelkash with a hopeless gesture of his hand. "Have you fallen in love with me or what? He's like a girl who doesn't know what to say! . . . Or are you so sick at the thought of our separation? Hey, you suckling babe! Spit it out, will you! Or I'll go my way!"

"You're going?" Gavrila yelled suddenly in a ringing voice.

The deserted, sandy beach shuddered at his shout, and the yellow, surf-washed waves of sand seemed to stir. Chelkash was startled. Gavrila, suddenly breaking away from where he stood, threw himself at Chelkash's feet, put his arms around them, and jerked them to him. Chelkash staggered, sat down heavily on the sand and, gritting his teeth, abruptly raised the clenched fist of his long arm in the air. But arrested by Gavrila's apologetic, imploring voice, he didn't have time to strike.

"Be an angel . . . and give me that money! Give me it, all of it, for Christ's sake! It's nothing to you. . . . You can get as much in a night . . . a single night. . . . But it would take me years to— Give it to me—I'll pray for you! Eternally—in three churches—for the salvation of your soul! . . . You'd only chuck this money to the winds . . . but I'd put it into the soil! Oh, do give it to me! It's nothing to you. . . . Or is that too much for you? You can strike it rich in just one night! Do a good deed for once! You're a lost soul anyway. . . . There's no way out for you. . . . But I would . . . Oh! Give me that money!"

Chelkash, frightened, astonished, and angry, sat on the sand, leaning back and straining to push him off with his hands; he sat there in silence and stared goggle-eyed at the lad whose head was pressed against his knees and who gasped his prayers in a whisper. He pushed Gavrila away, finally scrambled to his feet and, thrusting his hand in his pocket, threw the notes at his feet.

"Here you are! Gobble them up," he cried out, trembling in his agitation, feeling both acute pity and hatred for this greedy slave. And he felt himself a hero once he had thrown down the money.

"I myself wanted to give you more. I was moved to pity yesterday, remembering what life's like in the village. . . . I thought to myself, 'I'll help the lad.' I waited to see what you'd do—ask me for the money or not? And you . . . Ah, you lump of felt! You beggar! . . . How can you torture yourself so for money? Idiot! Ah, greedy devils! . . . They have no respect for themselves. . . . Sell themselves for a copper coin!"

"You're an angel! . . . May Christ save you! Look at me now! I'm . . . rich . . . now! . . ." Gavrila squealed with delight, shaking all over as he stuffed the money under his shirt. "Ah, you're so good! . . . I shan't ever forget it! . . . Never! . . . I'll instruct my wife and children. 'Pray for him,' I'll say!"

Chelkash listened to his sobs of joy, stared at his glistening face distorted by the elation of greed, and felt that he himself—thief and idle fellow that he was, a man uprooted from the soil—could never sink so low, be so greedy and so unself-respecting. He could never be like that! . . . And this thought and feeling, filling him with awareness of his own freedom, kept him on the deserted seashore near Gavrila.

"You've brought me happiness!" Gavrila shouted and, seizing Chelkash's hand, pressed it to his face.

Chelkash held his tongue, grinning like a wolf. Gavrila went on gushing: "And what was I thinking? On the way here . . . I thought . . . I'll whack him—you—with an oar . . . just one whack and all the money would be mine, and I'd dump him—you, I mean—into the sea . . . eh? 'Who'd miss him?' I said. 'And even if they did find him, they wouldn't bother investigating—how it happened and who did it. He's not the sort of man,' I said, 'they'd kick up much fuss about! . . . A man no one needs on this earth! Who'd take his side?' "

"Give me back the money!" Chelkash snarled, gripping Gavrila by the throat.

Gavrila tried to wrench himself away, once, a second time, but Chelkash's other arm encircled him like a snake. . . . There was the rending sound of a shirt being torn, and Gavrila lay sprawling on the sand, his eyes bulging madly, his fingers snatching at the air, and his feet kicking. Chelkash—straight, lean, rapacious—grinned malevolently as he went off into a sarcastic staccato laugh, and the mustache on his keen, angular face bristled. Never in his whole life had he been so painfully punished, and never had he been in such a rage.

"Are you happy now?" he hissed at Gavrila through his laughter and then, turning his back on him, strode away in the direction of the town. But he had not taken five paces when Gavrila, hunching himself like a cat, jumped to his feet and, with a wide sweep of his arm, aimed a round stone at him.

"Take that!" he shouted angrily.

Chelkash grunted, put his hands to his head, tottered forward, spun around toward Gavrila, and fell face down in the sand. Gavrila froze, staring at him. Chelkash moved one of his feet, tried to raise his head and, quivering like a string, suddenly went limp. Then Gavrila started to run toward the distant horizon, where a black tousled cloud hung over the misty steppe and where it was already dark. The waves ran rustling up the sand, merging with it, retiring, and then running back again. The foam hissed, and spray flew through the air.

A drizzle set in, turning quickly into large, solid rain, pouring in thin rivulets out of the sky. These rivulets wove a whole net from the threads of water—a net which at once blotted out the horizons of both steppe and sea. But then Gavrila came running out of the rain again, flying like a bird; running up, he fell on his knees beside Chelkash and tried to turn him over. He suddenly dipped his hand into warm, red, sticky blood. . . . He shuddered and started back; his face looked pale and crazed.

"Brother, try and get up!" he whispered into Chelkash's ear, beneath the drumming of the rain.

Chelkash came to and pushed Gavrila from him, exclaiming in a hoarse voice: "Get out of here!"

"Brother! Forgive me! It was the devil," Gavrila whispered, trembling and kissing Chelkash's hand.

"Go . . . Take yourself off," croaked the other.

"Take the sin of my soul! . . . Forgive me, my brother. . . ."

"Damn you . . . will you get away, you! Go to the devil!" Chelkash suddenly shouted, sitting up on the sand. His face was pale and angry, his eyes were blurred and closed as though he were very anxious to fall asleep. "What more do you want? You've done your bit . . . Go! Off with you!" And he tried to push the now remorseful Gavrila with his foot, but failed to do so; he would have collapsed once more if Gavrila had not held him up by the shoulders. Chelkash's face was now level with Gavrila's. They both looked pale and ghastly.

"Tfu!" Chelkash spat into his hired man's wide-open eyes.

The latter humbly wiped his face with his sleeve and whispered back: "Do what you will. . . . I won't say a word. Forgive me, for Christ's sake!"

"Sniveler! . . . You don't even know how to whore!" Chelkash exclaimed with contempt as he tore off the shirt from under his jacket and, now and then gritting his teeth, began to bandage his head. "Did you take the money?" he squeezed through his teeth.

"I didn't take it, brother! I want nothing of it now! . . . It only brings trouble! . . ."

Chelkash, reaching into the inner pocket of his jacket, pulled out a wad of notes, replaced one of the rainbow notes in his pocket, and tossed the rest to Gavrila.

"Take them and get out!"

"I won't take them, brother. . . . I can't! Forgive me!"

"Grab them, I tell you!" roared Chelkash, his eyes rolling in a terrifying way.

"Forgive me! . . . I will take them then," Gavrila replied timidly, falling on the rain-drenched sand at Chelkash's feet.

"I knew you'd take the money, you sniveling liar!" Chelkash said with conviction and, with an effort, lifting up Gavrila's head by the hair, he thrust the money into his face.

"Take it! Take it! You didn't work for nothing! Grab it. Don't be afraid! Don't be ashamed of having nearly killed a man! You wouldn't have to answer for a man like me. They'd only say 'thank you' if they found out. Here, grab it!"

Gavrila noticed Chelkash laughing, and felt easier. He clutched the banknotes.

"Brother! You'll forgive me, won't you? You won't? Ah," he whined.

"My brother!" Chelkash replied, mimicking his tone as he stood up swaying. "What for? For nothing at all! It's me today, your turn tomorrow. . . ."

"Ah, brother, brother!" Gavrila sighed, sadly shaking his head.

Chelkash faced him with a strange smile, and the rag round his head, growing redder, began to resemble a Turkish fez.

It was raining buckets. The sea growled dourly, and the waves madly thrashed the shore.

The two men stood silent for a time.

"Well, good-by!" Chelkash exclaimed with irony as he walked away. His legs were unsteady as he staggered forward, holding his head strangely as if afraid of losing it.

"Forgive me, brother!" Gavrila implored once more.

"Don't bother!" Chelkash answered coldly, walking on.

He staggered on, supporting his head with the palm of his left hand and pulling at his mustache with the right.

Gavrila watched him depart until he was swallowed up in the rain, which poured down ever more steadily in thin, endless rivulets from the clouds and enveloped the steppe in steely, impenetrable darkness.

Then Gavrila pulled off his soaked cap, crossed himself, glanced at the money clutched in his fist, took a deep, free breath, tucked the money into his shirt, and, with long, firm steps, strode along the seashore in the opposite direction to that taken by Chelkash.

The sea howled, casting up large, heavy waves upon the sandy beach and breaking them up into spray and foam. The rain zealously thrashed both sea and earth . . . the wind sobbed. . . . All around was a steady roaring. . . . Neither sea nor sky could be seen for the rain.

The rain and the spray of the waves very soon had washed away the red stain from the spot where Chelkash had fallen, had washed away from the beach any trace of either Chelkash or the young country boy. . . . And nothing remained on the deserted seashore to remind one of the small drama that had just been enacted between two human beings.

ON THE RAFTS

An Easter Story

Slowly the massive clouds crept over the drowsy river; they seemed to drop lower and lower; on the horizon, their gray wisps seemed to touch the very surface of the rapid and turbid springtide waves and, whenever they touched the water, an impenetrable wall of cloud rose up as though to bar the flow of the river and the passage of the rafts.

And the waves, washing ineffectively against this wall, struggled against it with a low, plaintive moaning, struggled and, thrown back again, scattered left and right into the damp gloom of the fresh spring night.

But the string of rafts glided on, and the horizon shifted before them into a space full of concentrated clouds.

The river banks could not be seen—the night had swallowed them, and the widespread waves of the inundation had pushed them somewhere else.

The river now was like a sea. The sky above it, muffled in clouds, loomed massive, moist, and dreary.

Rapidly the noiseless rafts slid through the water. Then, advancing out of the darkness toward them, a steamer appeared, its funnel ejecting a swarm of bright cheerful sparks and its paddle wheels dully striking the water. . . .

The two side-lanterns on the spreader loomed larger and more bright, while the lantern on the mast itself swayed gently from side to side, winking mysteriously into the darkness.

The intervening space was filled with the noise of churning water and the heavy grunting of the engines.

"Ahoy! Look sharp!" a powerful, chesty voice called out from the rafts.

At the steering oars at the tail end of the raft stood two men: Mitya, the raftman's son, a fair-haired, weakly, thoughtful youth of about twenty; and Sergey, a hired laborer, a morose, healthy fellow with a reddish beard framing a protruding row of strong, large teeth.

"To port!" A loud shout from the forward raft again shook the darkness.

"We know that ourselves! Why yell?" Sergey grumbled as, sighing, he pressed his chest against the steering oar.

"O-ouch! Tug harder, Mitya!"

Mitya, his feet pressed against the wet logs, tugged with his thin arms at the heavy pole of the rudder and coughed in a hoarse way.

"Pull . . . more to port! . . . Hey you devils!" came the anxious, angry shouts from forward.

"Go on yelling! Your shriveled, ailing son couldn't snap a straw over his knees, but you put him at the helm and then yell all over the river. You couldn't hire an extra laborer, you rapacious father-in-law. So, go on straining your gullet now! . . ."

Sergey was now grumbling out loud, apparently having no fear of being overheard, even wishing that he would be.

The steamer sped past the rafts, thudding and sweeping the foaming waves from under the paddle wheels. The logs swayed in the water and the osier branches binding them creaked plaintively, emitting a sort of damp sound.

The lighted portholes of the steamer glared, like a row of fiery eyes, at the river and the rafts, glimmered in bright quivering patches on the agitated water, and then vanished.

The wash splashed strongly against the rafts, the logs leapt, and Mitya, swaying unsteadily and afraid of falling, hung on grimly to the rudder.

"Well, well!" Sergey murmured ironically. "You're doing a dance! Your father will take you to task again . . . Or he'll walk over and give you a few punches in the ribs, and then you'll dance in another way! To starboard now! Pull! . . ."

Sergey, with his arms resilient as steel springs, wielded his oar with great power, dividing the water deeply with it.

Energetic, tall, rather spiteful and mocking, he stood there as if his bare feet were growing out of the logs and, in an attitude of concentration, he peered keenly ahead of him, ready at any moment to change the direction of the rafts.

"Some father you've got! Look at the way he's cuddling Maria! What a devil! He has no shame or conscience! And why don't you go off somewhere, Mitya, and leave these pagan devils? . . . Eh? D'you hear me?"

"I hear you!" Mitya said in a low voice, not looking in the direction where Sergey had seen his father.

" 'I hear!' Ah, you sour brew!" Sergey teased him, laughing. "What a business!" he continued, egged on by Mitya's apathy. "What a devil he is—that old man! Married off his son and walked off with his daughter-in-law, and—he was right! The old bastard!"

Mitya kept silent, staring back at the receding river, where a wall of thick clouds had also formed.

There were clouds everywhere now, and the rafts looked as though they had stopped floating and were standing motionless in that concentrated black water, crushed down by heavy, dark-gray mounds of clouds that, falling from the sky, had obstructed the path.

The river looked like a bottomless pit, girded on all sides by hills reaching up to the sky and cloaked in a close shroud of mist.

It was oppressively quiet all around and the water, as though waiting for something, splashed gently against the rafts. A lot of sorrow and a sort of shy questioning could be detected in that plaintive sound, the only audible one in the night and the one that made the stillness even more marked. . . .

"If only a breeze would blow," Sergey said. "No, we don't need a breeze—a breeze would only bring rain," he contradicted himself, filling his pipe.

A match sputtered, and the sound of hoarse breathing could be heard as he sucked at the stem of his pipe, the passage of which was clogged, and a red light, now brighter, now dimming, lit up Sergey's broad face as it loomed and vanished in the darkness.

"Mitya!" he called again. Now he sounded less gloomy, and a mocking note was more clearly discernible.

"Ah?" Mitya answered softly, with his gaze fixed into the distance, where he was examining something with his large, sad eyes.

"How can that be, brother, eh?"

"What?" Mitya responded grumpily.

"You got married?! And the fun of it! How was it all? So you went off with your wife—to bed? And what then?"

"Ahoy there, look out!" a voice boomed over the river.

"Yelling again, that anathema of a father-in-law!" Sergey commented before resuming his topic. "Well, tell me, won't you? Mitya! Tell me, I say! Eh?"

"Leave me alone, Sergey! I've already told you!" Mitya implored in a whisper; but evidently realizing that he couldn't get rid of Sergey, hurriedly began: "Well, we came to the bedroom. And I said to her: 'I can't be a husband to you, Maria. You're a healthy girl, but I'm a frail, sickly man, and I didn't want to get married at all, but father, as it were, forced me—'Get married,' he says, 'and that's all!' 'I,' I said to him, 'don't like the sister-sex, and Maria less than any of them.' It's painful, I know. . . . But I'm no good at this . . . you understand . . . It's filthy and sinful. . . . And children too. . . . One must be responsible to God for them. . . ."

"Filthy!" Sergey squealed out, guffawing. "Well, and what did she do then, your Maria? Eh?"

"Well . . . And she said, 'What am I to do now?' She sits crying there. 'Why don't I please you,' she asks. 'Or am I a monster?' She's a shameless hussy, Sergey! . . . 'With all my health, am I to go to the father-in-law or what?' And I say to her: 'As you will,' I says . . . 'Go where you want. As for me, I can't go against my soul. . . . Granddad Ivan used to say, "It's a sinful business, this." Are we beasts, you and I, or what?' . . . And she goes on crying. 'You're the ruin of my maiden beauty,' she says. I felt pity for her. 'It's nothing,' I say, 'we'll manage somehow. Or go into a convent,' I says. Then she starts abusing me: 'You're a fool, Mitya,' she says, 'a scoundrel.' "

"Oh Lord!" Sergey hissed admiringly. "So you cut her off—told her to go into a convent?"

"That's what I told her," Mitya replied simply.

"And she called you a fool?" asked Sergey, raising his voice.

"Yes . . . she abused me."

"She had reason to, brother! She had reason! You should have been trounced too!" Sergey said, changing his tone. Now he was speaking both severely and suggestively. "How can you go against the law? But you did go against it! It's established, and you cut right across it! You couldn't argue, but had to cut it off! So you turned it inside out! Into a convent! Fool that you are! And what does a girl need? A convent? What sort of people have we today? Just think what's come of it! You haven't much to say, but you've ruined a girl. . . . She went over to the old man—and you've led him into sin. How many laws have you broken? What a fool!"

"The law's in the soul, Sergey. There's one law for all: don't do what is against your soul, and you will do no wrong on earth," Mitya said softly and pacifyingly, with a shake of his head.

"So you did it!" Sergey retorted energetically. "In the soul! That's something. . . . There's many a thing in the soul. You can't put a stop on everything. The soul, the soul . . . You must have some notion of it, brother, otherwise, you know . . ."

"No, you haven't got it right, Sergey!" Mitya began hotly, flaring up suddenly. "The soul, brother, is always pure, like a little dewdrop. She's inside a shell, that's what! She's deep too. If you listen to her, you won't go wrong. It will always be Godlike if it's done according to the soul. For God's in the soul, and the law is in her too. She's created of God, breathed into man by God. You only have to know how to see into her. . . . Only you mustn't feel sorry for yourself. . . ."

"Ahoy, you! Sleepy demons! Keep your eyes peeled!" The thundering voice came rolling and rippling over the river.

The very sound of the voice made one feel that it was

the voice of a robust, energetic man, well satisfied with himself and well able to take care of himself. He did not shout because he felt obliged to urge on the raftmen, but because his soul was full of joy and strength—and this joy and strength, demanding release, had finally burst forth in this thundering, energetic shout.

"Hear how he barks, the old devil!" Sergey commented with pleasure, staring keenly ahead. "They're cooing, the little doves! Don't you ever feel jealous, Mitya?"

Mitya gazed indifferently in the direction of the forward oars, where two figures ran over the raft from right to left, stopping close to each other and at times fusing into one dense dark mass.

"Not jealous?" Sergey repeated the question.

"What's it to me? It's their sin—their responsibility," Mitya gently replied.

"So-o!" Sergey drawled ironically as he stuffed some more tobacco into his pipe. Again there was a red gleam in the dark.

But the night thickened, and the gray clouds, the black clouds, dropped lower and lower over the wide, quiet river.

"Where did you pick up all that wisdom, Mitya, eh? Or were you born with it? You don't take after your father. Your father's a hero. Just look at him—he's going on fifty, but what a queen of a woman he's cuddling! That woman's pure sap. And she loves him—you can't deny that! She loves him, brother. You can't help loving an ace like that! A king of aces, that buzzard of a father of yours. It's a delight to see him at work. He has great quality, enough repute to spare some, and his head's in the right place. Y-yes! But you don't take after either your mother or your father. Mitya? What would your father do if your mother, the deceased Anfisa, were still living? A strange business it would be! I'd have watched her give it to him. . . . She was a woman too, a strong one, your mother. A match for Silan."

Mitya was silent, leaning on his oar and staring at the water.

Sergey also kept silent. From the rafts ahead came a woman's ringing laughter. A man's deep laugh blended

with it. In the patchy darkness their figures were hardly
visible to Sergey, who peered inquisitively at them
through the dark. One could make out that the man
was tall and that he was standing by his oar with his
legs wide apart, half-turned toward a small, rounded
woman who was leaning with her bosom against the other
oar some three yards away from the first oar. She was
shaking her finger at the man and laughing with a
bubbling eagerness. Sergey turned away with a sigh of
distress and, after a concentrated silence, spoke again:

"Ah! It's cosy for them there. Very nice! A rolling
stone like me wouldn't mind being in their place! Not
for the life of me would I have left such a woman!
Ah, you! I'd hold and fondle her and not let go. 'Here,
feel how much I love you.' . . . The devil! But I haven't
any luck with women. . . . Evidently they don't like
redheads, the women. Y-yes. She's capricious, that
wench. . . . Ah, the hussy! She's greedy for life. Mitya!
Are you asleep?"

"No," Mitya answered softly.

"S-so! How will you go through life, brother! To
speak the truth—you're as lonely as your little finger.
That's hard! What will you do with yourself now? You
won't be able to find a living for yourself among people
now. You're too strange. Is he a man who can't stand
up for himself? It's teeth and claws one needs, brother.
Every one will ride it over you. How can you defend
yourself? Defend yourself with what? Ah, you! You're
a strange one! Where are you going?"

"I?" Mitya asked, coming to life. "I'll go off, brother.
Off in the autumn—to the Caucasus, and that'll be the
end of it! Oh Lord! The sooner I get away from you all,
the better! Soulless people! You're a godless lot—to run
away from you is salvation! Why are you living?
Where is your God? You talk the same, all of you.
. . . Are you living according to Christ? Ah, you—
wolves that you are! But there are other people, their
souls alive in Christ, and their hearts bear love, and
they suffer for the salvation of the world. And you?
Ah, you! Wild beasts, roaring filth! There are other people. I have seen them. They called me. I am going to
them. They brought me the Holy Writ. 'Read it, man

of God,' they said, 'read the true word, our beloved brother! . . .' And I read it, and my soul was reborn of God's word. I shall go off. I'll abandon you, mad wolves that feed on each other's flesh. Damnation upon you!"

Mitya said this in a passionate whisper, choking with the overpowering emotions of contempt and rage against the mad wolves and of thirst for the people whose souls were concerned with the salvation of the world.

Sergey was staggered. He stood silent with his mouth wide open and holding his pipe in his hand; he thought for a while, glanced around him, and then said in a thick, gloomy voice: "See how you're biting into it! And angry too. Pity you ever read that book. Who knows what sort of thing it is? Well . . . be off, be off, lose yourself, or you'll spoil altogether. Ai-ai! Run away before you go wild. . . . And what sort of people are those in the Caucasus? Monks? Or maybe Old Believers? Are they Molokans or what? Eh?"

But Mitya's flame died down as quickly as it had flared up. He tugged at his oar, panting hard from the effort and whispering something rapidly and nervously to himself.

Sergey waited awhile for his answer, which was not forthcoming. The depressing, deadly still night weighed down on his healthy, uncomplicated nature; he felt like reminding himself of being alive by disturbing this stillness with shouts, by disturbing it in every way, and alarming this quiet, contemplative silence of the inert watery mass slowly pouring down toward the sea, and the motionless mounds of clouds drearily stuck there in the sky. Life was throbbing at the other end of the raft, and this made him want to live.

Ahead, he could catch the sound of gentle, contented laughter, broken exclamations, shaded by the silence and darkness of that night so full of the scents of spring, which stimulated a feverish desire to live.

"Stop it, Mitya. Where are you taking us? The old man will turn on you," Sergey said at last, unable to bear the silence and noticing that Mitya was aimlessly digging his oar into the water. Mitya stopped, wiped his perspiring forehead and stood still, leaning with his chest on the oar and breathing heavily.

"Not many steamers today somehow. . . . Only one's turned up so far, though we've been floating a good many hours. . . ."

Perceiving that Mitya was not going to reply, Sergey reasoned it out for himself: "It's because the navigation hasn't started properly yet. It's just beginning. We'll float down to Kazan in a jiffy—the Volga's got a mighty pull. She's got a heroic backbone—she can lift anything. What's struck you dumb? Angry, are you, Mitya? Eh?"

"Well, what is it?" Mitya asked grumpily.

"Nothing. You're such an odd fellow. . . . Why so silent, I say? Are you thinking all the time? Drop it. It's harmful. Ah, you, wise man, churning over your wisdom all the time, but you don't know you haven't got any common sense! Ha-ha!"

And Sergey, having laughed and heaved a noisy sigh, fell silent for a moment, then tried to whistle but cut it short, and finally proceeded to develop his thought further: "Thinking! Is that an occupation for a simple man? There, look, your father doesn't try to be wise— he just lives. He's being nice to your wife, and they laugh at you together—you wise fool. That's the way it is! And how are they making out? Blast them, you say! Sure Maria is already pregnant! You needn't be afraid; the child won't be like you. He'll be as much of a dare-devil, we must suppose, as Silan Petrov. But the child will be registered as yours. What a business! Ha! 'Daddy!' he'll call you. But you'll be no daddy to him, but his brother. And his real daddy will be his grand-dad! Really smart, that! Vile, isn't it? And yet they're daring folk! Isn't that so, Mitya?"

"Sergey!" came a passionate, agitated, almost sobbing whisper. "For Christ's sake, I beg you, don't tear at my soul, don't burn me, leave me alone! Keep your mouth shut! By the divine Christ I beg you, don't talk to me, don't poison me, don't suck my blood. I'll jump into the river, and then you'll have a great sin on your soul! I'll destroy my soul—don't touch me! For God's sake—I beg you!"

A painful screeching howl tore through the silence of

the night, and Mitya collapsed on the logs where he
stood, as though he had been hit by something heavy
that had fallen on him from above, out of the frowning clouds hanging over the black river.

"Well, well, well!" Sergey growled apprehensively,
watching his companion writhing on the logs as though
he had been scorched by fire. "You're a strange character! An odd fellow . . . you should have told me
. . . if you weren't . . . if it wasn't . . ."

"You've been tormenting me all the way—for what?
An enemy, am I, of yours? Ah? An enemy?" Mitya
asked in a heated whisper.

"You're an odd one, brother! Very odd!" Sergey muttered, hurt and confused. "How did I know? Your soul's
unknown to me!"

"I want to forget it, d'you understand! Forget it for
the rest of my life! My shame . . . my raging torment
. . . you're a savage lot! I'll go away! I'll go forever.
. . . I can't take it. . . ."

"Yes, go off with you!" Sergey blurted out for the
whole river to hear, fortifying his exclamation with a
thundering, cynical swear word. Then he stopped short,
hunching himself up and squatting down, evidently also
crushed by the spiritual drama that had unfurled itself
before him and that he now could not help understanding.

"Hey, you!" Silan Petrov's voice boomed over the
river. "What's going on there? What are you barking
at? Eh?"

Silan Petrov must have liked breaking the dense silence of the river with his deep, strong voice. The shouts
poured out, one after another, shaking the warm, moist
air, crushing with their vital force Mitya's puny figure,
which stood once again by the oar. Sergey, answering
his boss with full lungs, swore at him at the same time
in a lower voice, using all the salty expressiveness of
the Russian vocabulary. Two voices tore the silence of
the night, rousing and shaking it, now blending into one
dense note as rich as the sound of a big brass tuba,
now rising to a falsetto, and they floated in the air,
faded, and died away. Then silence again succeeded.

Through a rift in the clouds some heavy patches of

moonlight fell on the dark waters and, glimmering there for a minute, vanished, obliterated by the humid darkness.

The rafts floated on further in the darkness and the silence.

2

Silan Petrov stood by one of the forward oars; he was wearing a red shirt with the collar unbuttoned and displaying his powerful neck and his hairy chest, solid as an anvil. A cap of gray hair hung over his forehead, and from under it a pair of large, burning, hazel eyes smiled ironically. His sleeves rolled up to the elbow bared his muscular forearms and hands, which firmly gripped the oar, and with his body leaning slightly forward he keenly scrutinized the dark, distant horizon.

Maria stood sideways to the current, about three paces away from him, and kept smiling at the broad-chested figure of her man. They were both silent, concentrating on their scrutiny: his, of the horizon; and hers, on the play of his bearded, animated face.

"Must be a fisherman's campfire!" he exclaimed, turning to face her. "It's all right! Let's keep her straight! O-och!" He blew out a whole pillar of hot air, smoothly dropping his oar into the water on the left and pulling it strongly through the water. "Now, don't pull so hard, Mashka!" he commented, seeing that she had also applied herself smartly to her oar.

Round and full, with lively black eyes and pink cheeks, barefoot and wearing only a wet sarafan, which clung closely to her body, she now turned her face to Silan and said with a tender smile: "You're taking very good care of me! The Lord be praised!"

"I'm kissing you, not taking care of you!" Silan replied, shrugging his shoulders.

"That doesn't leave a trace!" she whispered provokingly.

They fell silent, looking greedily at each other.

The water murmured reflectively under the rafts. In

the distance, somewhere to the right, cocks began to crow.

The rafts, swaying barely perceptibly underfoot, glided forward into the thinning, melting darkness, while the clouds assumed sharper outlines and lighter hues.

"Silan Petrovich! Do you know what they were squealing about over there? I know, on my word, I know! That Mitya was complaining about you to Sergey, and he moaned so pitifully that Sergey swore at us."

Maria stared searchingly into Silan's face, which now, after her words, looked severe and coldly stubborn.

"Well, and what about it?" he asked curtly.

"Just so. Nothing."

"If it's nothing, you shouldn't have spoken."

"You mustn't be angry!"

"At you? I'd like to be sometimes, but I haven't the guts."

"Do you love your Mashka?" she asked him in a teasing whisper as she bent over him.

"Akh!" Silan grunted expressively and, stretching out his strong hands toward her, gritted through his teeth: "Go off with you. . . . Don't play about. . . ."

She arched like a cat and clung to him softly.

"We'll get the rafts all piled up!" he whispered, kissing her face as it burned under his lips.

"Enough now! It's getting light. . . . They can see us already from that end," she said.

She tried to push herself away from him. But he held her all the more firmly with his hand.

"See us? Let them see us! Let them all see us! I spit on all of them. It's as if I were sinning. I know that. But what about it? I'll answer for it to the Lord. Anyway you weren't his real wife. You're free, that's what, you're on your own. . . . It's hard for him! I know that. But what about me? It isn't so flattering to be entangled with one's daughter-in-law. Supposing even you're no wife to him . . . and yet! How am I to be now—with my self-respect? And isn't it sin before God? Sin! I know it all! And yet I transgressed. Because—it was worth it. One lives in the world only once, and one may die any day. Ah, Maria! If I'd only waited a month before marrying off Mitya, this wouldn't have come about! No, after

Anfisa's death I would have sent the matchmakers to you—and that would have been that! Everything within the law, without sin, without shame! It was my mistake. It'll take five—ten years off my life, it will, this mistake. I'll die before my term. . . ."

"Well, all right, don't work yourself up. We've spoken about this more than once," Maria whispered and, quietly disengaging herself from his embraces, walked over to her oar. Silan began to apply himself to work powerfully and impulsively, as if wishing to rid himself of a burden that had fallen on his chest and had cast a shadow on his handsome face.

It was growing light.

And the thinning clouds spread lazily over the sky as though they wished to obstruct the rising sun. The waters of the river assumed the cold, glittering appearance of steel.

"He talked to me again awhile ago. 'Father,' he said, 'isn't this a shame and a disgrace to both you and me? Give her up!' He meant you, of course," Silan Petrov said with an ironic smile. " 'Give her up,' he said, 'be reasonable.'—'Son,' I said, 'my dear son, get out of my way if you want to remain alive! Or I'll tear you to bits like a rotten rag. There will be nothing left of your virtue. Were you born to torment me, you degenerate?' There he was trembling. 'Father,' he says, 'am I to blame?' —'You're to blame,' I says, 'you squeaking mosquito, because you're a stone in my path. You're to blame,' I says, 'because you don't know how to stand up for yourself. You're just dead matter,' I says, 'rotten carrion. If,' I says, 'you was healthy, I could at least have killed you, but I can't even do that. It's pity I have for you, you unfortunate manikin.' He began to howl. Akh, Maria! People are no good these days! Another man would have acted! Got himself out of that noose quick enough. But we're still stuck there! Yes, and maybe we'll end by strangling each other."

"What are you talking about?" Maria asked timidly, looking with apprehension at this severe, powerful, and cold man.

"Just so . . . If he died . . . That's it. If he died . . . it would be a smart thing! Everything would fall into place. I'd give your folks the ground I own; I'd stuff their throats with it, and go off with you . . . to Siberia . . . or the Kuban! 'Who's she?' 'My wife!' D'you understand? We'd obtain the necessary document—a paper. I'd open a shop somewhere in a village. And we'd live together. And we'd wipe away with prayers our sin before the Lord. How much do we need? We'd help people to live their life, and they'd help to quiet our conscience. . . . That would be good! Wouldn't it, Masha?"

"Y-yes!" she sighed and, shutting her eyes, plunged into deep thought.

They were silent for a while. . . . The water made a rippling sound.

"He's got no life in him. . . . Maybe he'll die soon," Silan Petrov said gruffly.

"May it be soon, O Lord." Maria breathed a prayer and made the sign of the cross.

The beams of the spring sun splashed forth and shimmered on the water in gold and rainbow hues. A breeze blew; everything quivered, came to life, and looked happy. The blue sky amid the clouds also smiled at the sun-painted water. The clouds had now been left behind the rafts.

There, gathering in a dark, weighty mass, they stood pondering and motionless over the wide river, as if picking a path that would lead them more quickly away from the living spring sun, so rich in gleaming joy and so hostile to them, the mothers of winter blizzards, delaying now their retreat before the onset of spring.

Ahead of the rafts shone a pure, clear sky, and the sun, still cool in the early morning air, but already springtime bright, was climbing imposingly and gracefully ever higher into the azure desert of the sky out of the purplish-golden waves of the river.

To the right of the rafts could be seen a brown, hilly shore hemmed in by a green forest; to the left, a pale emerald carpet of meadows glittered with the diamonds of the dew.

Through the air was wafted the juicy smell of earth, of newly born grass, and the resinous aroma of the conifers.

Silan Petrov glanced back at the steering oars on the
rear raft.

Sergey and Mitya looked as though they were part of
the oars. But it was still difficult to distinguish their features in the distance.

He shifted his eyes to Maria.

She was feeling the chill. Standing by her oar, she had
squeezed herself into a ball and looked completely round.
All glowing in the sunshine, she stared thoughtfully ahead
of her, while on her lips played that enigmatic and en-
chanting smile that can make even an unattractive woman
look charming and desirable.

"Keep your eyes peeled, lads-o! O-o! . . ." Silan Petrov
thundered forth with all his might, feeling a great flow of
energy in his broad chest.

And everything around him seemed to stir at his shout.
On the hilly shore the echo sounded for a long time.

IN THE STEPPE

We strode out of Perekop in the worst of tempers—as famished as wolves and raging against all the world. For the last day and a half we had fruitlessly applied all our talents and efforts either to earn or steal something; and when we finally became convinced that we would succeed in neither endeavor, we decided to go on further. Where? Further—that was all we knew.

We were ready in every respect to continue further on that road of life, which we had already trodden for some time—such was the silent resolve of each of us, and it was brightly reflected in the grim glitter of our hungry eyes.

There were three of us. We had met but recently, having stumbled across each other in Kherson—in a tavern there on the banks of the Dnieper.

One of us, formerly a soldier of the railway battalion and later apparently a railway employee, was a red-haired, muscular man with steely gray eyes; he spoke some German and possessed a very detailed knowledge of prison life.

The likes of us have no fondness for talking much about the past, and we always have more or less solid reasons for this. Thus we all believed each other—at least we believed each other on the face of it, for, inwardly, each of us had very little belief in himself.

Whenever our second companion, a small shriveled man with thin lips always skeptically compressed, spoke of himself as a former student of Moscow University, the soldier and I took this for granted. Fundamentally, we didn't care a damn whether he had been a student, a detective, or a thief. What mattered to us was that, at the time we knew him, he should be on a footing of equality with us: that he should have experienced hunger, received special attention from the police in the towns, and been looked on askance by the peasants in the villages; that he should have hated both the police and the peasants with all the hatred of a homeless, famished beast; and that he should dream of universal revenge toward one and all—in a word, that he should be, both by his position among the kings of nature and the rulers of life, and by his temperament, a berry from the same bush as ourselves.

The third was myself. Out of modesty, so characteristic of me since I first grew my nails, I shall say nothing about my qualities and, unwilling to appear naïve, shall pass over my feelings in silence. But perhaps, by way of some material for a character sketch of myself, I might mention that I have always considered myself to be better than others and have successfully insisted on this up to the present time.

Thus, we walked out of Perekop and marched on further, bearing in mind the shepherds whom one could always ask for a crust of bread. They very seldom refused this to wandering folk.

I walked beside the soldier; the student strode behind us. He had around his shoulders something that reminded one of a jacket; on his head—pointed, angular, and smoothly shaved—there rested the remains of a broadbrimmed hat; his legs were encased in a pair of gray trousers with many-colored patches, and he had fixed to his feet, with the help of string twined from the lining of his clothes, the top of a boot he had found on the way. He gave the name of "sandals" to this construction. He walked on in silence, kicking up a great deal of dust, his small greenish eyes glittering. The soldier wore a red fustian shirt that, according to his words, he had "personally-handed" acquired in Kherson; over his shirt he wore, in addition, a warm woolen vest; on his head, according to all the army regulations—"with the top crown

of the cap bent over the right brow"—a soldier's peaked
cap of indeterminate color; on his legs dangled a pair of
wide *sharovary*.[1] He was barefoot.

I too was clothed but barefoot.

On every side the steppe unfurled in a heroic gesture
and, covered with the blue sultry dome of cloudless sky,
lay there like a vast, round, black dish. The gray dusty
road crossed it in a wide band and scorched our feet.
In places, we came across prickly strips of stubble where
the wheat had been already harvested, and these strips
bore a strange resemblance to the soldier's long unshaven
cheeks.

The soldier walked on, singing in a hoarse bass voice:

"And three of us chant and praise your holy
    resurrection. . . ."

While doing his military service he had acted as a sort
of sexton to the battalion church, and he knew by heart
a countless number of troparions,[2] the opening verses
of hymns, and short hymns in praise of saints, and took
advantage of this knowledge each time our conversation
flagged.

On the horizon in front of us some shapes loomed up,
delicately outlined and tenderly shaded in lilac and pale
pink.

"Must be the Crimean mountains," the student suggested.

"Mountains?" the soldier questioned. "You saw them
much too soon, my friend. Those are . . . clouds. Look at
them—they're like cranberry syrup with milk. . . ."

I remarked that it would have been very pleasant if
the clouds had indeed been made of cranberry syrup.

"Ah, the devil!" the soldier cursed, spitting. "If only
we'd come across one living soul! But there's no one
here. . . . We'll have to suck our own paws, like the
bears do in winter. . . ."

"I said we should move through inhabited places," the
student remarked didactically.

1 *Sharovary*—a type of baggy oriental trousers sometimes worn in
the Ukraine.
2 *Troparion*—a short hymn in the offices of the Greek Church.

"You said!" the soldier retorted indignantly. "That's why you're so learned—just to talk. Where are the inhabited places here? The devil alone knows where they are!"

The student stopped talking and compressed his lips. The sun was setting and the clouds on the horizon shimmered in a variety of hues that escaped description. There was a smell of earth and salt.

This dry, savory smell whetted our appetites still more. There was a sucking void in our bellies. It was a strange and unpleasant sensation: it was as if the juices were slowly flowing out somewhere from all the muscles of the body and were evaporating, and the muscles themselves were losing their vital elasticity. The sensation of prickly dryness filled the palate and the throat, the head felt dizzy, and dark spots danced before the eyes. At times the spots assumed the appearance of smoking pieces of meat and loaves of bread; memory provided these "visions of the past, mute visions," with their appropriate smells, and then it felt as though a knife were being twisted in one's guts.

Nevertheless we strode on, sharing our sensations and keeping a sharp lookout on all sides—in case we might catch sight of a flock of sheep—and listening for the possible creaking of a Tartar wagon loaded with fruit for the Armenian bazaar.

But the steppe was empty and silent.

On the eve of this heavy day the three of us had eaten, between us, four pounds of rye bread and about five watermelons, but we had since then tramped about twenty-six miles—an expenditure of energy over and above our income! Falling asleep then in the market square of Perekop, we had awakened from hunger.

The "student" had very justly advised us not to go to bed, but to occupy ourselves during the night with— But in respectable society it is not customary to talk aloud about projects to violate the rights of property. Therefore I am silent. I only wish to be truthful. It is not in my interest to be crude. I know that people in our highly cultured days are becoming ever more tender of soul and, even when they take their fellow man by the throat with the obvious intention of throttling him, they try to do so with every possible courtesy while still preserving all the conventions appropriate to the occasion. The experience of my own windpipe obliges me to take note of this progress in our behavior; and with a pleasurable feeling of certainty I confirm that everything in this world is evolving and being perfected. In particular, this remarkable process is impressively confirmed by the annual increase in the number of prisons, taverns, and houses of prostitution. . . .

Thus, swallowing our hungry saliva and trying with our friendly conversation to crush the pains in our bellies, we strode on through the deserted, noiseless steppe, in the reddish beams of the sunset. In front of us the sun was quietly dropping down into the soft clouds, which its beams had so generously painted, while behind us, and also on our flanks, the light-blue dusk, rising from the steppe toward the sky, was narrowing down the forbidding horizons.

"Time to gather material for a campfire, brothers," the soldier warned, picking up a stray chip of wood from the roadway. "We'll have to spend the night in the steppe—the dew is out! Thorns, twigs—anything will do!"

We scattered on both sides of the road, gathering up tall dry weeds and everything that would burn. Every time we had to bend to the ground, a passionate desire arose in the body to fall down and eat the earth, the black, fat earth, to eat a lot of it, to eat to the point of exhaustion and then fall asleep. Even to fall asleep forever as long as one could chew and feel the warm, thick mixture slide down slowly from the mouth through the parched alimentary canal into the stomach, which was consumed with desire to absorb something into itself.

"If only we could find some roots," the soldier said with a sigh. "There are such edible roots. . . ."

But in the black, recently plowed earth there were no roots. The southern night advanced rapidly and no sooner had the last sunbeam been extinguished than stars began to gleam in the dark blue sky, while all about us the shadows gathered ever more densely, narrowing down the endless, smoothly spreading steppe. . . .

"Brothers," the student said in a low voice, "there's a man lying down there to the left. . . ."

"A man?" the soldier repeated doubtingly. "And why should he be lying there?"

"Go and ask him. He surely has bread, since he's camping on the steppe."

The soldier glanced in the direction where the man was lying and spat decisively.

"Let's go to him!"

Only the "student's" sharp green eyes could have identified as a man that dark bulk some hundred yards from us to the left of the road. We headed in his direction, stepping briskly over clods of plowed earth, and sensed how the newborn hope of food sharpened the pangs of our hunger. We were getting near, but still the man did not budge.

"Maybe it isn't a man," said the soldier, expressing our general impression.

But our doubts were dispelled at that very moment, for the inert bulk on the ground suddenly stirred, rose up, and we saw that it was really a man, a living man, kneeling with his arm stretched toward us. In a dull, quavering voice he called out: "Keep away or I'll shoot!"

A dry, short click sounded in the turbid air.

We stopped as though by command and were silent for several seconds, staggered by this unpleasant encounter.

"What a son of a gun!" the soldier muttered expressively.

"Yes," the "student" drawled thoughtfully. "He goes about with a revolver . . . evidently a fish well stuffed with roe. . . ."

"Hey!" the soldier shouted, apparently making up his mind.

The man, without changing his attitude, was silent.

"Hey, you! We won't touch you—only give us some bread—do you have any? Give it to us, brother, for Christ's sake! . . . May you be cursed, anathema!"

The soldier spoke these last words into his mustache. The man still kept silent.

"Do you hear?" the soldier called out again with a

quiver of anger and despair. "Give us some bread, I say!
We won't go near you. . . . Just throw it to us. . . ."

"All right," the man answered briefly.

He might have said "My dear brothers!" But even if
he had poured into these three words all the purest and
most sacred emotions, they would not have excited us
as much and made us so human as this brief, dull-sound-
ing phrase, "all right."

"Don't you be afraid of us, my good man," the soldier
said with a gentle smile, even though the man could not
see his smile, since he was now at least twenty paces
away from us.

"We are peaceful folk. . . . We're tramping from Russia
to the Kuban. . . . We got rid of all our money on the way;
we've eaten everything off our backs. . . . And we haven't
had anything to swallow now for the last two days. . . ."

"Catch!" the good man cried out, swinging his arm
through the air. A black hunk flashed by and fell on the
plowed land not far from us. The "student" made a dash
for it.

"Here, catch again! I haven't any more. . . ."

When the "student" had picked up this peculiar offering, it turned out that we now had between us four
pounds of dry wheat bread. It was earth-stained and very
dry. Dry bread is more nourishing than fresh; it contains
less moisture.

"Here . . . and here . . . and here!" said the soldier
as he distributed hunks of bread to us. "Wait . . . that's
not an equal portion! We'll have to pinch off a piece of
yours, professor, or he won't have enough. . . ."

The "student" submitted without demur to the loss of
a piece of bread about an ounce in weight; I, the
recipient, thrust it into my mouth.

And I began to chew on it, chew slowly, barely restraining the convulsive movements of my jaws, which would
have reduced a stone to powder. It gave me acute pleasure
to feel the contractions of the alimentary tract and
satisfy it gradually, drop by drop. Gulp by gulp, the
warm, indescribably succulent drops penetrated into the
stomach and, it seemed, they immediately became transformed there into blood and brain. Joy—such strange,
quiet and revitalizing joy—warmed the heart as the stom-

ach was filled. I forgot about the accursed days of
chronic hunger, forgot about my companions, who were
also immersed in enjoying the sensations I myself experienced.

But when I had pitched the last crumbs from the palm
of my hand into my mouth, I felt a mortal need to eat
more.

"Curses! he must have some lard left there, or meat of
some sort," the soldier growled, sitting on the ground
opposite me and rubbing his belly with his hands.

"That's why the bread had a smell of meat. . . . Yes,
and he must have some bread left over, too," the
"student" said. And then he added softly, "If it hadn't
been for the revolver . . ."

"Who is he?"

"Evidently our brother Isaiah. . . ."

"A dog!" the soldier decided.

We sat close together, staring in the direction where
our benefactor was sitting with his revolver. From
there came no sound, no sign of life.

Night was marshaling its dark forces around us. It was
deadly still in the steppe—and we could hear each other
breathe. Now and then a gopher whistled a melancholy
note. . . . The stars, those living flowers of the steppe,
flamed above us. But we wanted to eat.

I'm proud to say that I was no better or worse than
my chance companions on that rather strange night. I
myself suggested that we get up and go after the man.
We needn't hurt him, but we would eat everything we
could find. If he shot at us—let him! He'd only get one
of three if he hit anyone at all; and even if he did hit,
a revolver bullet would hardly kill one.

"Let's go!" the soldier exclaimed, jumping to his feet.

The "student" rose more slowly.

And off we went, almost running. The "student" kept
behind us.

"Comrade!" the soldier called out to him reproachfully.

Then we heard a dull muttering sound and the click of
a revolver hammer being cocked. There was a flash of
fire, followed by the dry sound of a shot.

"Missed!" the soldier cried joyfully, reaching the man

in one leap. "Ah, you devil, I'll give it to you now. . . ."

The student threw himself toward the knapsack.

The "devil" fell on his back from a kneeling position and, throwing out his arms, groaned hoarsely . . .

"What the hell!" the soldier exclaimed in surprise as he drew back his leg to kick the man. "Did he shoot himself or what? You! Hey, you! Did you shoot yourself or what?"

"There's meat, and buns, and bread . . . lots of it, brothers!" came the student's exulting voice.

"Well, the devil take you, perish then. . . . Let's eat!" the soldier shouted.

I took the revolver from the man's hand; he had already stopped wheezing and now lay immobile. There was a bullet still in the breech.

We ate again in silence. The man lay there in silence, too, without moving a limb. We paid no attention to him.

"Is it only for the sake of bread you did this, brother?" a coarse, trembling voice then suddenly inquired.

We all shuddered. The student even choked and, bending over to the ground, began to cough.

The soldier, chewing his morsel to the end, began to curse.

"Dog's soul that you are! May you break like a dry stick! Shall we flay you or what? What need have we of your skin? You stupid mug, you. Unclean spirit! You arm yourself and shoot at people! Damnation on you! . . ."

He swore and went on eating, and for that reason his swearing lost some of its expressiveness and force. . . .

"You just wait, we'll finish eating and then we'll settle accounts with you," the student spitefully promised.

Then, frightening us, a sobbing howl tore the stillness of the night. "Brothers, and how did I know. I fired because I was afraid. I've been walking all the way from New Athens . . . to get to the Smolensk province. . . . Oh Lord! Fever has worn me out. . . . As soon as the sun sets—I'm done for! It's because of the fever I left New Athens. . . . I was carpentering there. I'm a carpenter. . . . Have a wife at home . . . two daughters . . . haven't seen these two or three years . . . brothers! Eat all you want. . . ."

"We'll eat it up, without your leave," the student said.

"Oh Lord! Had I but known you were peaceful folk, good folk . . . would I have fired at you? But it's the steppe here, nighttime. . . . Am I to blame?"

He talked and sobbed or, rather, uttered a trembling, frightened howl.

"What a whine!" the soldier exclaimed contemptuously.

"He must have money on him," the student declared.

The soldier narrowed his eyes, stared at him, and smiled ironically. "You're a shrewd one. . . . Well, let's start a campfire and turn in. . . ."

"What about him?" the student asked.

"The devil take him! Are we to roast him or what?"

"We should," the student said, nodding his angular head.

We now went off to fetch the firewood, which we had been carrying and which we had dropped when the carpenter stopped us; we carried it over and were soon seated around a fire. It was a windless night and the fire burned quietly, lighting up the small space we occupied. We felt drowsy, although we could have supped again.

"Brothers!" the carpenter called out to us. He lay some three paces away from us, and it seemed to me that he kept whispering to himself from time to time.

"Yes?" the soldier asked.

"Can I move closer . . . to the fire? My death is upon me. . . . My bones are creaking! . . . Oh Lord! Looks as if I won't reach home. . . ."

"Crawl over here," the student said, giving him permission.

Slowly, as though afraid of losing an arm or a leg, the carpenter edged his way over the ground toward the fire. He was a tall man and terribly gaunt; everything seemed to hang loosely on him; and his large turbid eyes reflected his gnawing pain. His distorted face was bony and, even by the light of the campfire, had an earthy yellow, corpselike tint. His whole body trembled, exciting contempt and pity. Holding out his long thin hands toward the fire, he massaged his fingers and their stiff joints yielded slowly, lifelessly. He was, to us, a revolting sight.

"What are you up to . . . in a condition like yours . . . tramping on foot? Are you a miser or what?" the soldier grimly asked.

"They advised me . . . don't cross by water, they said . . . but walk through the Crimea . . . the air there, they said. But I can't go on walking. . . . I'm dying, brothers! I'll die alone in the steppe . . . the birds will peck me to bits, and no one will recognize me after. . . . My wife . . . my daughters will be waiting for me—I wrote them—but the rains of the steppe will wash my bones . . . Oh Lord, Oh Lord!" And here he howled as dismally as a wounded wolf.

"Oh, you devil!" the soldier exclaimed in a rage, and jumped to his feet. "What are you whining for? Why don't you let people rest? You say you're perishing? Well, perish then, but hold your tongue. . . ."

"Let's sleep," I suggested. "And you, if you want to stay by the fire, then don't howl. . . ."

"Do you hear?" the soldier savagely added. "Get that into your head. You think we're going to look after you because you chucked bread and fired your bullets at us? Sour devil! Others would—Tfu! . . ."

The soldier fell silent and stretched himself out on the ground.

The student was already lying down. I lay down too. The frightened carpenter curled up in a ball and, moving nearer the fire, began to stare into it. I could hear his teeth chattering. The student lay down to the left of him and, also rolled up in a ball, seemed to fall asleep at once. The soldier, his hands tucked behind his head, stared at the sky.

"What a night, eh? What a number of stars," he commented, turning to me. "This sky's a quilt, not just a sky. I love this vagrant life, my friend. It is a cold and hungry life, but it is also very free. . . . There is no authority over you. . . . You could bite off your own head, even, and no one would say a word. I've starved plenty these days and felt angry . . . but here am I lying down now and looking up at the sky. . . . The stars are winking at me; 'Take it in your stride, Lakutin, they say, walk the earth and don't give in to anyone.' And the heart feels good. . . . And you—what's your name?

Hey, carpenter! Don't you be angry with me now and don't fear anything. . . . That we've eaten your bread, that's nothing. You had some bread; we had none; so we ate yours. . . . But you, savage man, you shoot bullets at us. . . . Don't you understand that a bullet can do harm to a man? I got very angry with you awhile ago and, if you hadn't fallen, I'd have whacked you real hard, brother, for your insolence. And as for bread, you'll reach Perekop by tomorrow and you'll buy yourself some bread there—you have money, of course. . . . How long have you had that fever of yours?"

For a long time the soldier's deep voice and the quavering voice of the carpenter buzzed in my ears. The dark, almost black night descended lower and lower upon the earth, while the fresh, juicy air flooded into the lungs.

The campfire gave off a steady light and invigorating heat. . . . Our eyes simply stuck together.

"Get up! Quick! Let's go!"

I opened my eyes in alarm and leapt quickly to my feet, which the soldier helped me to do by seizing my hand and jerking me off the ground.

"Quick now! March!"

His face was set and anxious. I glanced around me. The sun was rising; a rosy sunbeam lay upon the carpenter's blue, immobile face. His mouth was open; his eyes bulged from their sockets, fixed in a stare of glassy horror. The clothes on his chest were torn, and he lay in an unnaturally crumpled pose. There was no sign of the "student."

"What are you staring at! Come along, I say!" the soldier urged me imperiously, dragging me off by the hand.

"Is he dead?" I asked, shuddering in the fresh morning air.

"Of course! And you'd be dead too if you'd been strangled," the soldier explained.

"Did . . . the 'student' . . . ?" I cried out.

"Who else? Or was it you? Or me? There's a scholar for you. . . . A cunning way he had with men . . . and he's got his chums into a mess, too. If I'd gotten wind of it,

I'd have killed that 'student' myself yesterday. Cracked him on the temple with my fist . . . and there would have been one scoundrel less in the world! D'you realize what he's done? Now we must make our way through the steppe in such a way that not a soul can catch sight of us. Do you understand? Because—they'll find the carpenter later today, and they'll see at once that he's been strangled and robbed. And they'll start looking for us . . . 'Where are you from and where did you sleep last night?' Though we haven't got anything of his on us —but, yes, I do have his revolver under my shirt! That's a fine business!"

"You'd better throw it away," I advised him.

"Throw it away?" he asked thoughtfully. "But it's a thing of value. . . . Maybe they won't catch us yet? . . . No, I'll not throw it away. . . . Who knows the carpenter had a weapon? I won't throw it away. . . . It's worth about three rubles. And there's a bullet in it too . . . eh! I'd sure like to put the bullet into the 'student's' ear! How much money did that dog scoop up—eh? Anathema!"

"So much for the carpenter's daughters," I said.

"Daughters? What daughters? Ah, you mean *his*. Well, they'll grow up. It's not us they'll marry. So we needn't bother about them. . . . Let's go, brother, go quickly. . . . But where shall we go?"

"I don't know. . . . It's all the same."

"I don't know either, but I know it's all the same. Let's go to the right: that's where the sea should be."

We walked on to the right. Far ahead in the steppe rose a dark hillock with the sun shining above it.

"You're looking back to see if he's been resurrected? Don't be afraid—he won't come chasing after us. . . . Our professor, one can see, had a few tricks up his sleeve; he made a good job of it. . . . There's a comrade for you! He's got us into trouble all right! Eh, brother? People go to rot, every year they go more to rot," the soldier concluded mournfully.

The steppe was silent and deserted, saturated with the bright morning sunshine; and it spread all around us, merging with the sky on the horizon, in such a clear, tender, and generous light that every dark and unjust deed seemed impossible here amid the great expanse of this free plain covered by the blue dome of the heavens.

"My belly aches for food, brother!" my companion exclaimed, rolling a cigarette.

"What'll we eat today? Where and how?"

That was the problem.

At this point the narrator—my neighbor in the hospital ward—concluded his tale, adding: "That's all. I became fast friends with that soldier. We tramped together as far as the Kars region. He was a good-natured, experienced little fellow—a typical tramp. I respected him. We tramped together as far as Asia Minor, and there I lost him. . . ."

"Do you sometimes recall the carpenter?" I asked him.

"As you see, or—as you've heard . . ."

"And . . . you're not disturbed?"

He laughed.

"And what should I feel? I'm not to blame for what happened to him, just as you are not to blame for what has happened to me. . . . And nobody is to blame for anything, because—we are all beasts."

TWENTY-SIX MEN AND A GIRL

Poem

There were six and twenty of us—twenty-six animated machines, cooped up in a damp basement where, making butter pretzels and cracknels, we kneaded dough from morning till night. The windows of our basement were on the level of a hole that had been excavated and then built over with now moldy brick; the window frames were barred on the outside with a fine iron screen, and the light of the sun could not penetrate to us through panes clotted with flour. Our boss had iron-barred the windows in order to make it impossible for us to hand out morsels of bread to beggars or those of our comrades who were out of work and starving. Our boss called us swindlers and gave us putrid offal instead of meat for our midday meals.

It was stifling and stuffy living in that stone box under the low, smoke-yellow ceiling completely covered with soot and cobwebs. We felt depressed and sickened inside the stout walls splotched with stains of filth and mold. . . . We used to get up at five in the morning without our fair share of sleep, and by six o'clock—dull-witted and lethargic—we were already sitting down at a table to fashion butter pretzels from dough prepared overnight for us by other assistants. All day long, from early morning till ten at night, some of us sat at the table with sleeves rolled up, kneading the tough dough and rocking our bodies to fight the creeping stiffness; others, in the meantime, were busy mixing flour and water. All day long the water, bub-

112

bling in the big cauldron where the pretzels were being
boiled, purred in a mournful, melancholy way, and our
baker's wooden shovel scuffled in quick and fierce thrusts
to and fro on the floor of the oven furnace, throwing slippery lumps of boiled dough onto the red-hot brick. From
morning till night logs burned in one section of the oven,
and the red reflections of the flame quivered on one of
the walls of the bakery as if in mute mockery of us. The
huge oven resembled the deformed head of a fabled monster. It seemed to project from under the floor, its gaping
jaws bristling with bright fire, to breathe scorching heat
upon us, watching our endless labors through a pair of
black, hollow vents above the mouth of the oven. These
two deep hollows were like the eyes—the pitiless and dis-
passionate eyes—of a monster: they always stared at us
with the same dark gaze, as if tired of watching slaves at
work and expecting nothing human from them; and they
hated the slaves with all the frigid contempt of wisdom.

Day after day, covered in flour, spattered with the mud
our boots brought in from the outside, we kneaded
dough and made pretzels saturated with our sweat in that
thick, badly smelling, overheated atmosphere; we detested
our work with a keen hatred, and never ate what came
from our hands, preferring black rye bread. Sitting opposite one another at a long table—nine men on each side—
we moved our hands and fingers mechanically for hours
on end, and we had grown so accustomed to our work
that we no longer kept track of our movements. We had
seen each other so often that we knew all the wrinkles
on each other's faces. We had nothing to talk about and
were used to that, and kept our mouths shut unless we
swore—for there is always a reason for abusing a man
and especially a comrade. But we abused each other very
rarely—for what can a man be blamed if he is half dead,
or if he is like a stone statue, all his feelings crushed by
the burden of his labor? But silence terrifies and torments
only those who have already spoken all they had to say
and have nothing left to add; on the other hand, silence
is simple and easy for those who have not yet begun to
speak. Sometimes we sang, and our song would begin as
follows: in the middle of work, someone would suddenly
sigh deeply like an exhausted hack and would then softly

take up one of those long-drawn-out, plaintively tender airs that always lighten the pressure on the singer's soul. One of us would sing, and we would listen at first in silence to his single song as it died away and faded under the oppressive basement ceiling, like the flickering flame of a bonfire in the steppes on a damp autumn night when the gray skies blot out the earth with their leaden roof. Then another singer would join in, and there would now be two voices floating gently and nostalgically in the stifling atmosphere of our stuffy hole. Next, several voices in unison would suddenly pick up the song—it would swell like a wave, growing stronger and louder, and shift apart the damp, massive walls of our stone prison. . . .

All twenty-six of us would be singing now. The loud, well-practiced voices filled the bakery; the song, hemmed in, beat against the stone walls, moaned, sobbed, and stirred our hearts with a gently tickling pain, making old wounds smart, and awakening our longing. . . . The singers would utter deep, heavy sighs; one of them would unexpectedly break off his song and listen for a long while to his comrades' singing, then pour his voice again into the general wave. Another, dismally exclaiming "Ekh!" would sing with his eyes closed; and the dense, broad wave of sounds would, perhaps, loom before him like a road, brightly illumined by the sun, stretching somewhere into the far distance—a spacious road along which he saw himself walking. . . .

The flame in the oven furnace would still be throbbing, the baker's wooden shovel would still be scraping on brick, the water in the kettle would be purring, and the reflections of the fire on the wall would be flickering as always, mocking us in silence. . . . And we would go on singing our blunted sorrow in words composed by other men, expressive of the heavy longing of living men deprived of the sun, the longing of slaves. That is how we lived, the twenty-six of us, in the basement of a large stone house; and our life was so oppressive that all the three stories of this house might well have been built right on top of our shoulders. . . .

But, besides our songs, we possessed something else that was good, that we loved, that was, perhaps, a substitute for the sun. There was a gold-embroidery work-shop on the second floor of our house and there, among the many seamstresses, lived Tanya, a sixteen-year-old housemaid. Every morning, her small rosy little face with its light-blue twinkling eyes would be glued to the pane of a small window cut in the door to the entrance hall, and she would shout to us in her tender voice: "Little convicts! Let me have my little pretzels!"

We all turned at the sound of this clear voice, gazing with pleasure and good nature at this pure, girlish face smiling so gloriously at us. It gave us pleasure to see her nose squashed against the glass and her small, white teeth glittering between her rosy lips parted in a smile. We rushed to open the door for her, pushing each other, and she, the bright darling, would take a step forward and hold out her apron, standing before us with her head slightly to one side and smiling all the time. The long thick plait of her chestnut hair fell over one shoulder and rested on her breast. We, dirty, ignorant, deformed men, looked up at her from below—the threshold of the door was four steps higher than the floor—we looked up at her with raised heads and greeted her with "Good morning!" and spoke some very special words to her—words we had found only for her. Our voices were softer and our jokes lighter when we talked to her. Everything we gave her was very special. The baker pulled out a shovelful of the crispest, most golden pretzels from the oven furnace and tossed them deftly into Tanya's apron.

"Be careful and don't let the boss see you!" we warned her. She only laughed mischievously and shouted gaily as she disappeared swiftly, like a little mouse: "Good-by, my little convicts!"

That was all. . . . But long after her departure we discussed her pleasantly amongst us; and we repeated the same things we had said yesterday and the day before, because she, and we, and everything around us, were the same as they had been the previous day and the day before. . . . It is a hard and torturing thing when a man goes on living and nothing around him ever changes; and if that fails to kill his soul, then the immobility of his environment becomes all the more tormenting to him. . . . We always spoke of women in a way that was repugnant even to ourselves when we heard our coarse, shameless, lewd talk; and that was understandable because the women we knew may, perhaps, have deserved no better comment. But our references to Tanya were never lewd; not one of us ever allowed himself even to put a hand on her, still less to utter a dirty joke in her presence. Perhaps this was due to the fact that she never stayed with us any length of time: like a falling star she would flash before our gaze and then vanish; and, perhaps, it was also due to her being so small and so very beautiful, for every form of beauty evokes respect even from the coarsest people. Moreover, even though our hard, convictlike labor had made us as dull as oxen, we yet managed to remain human beings and, like all human beings, could not live without having something to worship. We had no one better than Tanya, and no one but she had ever paid any attention to us stuck in that basement—no one at all, even though dozens of other people lived in the house. And finally, and this is probably the main reason, we regarded her as something very personal, something that existed only thanks to our pretzels. We had made it our duty to give her freshly baked ones every day, and that was the daily sacrifice we offered to our idol; it became an almost sacred ritual and with every day it bound us even more closely to her. Besides the pretzels we gave Tanya many pieces of advice—to dress more warmly, not to run up and down stairs so fast, not to carry any heavy loads of logs. She listened to our advice with a smile, replied to it with a laugh, and never heeded us, but this did not offend us: we only wanted to show that we were concerned about her.

She often turned to us with various requests, asking us, for example, to open the heavy door of the ice-cellar and to chop wood for her. We did this, and anything else she asked, not only with delight, but with a sort of pride as well.

But when one of us asked her to repair his only shirt, she replied with a contemptuous snort: "What more! You expect me to do that!"

We laughed a lot over this odd fellow, and no one ever asked her to do anything again. We loved her—that

was the long and the short of it. Man always desires to
impose his love upon someone, even if it becomes a crushing burden sometimes or proves soiling; with his love he
may poison the life of one he holds most dear, because,
in loving, he fails to respect the beloved. We were obliged to love Tanya because we had nobody else to love.

At times one of us would suddenly, and for some reason, begin to argue as follows: "And why are we spoiling this girl? What's she got? Eh? We're too stuck on
her!"

The man who ventured to say such things was swiftly
and rudely put in his place. We needed to have
something to love: we had found it, and we loved it;
and what we loved, all twenty-six of us, must be as permanent as a holy of holies to any one of us; and everyone
who went against us in this was our declared enemy. We
loved what was, perhaps, not so very beneficial for us;
but since there were six and twenty of us, we always
wished for this very reason to ensure that the rest of us
also held sacred what was precious to each of us in-
dividually.

Our love weighs no less than our hatred, and, for this
very reason perhaps, certain proud characters affirm that
our hatred is more flattering than our love. . . . But why
do they not run away from us in that case?

In addition to the pretzel bakehouse our boss also had
a bakery for rolls; it was situated in the same house, with
only a wall dividing it from our hole; but the bakers who
made rolls—there were four of them—held themselves
aloof; regarding their work as cleaner than ours, and
themselves as our superiors, they avoided our premises
and sniggered contemptuously whenever they met us in
the yard. We did not visit them either: our boss forbade
us to do so for fear we might steal some of the white
rolls. We disliked these bakers because we envied them:
their work was easier than ours, they received more pay,
they were better fed, they had bright spacious premises,
and they were all so very clean, healthy, and repugnant.
We ourselves looked a sort of dirty yellow-and-gray;
three of us were syphilitic, several had the itch, and
one was completely twisted with rheumatism. On holi-

days, and in their spare time, the bakers of rolls wore
jackets and creaking boots; a couple of them owned accordions; and they all used to go promenading in the
park. We, on the contrary, were dressed in filthy rags,
shoes made of bast or worn-out leather, and the police
would not admit us into the park. So how could we like
the bakers?

We learned one day that their chief baker had gone
on the booze; the boss had dismissed him and engaged
a substitute, a former soldier, who walked about in a
satin vest and with a gold watch and chain. We were
very anxious to see such a dandy; in the hope of catching
sight of him we began taking turns to run out into the
yard.

But he paid us a visit in person. Kicking open the door
and leaving it ajar, he paused on the threshold and called
out with a smile: "God bless! A fine day to you, lads!"

The frosty air, bursting through the door in a cloud of
steam, wreathed around his feet as he stood on the
threshold looking us up and down; a row of large yellow
teeth glittered from under his fair, smartly twirled mustaches. The vest he wore was, indeed, very unusual: blue
and embroidered with flowers, it shone brightly, and its
buttons were of some sort of red stone. There was a gold
chain too. . . .

He was handsome, this soldier, tall, healthy, pink-
cheeked; and his large bright eyes—amiable and clear—
made a good impression. On his head he wore a white,
stiffly starched baker's conical hat, while the tips of a
pair of pointed, fashionable, highly polished boots peeped
from underneath his spotlessly clean apron.

Our baker respectfully requested him to shut the door;
this he did without haste and then started to question us
about the boss. Interrupting each other, we told him that
our boss was a cunning rogue, a scoundrel, a rascal and a
bloodsucker—all the things that we could and should say
about the boss, but that cannot all be reported here. The
soldier listened, his mustaches quivering, and scrutinized
us with his soft, clear gaze.

"And do you have many girls here?" he suddenly inquired.

Several of us tittered respectfully; others made sweet

faces, and one of us finally explained that there were nine girls in the house. . . .

"D'you profit by them?" the soldier asked with a wink.

We laughed again, not very loudly, in an embarrassed way. . . . Many of us would have liked to show ourselves as devil-may-care as this baker, but none of us, not a single one, could carry it off. Someone even admitted this, saying quietly: "That's not for us. . . ."

"Y-yes, it's difficult for you!" the soldier commented with assurance, examining us closely. "There's something . . . not quite so . . . about you . . . You haven't got the bearing . . . a decent manner . . . appearance, I mean! And as for women—they love a man's appearance! The body frame has to be just right for her . . . so that everything . . . is in its place! And moreover she respects strength. . . . A man's arm must be . . . like this!"

The soldier thereupon pulled out his right hand from his pocket and showed us his arm with sleeve rolled up to the elbow. . . . His arm was white, muscular, and covered with glistening golden hair.

"The leg, the chest—they should all be firm. . . . And again—a man should be dressed according to form . . . as the beauty of things demands. The women—they just love me. I don't call or lure them—they just come five at a time and hang around my neck. . . ."

He sat down on a sack of flour and gave us a detailed account of how much women loved him and how cavalierly he treated them. Then he departed. When the creaking door had shut behind him, we were speechless for a long while, pondering on him and his stories. Then, of a sudden, we all began to talk, and it became clear that all of us had taken a liking to him. He was so simple and friendly—he had come in, sat about, and chatted. No one had ever visited us, no one had ever talked to us in such an amiable manner. . . . And we continued to discuss him and his future exploits with the women embroiderers, who, whenever they met us in the yard, either avoided us with pursed lips or marched right past us as if we did not exist. We had always admired them as they passed by our windows—in the winter, wearing some sort of special hats and fur-lined coats, and, in the summer, dressed in flowered hats and carrying bright parasols. But, in private among ourselves, we spoke of those girls in a way that, had they heard us, would have made them furious with shame and a sense of outrage.

"However, I hope he doesn't spoil . . . our Tanya!" the baker suddenly exclaimed with concern.

We stopped talking, flabbergasted at these words. Somehow we had forgotten about our Tanya: the soldier's sturdy, handsome figure had fenced her from us. A heated discussion followed: some argued that Tanya would never sink so low; others affirmed that she would be unable to resist the soldier; others again suggested that, if the soldier tried to annoy her, we'd break his ribs. Finally, we all resolved to keep an eye on both of them, and to warn the girl to be on her guard against him. . . . This ended the discussion.

About a month elapsed. The soldier went on baking bread, walking out with the women embroiderers, dropping in quite often to see us, but now he made no mention of his conquests and only twirled his mustaches and smacked his lips.

Each morning Tanya came to fetch her "little pretzels" and, as always, she was cheerful, tender, and affectionate toward us. We tried to talk to her about the soldier, but she merely referred to him as "a pop-eyed calf" and bestowed many other funny nicknames on him, which reassured us. We took pride in "our" girl. Observing how much fuss the women embroiderers made over the soldier, we felt elevated by Tanya's attitude to him and, as if guided by her attitude, began to treat the soldier with scorn. As a result we loved her all the more, welcoming her with even greater joy and amiability in the morning.

But one day the soldier came to see us a little the worse for drink; he sat down and began to laugh. When we inquired as to the cause of his laughter, he explained:

"Two of them—Lydka and Grushka—had a fight over me. . . . They really damaged themselves! Ha-ha-ha! One of them pulled the other's hair, got her down on the floor in the passage, and then sat on top of her. . . . Ha-ha-ha-ha! They clawed each other's faces and ripped their clothes—you'd die laughing to see it! And why can't women fight fair? Why do they scratch, tell me that?"

He sat on the bench there, in the pink of health, clean-cut, beaming—sat there and couldn't stop laughing. We remained silent. On this occasion we found him unpleasant.

"Say, don't I have all the luck with the girls, eh? I'll die laughing. I need only wink, and the girl's ready! The devil!"

He raised and then let drop his white hands with their glistening hair with a loud slap upon his knees. And he stared at us with a look of delighted astonishment as if genuinely puzzled at being always so lucky in his affairs with women. His pink, stolid dial of a face shone with uninhibited self-satisfaction and happiness as he smacked his lips with juicy gusto.

With violent fury our baker thrust his shovel into the hearth of the oven and remarked with sudden irony: "It doesn't need great strength to topple a sapling, but just you try toppling a full grown pine. . . ."

"What do you mean? Are you talking to me?" the soldier asked.

"And you . . ."

"What are you saying?"

"Nothing . . . it's passed!"

"No, just a minute! What is it about? What pine?"

Our baker made no reply as he worked rapidly with his shovel in the oven: into it he would thrust the boiled dough of the pretzels, hook the already baked ones out, and noisily chuck them on the floor for his young assistants, who then threaded them on bast strips. He seemed to have forgotten the soldier and his conversation with him. But the soldier grew very restless of a sudden. He rose to his feet and stepped toward the oven, at the risk of running his chest against the end of the handle of our baker's shovel, which was feverishly darting in and out of the oven.

"Now, tell me . . . who's she? You annoy me . . . I? Not one of them can shake me off, no! And you're casting such aspersions . . ."

He seemed genuinely hurt. Evidently he had no reason to respect himself except for his ability to seduce women. Perhaps this ability of his was the only vital virtue he possessed and it alone qualified him to feel himself alive. There are people who cherish some disease of mind or body as their greatest and highest asset in life. They put up with the disease all their lives, and it provides them with their only vitality; suffering from it, they nourish themselves upon it, complain of it to others, and in this way attract the attention of their neighbors. In this way they exact the compassion of others, and it is all they have. Deprive them of their disease, cure them, and they will feel very unhappy; they will thus lose their only reason for living—they will become empty. Sometimes a man's life is so wretched that he is involuntarily compelled to value some particular vice of his and to live by it; and it can also be said that boredom makes such people vicious.

The soldier, offended, pushed against our baker, yelling: "No, you tell me—who?"

"Want me to tell you?" the baker asked, turning suddenly.

"Well?"

"D'you know Tanya?"

"Well?"

"That's it! Try her. . . ."

"I?"

"You!"

"Her? For me—that's nothing!"

"We'll see!"

"You'll see! Ha-ha!"

"She'll fix you. . . ."

"A month is all I need!"

"You're a real braggart, soldier!"

"Two weeks, then! I'll show you! Who's she? Tanka! Tfu! . . ."

"Now off with you. . . . You're getting in the way!"

"A couple of weeks and the thing will be done! Ah, you . . ."

"Off with you, I say. . . ."

Our baker, suddenly furious, raised his shovel. The soldier backed away in astonishment, glared at us, and, after a short silence, exclaimed in a sinister tone, "Very well then!" and left us.

Fascinated, we had not said a word during the dispute.

But when the soldier was gone, we all began to talk with noisy animation.

Some shouted to the baker: "That wasn't a good thing you started, Pavel!"

"Get on with your work!"

We felt that the soldier had been hurt to the quick, and that danger now threatened Tanya. We felt this, but at the same time we were gripped by a burning, pleasing curiosity as to the outcome. What would come of it? Would Tanya hold out against the soldier? Almost all of us declared with conviction:

"Tanya? She'll hold out. You can't take her with bare hands!"

We were terribly eager to test the fortitude of our idol: with great intensity we demonstrated to each other that our idol was a strong idol, that it would emerge victorious from this conflict. In the end, we began to think that we had not baited the soldier enough, that he would forget the dispute, and that we should try to arouse his vanity more thoroughly. From that day we began to live a very peculiar, highly strung, nervous life, such as we had never lived before. For whole days we argued with each other, became more intelligent, all of us, and began to talk better and at greater length. It seemed we were playing some sort of a game with the devil, with Tanya as our big stake. And when we learned from the bread bakers that the soldier had begun "to try and make" our Tanya, we felt elated and so glad to be alive that we failed to notice that our boss, profiting by our excitement, had added an extra five hundred pounds of dough a day for us to knead. Work did not even seem to tire us. Tanya's name was on our tongue all day. And every morning we awaited her arrival with a very particular impatience. Sometimes we imagined her entering—no longer the same Tanya, but somehow a very different person.

However, we never told her of our dispute. We asked no questions, and treated her as before, with every affectionate regard. But a new element alien to our former feelings had already crept into our attitude toward Tanya —and this new element was a keen curiosity, cold and sharp as steel. . . .

"Brothers! Time's running out today!" the baker announced one morning as he began work.

We knew this very well ourselves even without being reminded, but we were now on the alert.

"Look closely at her . . . when she comes in . . . as she will in a moment!" the baker suggested.

Someone exclaimed with regret: "But can you spot anything with your eyes! . . ."

Again a lively, noisy argument broke out between us. This day we would finally learn how pure and unsullied was the vessel into which we had poured our best. For the first time that morning we suddenly felt that we were actually playing for big stakes, that our idol's test of purity might also prove her undoing in our eyes. In all these past days we had heard that the soldier had been pursuing Tanya persistently, closely, and without any let-up but, for some reason, none of us had questioned her as to her attitude. And she had continued to call on us punctually every morning for her order of pretzels, and she looked the same as ever.

It was not long before we heard her voice: "Little convicts! Here I am. . . ."

We hastened to let her in, and as she entered we met her—contrary to our custom—in silence. With all our eyes fixed upon her, we were at a loss what to say and what to ask. And we stood facing her, an opaque, silent crowd. She was evidently surprised at this unaccustomed confrontation, and we suddenly saw her turn pale and nervous. Fidgeting on one spot, she asked in a suppressed voice: "What's the matter with you all?"

"And with you?" the baker asked sullenly, without removing his eyes from her.

"What do you mean—I?"

"N-nothing . . ."

"Well, let me have the pretzels quickly. . . ."

She had never been impatient with us before.

"You've time enough!" our baker said, without budging or taking his eyes off her face.

Then, of a sudden, she turned and vanished through the door.

The baker picked up his shovel and, turning his back to us as he faced the oven, exclaimed in a low voice: "It's done! Ah, that soldier! . . . The scoundrel!"

Jostling each other like a flock of sheep, we made for

the table, sat down quietly, and set to work without any vim. Very soon someone remarked: "And maybe, still . . ."

"No, now! You can talk!"

We all knew that he was an intelligent man, more intelligent than the rest of us. And we understood his exclamation to mean that he was convinced the soldier had won. . . . We felt dejected and disquieted. . . .

During the midday meal the soldier came in. As always he was clean and dapper, and as always he looked us straight in the eye. We felt awkward returning his gaze.

"Well, honest sirs, would you like me to give you an example of soldierly valor?" he asked with a proud smile. "Then go out into the entrance hall and peep through the cracks. . . . D'you understand?"

We went out and, huddling together, fixed our eyes to the cracks in the wooden wall of the entrance hall giving on the yard. We did not have long to wait. . . . Very soon Tanya, with hurried step and troubled face, walked across the yard, jumping over the puddles of mud and thawing snow. She disappeared behind the door to the ice-cellar. Then the soldier, whistling, followed her there without haste. His hands were thrust deep in his pockets and his mustaches quivered.

It was raining, and we watched the raindrops falling into the puddles and the puddles wrinkling under their impact. It was a damp, gray day—a very dreary day. Snow still lay on the roofs, and dark muddy patches had appeared on the ground. The snow on the roofs was also covered with a dirty brown deposit. The rain fell slowly, making a dismal sound. We felt chilled, and it was unpleasant waiting. . . .

The soldier was the first to emerge from the cellar; he walked slowly the length of the yard, his mustaches quivering, his hands in his pockets. He looked the same as usual.

Then Tanya came out. Her eyes . . . her eyes were shining with joy and happiness and her lips were smiling. And she walked as if in her sleep, with staggering, uncertain steps.

This we could not quietly accept. We, all of us, made a dash for the door, leapt out into the yard and began loudly and savagely to whistle our spite at her.

She gave a start on catching sight of us and then stopped as though rooted in the mud at her feet. We crowded around her and wickedly, without restraint, started to swear at and abuse her with lewd words.

We did so without shouting or haste, for having barred her way and surrounded her we could mock her to our hearts' content. I shall never know why we did not beat her up. She stood in our midst, turning her head here and there, listening to our insults. And with ever increasing violence we pelted her with the mud and venom of our words.

The color had left her face. Her light-blue eyes, shining happily a minute before, were now wide open, her breath came with an effort, and her lips quivered.

And we, who had surrounded her, took our revenge because she had robbed us. She had belonged to us, we had spent our very best on her; and even though our "very best" was no more than a beggar's crumbs, yet there were six and twenty of us and she was all alone, and, for that reason, no torture was adequate for her! How we insulted her! She had not uttered a word, staring at us with wild eyes and trembling all over.

We laughed, roared, growled. . . . Other people came running up. . . . One of us snatched at the sleeve of Tanya's blouse. . . .

Suddenly her eyes flashed. Without undue haste she raised her hands to her head and, tidying her hair, addressed us very coolly and distinctly, looking us straight in the face: "Ah, you unhappy convicts!"

And then she walked straight at us, just walked as if we were not standing there at all in front of her, as if we were not barring her way. Thus, none of us did actually bar her way.

Having broken out of the encirclement, she, without turning around, exclaimed in a loud voice tinged with pride and contempt: "Ah, you rabble, you vipers!"

And she went off—upright, beautiful, and proud.

We were left standing in the middle of the yard, in the mud, beneath the rain and the gray sunless sky.

Then we went back in sullen silence to our bricked-in hole. As before, the sun never looked into our windows, and Tanya came visiting no more—never again!

A MAN IS BORN

This happened in '92, the year of the famine, between Sukhum and Ochemchiry, on one side of the River Kodor, not far from the sea—through the merry din of the sparkling waters of a mountain torrent I could clearly distinguish the hollow-sounding splash of the sea waves.

It was autumn. In the white foam of the Kodor, yellow bay leaves whirled and flashed like small, nimble salmon trout. I was seated on the rocks above the river, thinking that the seagulls and the cormorants must likewise mistake the leaves for fish and thus deceive themselves, and that was why they uttered such shrill screams of disappointment yonder to the right, beyond the tree, where the surf was breaking.

The chestnut trees overhead were dressed in gold, and at my feet lay a multitude of leaves resembling the severed palms of hands. The branches of the hornbeam on the other bank were already bare, and hung like a torn net in the air. As though caught in the net, a red-and-yellow mountain woodpecker leapt about and hammered at the bark of a trunk with his black beak, driving out the insects for the nimble titmice and the gray nuthatches —visitors from the far North—to peck at them.

To my left, misty clouds threatening rain lowered above the mountain peaks, and the shadows they cast crept over the green slopes where the boxwood trees grew, and one could still find in the hollows of the ancient beeches and lindens there the "heady honey" that, with

130

its intoxicating sweetness, had nearly undone the army of Pompey the Great by knocking out a whole legion of his iron Romans. The wild bees manufacture it from the blossoms of the bay and the azalea, and "journeying" folk can gather it from the hollows and eat it, spreading it on their *lavash*—thin flat millcakes of wheaten flour.

Badly stung by an angry bee, I was busy doing this as I sat on the stones under the chestnut trees, dipping morsels of bread into a pot full of honey, eating, and admiring the lazy shimmering effects of the weary autumn sun.

Autumn in the Caucasus resembles the interior of a resplendent cathedral built by great sages—they are always great sinners too—built by them in order to conceal their past from the probing eyes of conscience—a boundless cathedral of gold, turquoise, emerald; on the mountain slopes they had hung their best silk-embroidered carpets from Turkistan, Samarkand, and Shemaha; they had plundered the whole world and brought their spoils here, beneath the eye of the sun, as though wishing to say to it:

"This is Thine. . . . A gift from Thy people . . . for Thee alone."

I saw gray, long-bearded giants with the enormous eyes of children descending from the mountains to beautify the earth, lavishly sowing everywhere treasures of every color, covering the mountain peaks with thick sheets of silver and the terraces with the animated texture of a variety of trees; and, as a result, beneath their hands this portion of the earth assumed a madly beautiful appearance.

And what a wonderful duty it is to be a human being on this earth! How many wondrous things one can see! How torturingly sweet is the heart's emotion when admiring this beauty!

Well, naturally, there had to be hard times; all of one's hatred would boil up in one's burning breast, and bitter anguish suck greedily at the heart's blood. But such anger is not always given us. Even the sun must feel depressed at times, gazing at people: it had tried so hard on their behalf, but the little people had not turned out too well.

It goes without saying, there are not a few good people, but they need repairing or—better still—remaking anew.

. . . To my left, above the bushes, a number of dark heads bobbed up and down; the human voices were barely audible amid the noise of the breaking surf and the rumbling of the torrent. Those were the "starving ones" tramping on their way to Ochemchiry from Sukhum, where they had been working on the construction of a highway.

I knew them—they were all people from Orel; I had been working together with them, and only the previous day we had all received our discharge. But I had set out before them, in the night, so as to greet the rising sun on the seashore.

Four muzhiks and a peasant woman with high cheek-bones, young, pregnant, her swollen belly rising up under her nose, and with blue-gray eyes bulging with fear. Above the bushes I caught sight of her head in a yellow kerchief swaying like a ripe sunflower in the breeze. Her husband had died in Sukhum from eating too much fruit. I had lived in the workers' barracks with these people. In the good old Russian custom, they had talked about their misfortunes so volubly and vociferously that their complaints could probably be heard for a couple of miles in every direction.

They were dreary people, crushed by their grief. It had uprooted them from their exhausted, unproductive, native soil, and had carried them, like withered autumn leaves, to this region, where the luxuriant character of a nature unfamiliar to them had both astonished and dazzled them, while the exacting conditions of their labor had finally finished them off. They gaped at everything here, blinking their sad, faded eyes in perplexity and smiling miserably at one another as they made their subdued comments:

"Ah, what a countryside this is. . . ."

"Things just push up out of it."

"Y-yes . . . but there's a lot of stone here. . . ."

"It's not an easy land, one must say. . . ."

And they recalled Mare's Meadow, Dry Run, Dampart —their native places where each handful of soil represented the remains of their grandparents, and where everything was memorable, familiar, and precious—watered with their own sweat.

They had with them another peasant woman—tall, straight, flat as a board, with jaws like those of a horse, and a pair of black, squinting eyes, gazing darkly, like coals.

In the evening this woman would join the woman in the yellow kerchief and go off a little way behind the workers' barracks; sitting down there on a heap of rubble, she would prop her cheek with her hand, tilt her head to one side, and sing in a high-pitched, angry voice:

> Above the parish churchyard
>   in the green green bushes,
> On the sandy earth . . .
>   I'll spread out a white kerchief . . .
> I'll sit waiting, waiting,
>   for my dear friend to come
> And when he comes, my dear one,
>   I'll bow down to him.

The woman in the yellow kerchief was usually silent, craning her neck and staring at her belly, but every now and then she would—unexpectedly, lazily, and huskily— join in the song with sobbing words:

> Oh, my darling, my own,
>   oh, my darling dearest,
> It's not my fate
>   to see you ever again.

In the black, stifling darkness of the southern night these plaintive voices reminded me of the North, the snow-covered wastes, the screeching of the blizzard and the distant howling of the wolves. . . .

Then the woman with the squint was stricken with fever and was carried off to town on a canvas stretcher —she shook and moaned on the stretcher as if continuing to sing her song about the parish churchyard and the sandy earth.

Bobbing in the air, the head in the yellow kerchief disappeared.

I finished my breakfast, spread some leaves over the honey in the pot, tied up my wallet and, without haste, moved off after the others, tapping with my boxthorn stick on the beaten soil of the path.

Here I was on a narrow gray strip of the road. To my right was the rolling, dense blue sea, which looked as if a host of invisible carpenters were working with a thousand planes—a white shaving sped rustling to shore, pursued by a breeze as moist, warm, and fragrant as the breath of a healthy woman. A Turkish felucca, craning to port, glided toward Sukhum with swelling sails that reminded me of an important Sukhum engineer I knew who used to puff his cheeks out—a man of the most serious mien. For some reason he always used to say "quite" instead of "quiet," and "thou" instead of "though."

"Quite! thou you're velligerant, I'll hand you over at once to the police. . . ."

He loved sending people off to the police, and it's comforting to think now that grave-worms have probably long ago stripped him to the bone.

The going was easy—like swimming through the air. Pleasant thoughts, colorfully dressed memories, performed a quiet choral dance in the memory. This choral dance in the soul was like the white crests of the sea waves; the crests skimmed the surface, but it was peaceful in the depths; there, in the sea depths, the bright resilient hopes of youth swam like silver fish.

The road was drawn toward the sea; twisting, it crawled nearer to the sandy beach upon which the waves kept breaking; the bushes likewise longed to gaze into the face of a wave, and they bent over the ribbon of the road as if nodding to the blue expanse of the watery waste.

A gust of wind blew from the mountains: it was a sign of rain.

A low moan in the bushes—a human moan, the kind that always stirs the soul in kinship.

I pushed the bushes aside—there, with her back leaning against a walnut tree, sat the peasant woman in the yellow kerchief, her head resting on her shoulder, her mouth monstrously distended, her eyes madly bulging. Her hands clutched her enormous belly, and she breathed so unnaturally and horribly that her belly convulsively leapt up and down, and the woman, pressing it with her hands, uttered deep hollow moans and bared a row of yellow, wolflike fangs.

"What is it? Did they hit you?" I asked, bending over her. Like a fly, she rubbed her bare feet one against the other in the ash-gray dust and, her heavy head dangling from side to side, hoarsely said:

"Go away, you shameless man. . . . G-go away. . . ."

I grasped what was the matter—I had seen it happen once before—and, of course, started away in fright. The woman emitted a loud, long-drawn howl; turbid tears gushed from her eyes, which were ready to burst, and flowed down her purple, tightly swollen face.

This brought me back. I threw my bag, the kettle, and the pot to the ground, pushed the woman over on her back, and tried to bend her legs up at the knees. But she shoved me away, striking me in the face and chest, turned over and, growling and snarling like a she-bear, crawled on all fours further away into the bushes.

"Robber . . . devil," she screamed.

Her arms gave way under her; she fell, hit the ground with her face, and howled again, convulsively straining her legs.

In the heat of excitement, I tried to recall all I knew of such matters, turned her over on her back, and bent her legs up—the chorion was now visible.

"Stay there, don't move, you're giving birth. . . ."

I ran down to the seashore, pulled up my sleeves, washed my hands and, returning, became a male midwife.

The woman writhed like birch bark in the fire, beating the earth with her hands and tearing at the withered grass; she wanted to stuff the grass into her mouth and in trying to do so spattered earth all over her horrible, inhumanly distorted face with its wild, bloodshot eyes. But now the chorion burst, and a little head was thrusting its way out. I had to restrain the convulsive movements of her legs, assist the emergence of the newborn child, and try to prevent her from stuffing the grass into her twisted, moaning mouth. . . .

We swore a little at each other: she, through her gritted teeth; myself—not too loudly either; she, because of the pain and shame; myself, because I was embarrassed and racked with pity for her. . . .

"Oh Lord," she moaned huskily, biting her blue, foaming lips, while the abundant tears of a mother's unbearable suffering poured from her eyes, which suddenly looked faded in the sun, and the whole of her body seemed to be breaking as if split in two.

"Go away, you devil. . . ."

With her weak, twisted hands she kept pushing me away, while I tried to encourage her: "Go on, give birth, you fool, faster. . . ."

I felt a torturing pity for her, and my eyes seemed bathed in her tears; anguish gripped my heart and I wanted to shout, and did shout: "Come on, hurry up!"

Then I held a man in my arms—a little red man. Through my tears I saw a red little body, an infant already dissatisfied with the world, wriggling, raging, and squalling at the top of his voice, though still attached to his mother. He had light blue eyes, a droll squashed nose and a red, crumpled face. His lips stirred and mumbled: "Ya . . . ya . . . yaa . . ."

He was so slippery I had to be careful he didn't float out of my hands. I was on my knees, staring at him and laughing—I was so very glad to see him! And I'd forgotten what I ought to do next.

"Cut it," the mother whispered. Her eyes were closed, her face sunken, ashen as that of a corpse, and her blue lips could hardly move: "With a knife . . . cut it."

My knife had been stolen in the workers' barracks. Instead, I bit through the umbilical cord; the child yelled in a deep Orel voice, and the mother smiled. I noticed how wonderfully her fathomless eyes began to flower and kindle with a blue flame—her swarthy hand fumbled with her skirt, trying to find a pocket, and her bloody bitten lips moved.

"I . . . I haven't the strength. There's a string in the pocket . . . to tie up the navel . . ."

I pulled out the string and tied up the navel. Her smile grew brighter. She smiled so happily and brightly that I was almost dazzled.

"Tidy yourself. I'll go and wash him."

"Careful—gently . . . careful . . ." she muttered, uneasy.

This red thing of a man did not require such great care; clenching his fists, he yelled and yelled as though challenging me to fight: "Ya . . . Ya . . ."

"Ah, you, you! You must assert yourself, brother, do it strongly, before your neighbors tear your head off," I advised him.

He cried out especially seriously and loudly when, gaily lashing both of us, the foam of a sea wave bathed him for the first time; then, when I began to slap his chest and back, he closed his eyes, struggled, and uttered a piercing shriek, while the waves, one after another, kept pouring over him.

"That's right, my little man from Orel, be noisy. Yell for all you're worth . . ."

When I brought him back to his mother, she lay where I had left her with eyes closed again, biting her lips, discharging the afterbirth in a series of convulsions; but in spite of this I caught her faint whisper through her groans and sighs:

"Give him to me . . . give him to me. . . ."

"He can wait."

"Give him to me. . . ."

And with trembling, uncertain fingers she tried to unbutton her blouse at the breast. I helped to release her breast, fitted by nature to feed a whole score of children, and placed the rowdy little Orel man next to her warm body. He understood everything at once and said no more.

"Most Holy One, Most Pure . . ." the mother sighed, shuddering, and rolling her disheveled head of hair from side to side on the wallet.

Then, with a gentle cry, she suddenly stopped speaking and again opened her now impossibly beautiful eyes— the holy eyes of a mother who has just given birth. Those blue eyes gazed at the blue sky, and a smile of joy and gratitude burned and melted in them; raising a heavy hand, the mother slowly made the sign of the cross over the child and herself. "Glory be to thee, Mother of God Most Pure . . . oh . . . Glory be . . ."

Her eyes grew dim and distant. For a long while she was silent, barely breathing. . . . Then, of a sudden, she called out in a harder, efficient voice: "Help undo my bag, young man."

We undid it. Then she gazed fixedly at me with a weak smile, and a hardly perceptible blush lighted her sunken cheeks and perspiring forehead.

"Will you go aside for a moment. . . ."

"Don't try and do too much. . . ."

"All right, all right . . . go off. . . ."

I moved into the bushes not too far away. My heart seemed spent, but a flock of glorious birds sang gently in my breast; and this, together with the never silent surf, made me feel so good I could have gone on listening for a whole year. . . .

Somewhere nearby a stream murmured—it sounded like a girl telling her girl companion about her beloved. . . .

A head in a yellow kerchief, now properly arranged, rose above the bushes.

"Hey, hey, you there, it's rather early to be doing things," I cried out.

Holding on to the branch of a bush, she looked drained, without a drop of blood in her face, with great blue lakes in place of eyes, but she whispered with emotion: "Look at him sleeping there. . . ."

The infant slept soundly but, in my opinion, no better than other infants. If there was any difference, it was due entirely to the surroundings: on a heap of bright autumn leaves he lay under a bush, the like of which could not be found in the Province of Orel.

"You'd better lie down, mother. . . ."

"N-no," she replied, shaking her unsteady head. "I must tidy myself first, and then go on to— What d'you call it?"

"Ochemchiry, you mean?"

"That's it! The people I was with must be miles in front now. . . ."

"But you can't walk yet?"

"And what about the Holy Virgin? She'll help. . . ."

Well, if she was setting out in the company of the Holy Virgin, I'd better hold my tongue!

She gazed at the small, swollen, sulky face under the bush, and her eyes beamed with warm, tender light; she licked her lips, slowly stroking her breast with her hand.

I kindled a bonfire and laid down a few large stones as a base for boiling a kettle.

"I'll treat you to tea in a moment, mother."

"Oh? That will be good. . . . My breasts feel so dry. . . ."

"Why did your own people abandon you?"

"They didn't abandon me—why should they? I lagged behind, and they were a little drunk. But it's just as well, for how would I have given birth in front of them all?"

She glanced at me, shielding her face with her elbow. Then, spitting blood, she bashfully smiled.

"Your first?" I asked.

"The very first. And who are you?"

"A man, I would say . . ."

"Of course you're a man! Married?"

"I haven't yet qualified. . . ."

"You're lying."

"Why?"

She dropped her eyes and thought for a while: "How is it you know about female matters then?"

Now I had to lie. So I said: "I've studied these matters. I'm a student. Have you heard of students?"

"Of course I have! The eldest son of our priest was also a student; he was learning to become a priest. . . ."

"I'm one of those too. Well, I'll go and fetch the water now. . . ."

The woman stooped over her son and listened to make sure he was still breathing. Then she glanced in the direction of the sea.

"I ought to wash myself, but the water's strange. What sort of water is it? It tastes salty and bitter," she said.

"You can wash very well in it—it's good healthy water!"

"Oh?"

"It's true. And it's warmer than water in a stream. The streams here are as cold as ice . . ."

"You should know. . . ."

An Abkhazian in a cart drove past us at a walking pace, his head drowsily lowered on his chest. His small horse, all sinew, wagged its ears, squinted its round black eye at us, and snorted; the driver quickly raised his head, crowned with a shaggy fur cap, glanced in our direction, and once again dropped his head.

"The people you see in these parts—they're an odd lot and even rather frightening," the woman from Orel gently commented.

I walked away. A bright stream of water, lively as quicksilver, made a murmuring sound as the autumn leaves turned somersaults in it. It was wonderful! I washed my hands and face, filled a kettle, and, as I walked back, saw through the bushes the woman crawling on her knees over the stony ground. She was glancing uneasily about her.

"What are you doing?" I called out.

Startled, her face gone gray, she tried to hide something under her. I guessed what it was.

"Give it to me. I'll bury it. . . ."

"Oh, my dear! How can we bury it here? It ought to be buried in a bathhouse, under the floor. . . ."

"What an idea! It will take some time before they build a bathhouse out here!"

"You're joking, but I'm frightened! What if some beast should find and swallow it! The earth must claim its own. . . ."

She turned her head aside and handed me the moist, heavy bundle. Then, quietly, bashfully, she said: "Well, do the best you can, bury it deeply, for Christ's sake. Have pity on my little son, do it properly. . . ."

When I returned, I saw her walking away from the seashore with uncertain steps, one arm held out before her; her skirt was wet up to her waist and her face was slightly flushed as if from an inward glow. I helped her to approach the bonfire.

"There's animal strength for you!" I thought with astonishment.

Then we had tea with honey, and she began asking questions: "You've given up studying, have you?"

"Yes, I have."

"Was it because of drink?"

"The drink really did for me, mother!"

"So that's the sort you are! I remember you now. I noticed you in Sukhum when you were quarreling with the chief over the food, and I thought to myself then—'he must be a drinking man, he is, a fearless fellow.'"

She licked the honey from her swollen lips with gusto, and her blue eyes kept darting sideways at the bush beneath which the new man of Orel was peacefully sleeping.

"How will he make out?" she asked with a sigh, looking closely at me. "You've helped me—many thanks—but whether it will be good for him—that I don't know. . . ."

Having had her fill of tea and food, she made the sign of the cross, and while I was putting together my belongings she swayed drowsily, brooding, her faded eyes fixed on the ground. Then she started to rise.

"You don't mean you're going already?" I asked.

"I am."

"You'd better take care, mother!"

"But the Blessed Virgin . . . ? Will you hand me the child!"

"I'll carry him myself. . . ."

After an argument she yielded and we set off—shoulder to shoulder, the two of us.

"I'd better not trip!" she exclaimed with a guilty smile, placing her hand on my shoulder.

The new inhabitant of the Russian land, a man of unknown destiny, snorted persistently in my arms. The waves splashed and murmured, all furled in the white lace of shavings; the bushes whispered and the sun, past the meridian, shone.

We walked on carefully. Every now and then the mother would stop, sigh deeply, throw up her head, glance around on all sides—at the sea, the distant forest and mountains—and then peer into her son's face. Her eyes, washed by tears of suffering, were remarkably clear again; they flowered once more and burned with the blue flame of inexhaustible love.

Halting for a moment, she exclaimed: "O Lord, dear God! How good, how good it is! And so I'd like to keep on—going on and on, to the very edge of the world, and he—my little son—he'd go on growing and growing in the freedom of the open air, close to his mother's breast, the little dear. . . ."

Loud sounds the sea, sounds the sea. . . .

MUSIC

I was sitting in the office of a gendarme colonel. It was a small, dark, cluttered room, encumbered almost entirely with a wide desk, three dark leather armchairs, a leather sofa, and a large cupboard; the distressing impression I had of stuffiness was further strengthened by numerous photographs on the walls.

There were a great many photographs, representing groups of men in military uniforms, ladies, children, a military camp, an unfamiliar town on the steep bank of a river, a slightly built cadet holding a white horse by the bridle, and the full-length figure of a monk jutting like a rock in the steppe.

The colonel, a tall man with a slight stoop, wore a gray tunic. He had a rather gaunt and transparent face. His blue-gray eyes were large and handsome, but they looked sad and weary. He was probably just over forty, but his beard was already gray, his wavy hair thin, and his left cheek frequently quivered and made him blink.

With his hands thrust into the pockets of his tunic, he paced slowly on his long legs past the table, and addressed me in a feeble voice: "How will you explain that, eh? This must be explained. . . ."

There were two windows in the office, but their red curtains were closely drawn; between the colonel and myself there floated a reddish, stifling gloom, saturated with the smell of leather, medicine, and the acrid smoke of sweetish tobacco.

When the guards had conducted me here from the prison through the animated streets of the town I had felt myself a hero; all my memories of the injustices of life had fired my heart with a beautiful, youthful rage; and I had walked toward my interrogation as if about to face a trial of strength.

At first I had answered the colonel's questions energetically and rudely, provoking him to shout and threaten and trying to involve myself deeper in a dispute with an evil, hostile soul. But after I had examined his waxen face and sad eyes, had listened to his broken voice and his indifferent questions, the fire went out of my heart and all my energy evaporated. I felt irked, bored, and uncomfortable.

This weary man was no enemy, no evil spirit. What he should have done on that bright spring day was to have gone out into the fields, into the woods, and lain down there in the fresh grass with his face turned up to the sky; but here he was instead, pacing around the room, wasting his time with me, and always posing the same annoying question: "Why did you visit Yaroslavl?"

"I've already told you."

"One can't believe that," he would say, closely examining the ash of his cigarette and then starting again to shuffle in his slippers over the parquet.

He stared at everything around him with a strangely fixed expression, as though the objects in his office were unfamiliar or displeasing to him, or as though he had failed to find what he was seeking. At times he would nod his head so vehemently that his beard, as it touched his chest, spread over it like a fan. Indeed, he resembled a bird of the steppes circling over its ruined nest.

It was the first time I had ever seen a man like him, and it occurred to me that he might well be the only one of his kind on earth.

"Listen," he said, halting and pulling out his watch, "what's going to happen to us, eh? Time you stopped sitting still like a nightingale."

He snapped shut the watch-lid and continued to stare into a corner where a bust of Alexander II loomed pale in the twilight.

"You think I wish you ill, want to keep you in prison,

and so on?" he resumed. "Why should I? Why should you be stuck in prison?"

"Let me out then."

A shudder passed over his transparent face, and one of his eyes closed.

"I can't," he declared, coughing drily and stroking his cheek energetically. On the index finger of his right hand he wore a heavy wedding ring, apparently of solid gold. "We must have a plausible explanation for your journey. I'll leave the room now, just for a quarter of an hour, but you had better do some hard thinking and put it all down in writing. . . ."

He walked to the door, stopped and, holding the door handle, gently said: "I have a son, a student, in Petersburg. He's about your age. . . . At this very moment, perhaps, a gendarme officer may be interrogating him too. . . . Do you understand? That's how—"

I was left alone in the reddish dusk; his words about his son had touched me somewhere.

His "that's how" echoed in my memory, and these gently spoken words began to assume the form of a question:

"That's how?"

With puffed angry cheeks the monk stared at me from the wall; a smiling, plump lady inspected her bared left shoulder. The window curtains were moth-eaten—if one looked at them hard enough, one could detect the turquoise blue sky through the tiny holes.

The colonel had asked "why?" too often. His son must be feeling very ill at ease if he was really sitting, as I was, in a gendarme's office.

On leaving the room the colonel had left the door slightly ajar, and music now poured into the office in disturbing streams. Somewhere in the house someone was playing on a grand piano.

The room was unbearably tedious. The music summoned one to draw near. I stood up, approached the door, and peeped out into a bright, sunlit room.

An open window revealed a festive, noisy spring day; the trees cast ornamental shadows upon the window sill and the floor. Facing me was a small door; behind it I could hear the tinkle of spurs, men's voices, the rasping sound of paper being torn up. This interfered with my listening to the music, which was being played in another room to the left. The door to this room was hung with a gently swaying, pleasantly faded carpet of many colors. Music detaches one from reality; forgetting where I was, I raised the carpet and found myself in a small drawing room. A tall triple mirror with flowers in front of it stood near the door. I stationed myself between the mirror and the hanging—I could now hear the music very well and, through the leaves of the flowers, I could also make out the musician, a slender woman, sitting with her back to me, bare-necked and wearing a light, striped dressing gown of oriental silk. Her head was small, and her hair was dark and curly. She was playing by ear, softly and slowly, as if trying to remember a forgotten piece. Her slender fingers picked hesitantly at the bass keys; her right hand ran busily over the middle keys; and I watched for a long time the quivering motion of her hands, sensing in the variety of their movements something smothered, shy and sad. . . .

The keys seemed to laugh. At first I found it hard to catch the melody of the piece; the alto and tenor notes sounded disconnected; the heavy sighs of the bass notes spoke out insistently and severely; and the playing in general reminded me of an autumnal picture: a cold, humid wind was flowing over the scythed meadows, over the stubble, and a forest trembled under its chill impact, letting its last golden leaves fall to earth. In the distance the bell of an invisible church tolled monotonously.

Then a bare-headed man appeared in the middle of a field; raising his arms high he ran on, chased by the wind, like a "rolling stone," and went on running and glancing back. A dark, muffled roar kept pace with him, and the expanse of fields grew ever wider, deeper, until, diminishing before them, he vanished from the earth.

The woman stopped playing and, dropping her arms, remained sitting motionless. She sat like that for a long time.

I looked at her through the flowers, thinking of nothing, a beautiful echo still resounding in my ears. I remembered only one thing: I must not move.

Then, slowly and as it were reluctantly, she placed her

right hand upon the keys, and once again the solemn chords embraced me. I listened to them with eyes closed. It seemed as if a large throng of people were praying harmoniously and unanimously—praying with tears of rage and despair. It was a very massive and powerful piece, and it seemed strange that such a small woman could play with such vigor.

This piece had completely deprived me of any awareness of reality. . . .

"Will you stop thumping, Natalia!" the colonel's voice exclaimed gruffly nearby.

The woman turned her head without removing her hands from the grand piano. Her face was small and birdlike and very compressed around the temples. She had large blue eyes and a hooked nose.

"The prisoner has disappeared, do you understand?" the colonel said as he entered the drawing room, holding a cigarette in an amber holder and stroking his hair with a shaking hand.

"Run away?" the woman asked in alarm.

"Apparently."

I understood at once that they were referring to me, but I could not emerge immediately from behind the door-hanging and the triple mirror. I felt myself in an awkward and somewhat comic situation.

"But how did he manage it?" she asked.

"He must have climbed out of the window. . . . He's crazy. The devil take him!" the colonel replied, departing.

The lady got up and followed him, pulling her dressing gown over her bosom. Then I stepped out to meet them.

"You?" the colonel cried out, retreating. "What are you up to? Why are you here?"

"I was just listening to the music."

He blinked, glanced at the lady and, knitting his graying brows, raised his shoulders.

"If that was improper of me, then please excuse me," I said, resolved to say no more.

"H'm, yes," the colonel responded, lighting a cigarette. "I don't know how it was—proper or improper—but you should not have done it. . . ."

He stared straight at me in silence. The lady, leaning

against him, asked him softly but so that I could hear: "Will he be punished for that?"

"Please!" the colonel exclaimed, pushing her aside and motioning me toward the door.

When I walked out into the bright room, he said with an ironic smile:

"You gave me a fright, dear sir. You're an eccentric! You really love music that much, do you?"

"I seldom hear it. . . ."

"Ah . . . yes! I'll put an end to the interrogation for the day. . . ." And smiling ironically and winking twice, he added: "This incident does not dispose me to severities. . . . It seems you will be obliged to listen once again to my wife's music—she always plays at this hour. . . . Good-by!—Hey, Saltykov, hand him over to the guards. . . ."

Saltykov, a stout, sweaty gendarme, looked me over with his twinkling, inebriated eyes, and replied with a sense of relish: "It shall be done, sir!"

When Saltykov had led me into the outer office, he said to me in a reproachful tone: "Why do you go walking about the offices as if you were in a marketplace? It's damned impertinence on your part, and you have proved nothing by it. And what were you trying to prove?"

"I was simply listening to the music. . . ."

"One listens to music in a town park. . . ."

And shoving me forward, he strictly commanded the guards: "Take him away, men!"

THE NIGHTMARE

(From My Diary)

Small, shapely, elegantly dressed, she called on me one morning when the sun was peering through the window of my room; she came in and sat down in such a way that a sunbeam embraced her neck and shoulders and made her very fair hair shine like gold. She looked very youthful and, judging by her manners, was well brought up.

Her hazel eyes smiled the nervous smile of a child that is embarrassed and a little angry at not being able to overcome the embarrassment.

Pulling off a glove from her slender hand, she looked at me from under her brows and began in a soft voice: "I know that my intrusion is impertinent . . . You are so busy, so very busy."

"Yes."

"Of course," she said, nodding her head and moving her beautiful eyebrows. "But everything now feels as if all of us were moving into a new apartment. . . ."

She sighed and, staring at her little foot encased in an expensive buttoned boot, continued: "I shan't keep you long. All I need is five minutes. I should like you to save me."

Smiling, I replied: "If a human being thinks he can be saved in five minutes, he is very far from destruction. . . ."

But this woman, looking me straight in the face with her clear eyes, said in a matter-of-fact way: "You see, I

152

was an agent of the Secret Police. . . . Oh, how you . . . what an expression in your eyes. . . ."

I kept silent, smiling stupidly, not believing her, and tried to overcome some sort of dark feverish impulse. I was convinced that she had brought me some verses or a story.

"That's vile, isn't it?" she asked very quietly.

"You're joking."

"No, I'm not joking. Is that very vile?"

Crushed, I muttered: "You have pronounced your own judgment."

"Yes, of course, I know," she replied, sighing and settling more comfortably in the armchair. A grimace of disillusionment twisted her face. The small fingers of her refined hand were slowly playing with a medallion chain. A sunbeam made her ear glow like coral. She looked, all of her, so springlike and festive. Then she began to speak in a confused and careless way as if talking of a prank.

"It happened three years ago, a little less. I had a romance; I fell in love with an officer who then became an adjutant in the gendarmerie, and then it was . . . I had just finished the institute and had begun attending the higher courses. At home we used to have gatherings of all sorts of serious people, politicians. . . . I don't like politics, I don't understand them. He kept questioning me. Everything is possible for the sake of love—don't you agree? Everything is admissible if you are in love. I loved him very much. And those serious people were so unpleasant, they criticized everything. I didn't like my fellow students at the courses either. Except one . . ."

Her childish babbling convinced me even more that she had no notion of guilt, that crime to her was a mere prank—a prank she found unpleasant to remember.

"Did you get paid?" I asked her.

"Oh, no. However . . ."

She thought for a few seconds, examining the ring on her finger.

"He made me presents of various things—this ring here and the medallion and also . . . Perhaps this is pay, is it?"

Tears showed in her eyes.

"He's not an honest man, I know that. Listen," she

urged in a low voice, "if my name is published—what will I do then? You must save me. I am young, I love life so much—people, books."

I stared at this woman, and the spring sun suddenly seemed superfluous both for her and for myself. A gloomy day, mist outside, slush and mud in the streets, silent, depressed people—all this would have harmonized better with her story than the glittering spring sky and the kindly voices of people.

What could one say to a person like this? I could find nothing to penetrate the heart and mind of the woman in the bright blouse with a low-cut neckline. A gold ring set with a blood-red ruby squeezed her finger; she admired the play of sunshine on the facets of the stone and carelessly strung word after word on the capricious thread of her sensations.

"Love often leads to evil acts," her voice continued, as if repeating the vile clichés of some film. Then she bent toward me with a very strange look in her eyes.

"I can't help you in any way," I said.

"Yes?" she asked quietly.

"I am fully convinced I cannot."

"But—perhaps."

She spoke tender words about human charity, about man's sensitive heart, about Christ and others who had taught us to forgive sinners—all words extraordinarily inappropriate and revolting.

Her low-cut blouse revealed her breasts, and I involuntarily closed my eyes. The cad who had debauched this creature, that trader in human honesty, had fondled these breasts, had experienced as much delight as an honest man does when caressing his beloved. Stupid though it may be, I felt like demanding of someone whether such a thing were just?

"You see how young I am, but in the last few days I've felt myself an old hag. Everyone now feels gay and joyful, but I cannot. What is the reason?"

Her question sounded sincere. She shrank, pressing her hands against her knees, biting her lips; her face turned pale and the brightness of her eyes faded. She looked like a flower crushed by some man's heavy boot.

"Did you betray many men?"

"I didn't count them, naturally. I only reported on those whom I didn't particularly like."

"Do you know what the gendarmes did to them?"

"No, that didn't interest me. Of course, I heard that some were put in prison, sent into exile somewhere, but I wasn't involved in politics. . . ."

She talked of this with indifference as if referring to some remote and uninteresting past. She was fairly calm; she uttered not one hysterical cry, no howl of tortured conscience, nothing that indicated suffering. She would probably feel much worse, more perturbed, after a slight tiff with her lover.

After talking for two or three more minutes, she rose, nodded her head graciously to me, and, with the light step of a woman fond of dancing, walked toward the door. On the way she let fall: "How cruel people are, if one only thinks of it."

I wished to say to her: "You are a little late in thinking about that." But, with a tremendous effort of will, I controlled myself, disguising my smoldering rage.

Stopping at the door and gracefully turning her head, she asked over her shoulder: "But what will happen to my relatives and family when my name is published? Just think of that!"

"Why didn't you think of it yourself?"

"But who could suppose there would be a revolution?" she cried out. "So you can do nothing for me?"

"For you—nothing," I said quietly.

She went away.

I had known Gurievich, Aseff, Serebryakova, and a number of other traitors; from the lists of them published recently I've learned that over a dozen of them had been acquaintances of mine; they had called me "comrade" and, naturally, I had believed them. When their names were revealed, one after another, I felt as if some ruthlessly evil person had spat his irony at my heart. That had been one of the very basest mockeries directed against my faith in man.

But a child's crime is the most terrible crime in the world.

When this woman had gone, I thought to myself with

all the dull passivity of despair: "Isn't it time for me to shoot myself?"

In two or three days' time she appeared again, dressed this time in black and looking even more elegant. In mourning she looked even taller, and her charming, rosy face was more solid, stricter. She evidently loved precious stones; her blouse was pinned with a diamond brooch and a large ruby on a gold chain hung around her neck.

"I understand. You find it revolting," she argued, "but I have no one to advise me except you. I have grown accustomed to believe in you; it seemed to me that you loved human beings, even sinners, but you are so stiff and harsh. . . . It's strange!"

"Yes, it's strange," I repeated, laughing and thinking how shamelessly life violates human beings. And, in a way, I also felt guilty before this woman. In what way? I could not understand.

She began to explain that there was a man who was ready to marry her.

"He's elderly, an old man even, but what am I to do? If I change my name, I shall be able to disappear."

And smiling, almost gaily, she repeated: "Then I shan't be what I am now, isn't that so?"

I felt like saying: "Madam, even if the earth began to fall apart, crumbling into dust in space, and all men went mad with terror, I'd assume nevertheless that you would remain as you are. And if, by a miracle of our will, love and happiness hitherto unknown to us should descend upon the earth, I'd still think that you would remain as you are."

But it was useless talking to her—she was too convinced that everything could be forgiven a beautiful woman.

"If you think that will help you . . ." I said.

"Ah, I don't know what to think. I'm just afraid."

She talked capriciously, like a naughty child that wishes its pranks to be forgotten.

I said nothing.

Then she suggested: "Would you give me away at my wedding in place of my father? I have no father. That is, he's been separated from my mother. I don't love him and don't see him. Will you, please?"

I shook my head negatively. Then she fell on her knees, exclaiming: "But listen, won't you listen!"

There was something theatrical in her gestures, and she obviously wanted to remind me that she was a woman, wanted me to feel like a male. Throwing her head back gracefully, arching her bosom forward, she looked like a poisonous flower, her beautiful head resembling a pistil among the black petals of a lace blouse.

"Would you like me to be your lover, your *fille de joie*?" For some reason she put this question in French.

I walked away from her. Springing up lithely, she said: "All your speeches about love and compassion are just lies. All lies. All of them! You have written about women in a way . . . they were always right—but that also is a lie! Good-by!"

Then, as she was leaving, she said with spiteful conviction: "You have destroyed me!"

She vanished, having glued a black shadow to my soul. Perhaps the words I have just used are too beautiful, too inappropriate, but she had thrown me into a prickly thornbush of torturing thoughts about her and myself. There is no other way of expressing what I feel. A heavy, black shadow was stuck to my soul. These are probably stupid words. Like all words.

Am I not myself responsible for all this vileness which seethes in the life around me? Am I not myself responsible for this life, which has been so soiled at its very dawn by the filth of treachery?

There is the clamor in the streets of the newly liberated popular elements; hundreds of voices come buzzing like a swarm of bees through the window. The city is like a hive in the spring when the bees wake; and it seems to me that I hear the fresh, pungent smell of new words, sense everywhere the honey and wax of new thoughts being created.

This gives me joy, yes.

Yet I feel nailed down to some rotting wall, crucified to it by the piercing thoughts of violence done to a human being whom I cannot, simply cannot help, in any way, ever.

FIRST LOVE

. . . Then destiny, aiming to educate me, obliged me to experience the tragicomic tribulations of first love.

A group of my acquaintances had decided to go boating on the River Oka. I was asked to convey an invitation for this outing to Mr. and Mrs. K., who had recently returned from France; and, though I had not yet met them, I called on them in the evening.

They lodged in the basement of an old house; opposite it, spreading over the whole width of the street, was a large, filthy puddle, which never dried up during the spring and most of the summer; the crows and the dogs used it as a mirror, and the pigs as a bath.

Being rather preoccupied, I tumbled into the apartment of these strangers like a stone that has rolled downhill, producing a strange flurry among its inhabitants. A stoutish man of medium height with a broad, reddish beard and a benevolent expression in his blue eyes materialized in front of me after shutting the door to the next room.

Adjusting his dress, he inquired not very invitingly: "What do you want?"

And he added: "You should knock on the door before entering!"

In the twilit room behind his back, something resembling a white bird fluttered and quivered, and a gay ringing voice cried out: "Especially when you call on married people. . . ."

160

I asked them gruffly if they were the people I sought. And when the man, who resembled a prosperous shop-keeper, replied in the affirmative, I explained the reason for my visit.

"You say Clark sent you?" the man inquired straight-forwardly and thoughtfully, stroking his beard; and at the same instant he gave a start and whirled around like a top, ejaculating painfully: "Oi, Olga!"

Judging by the spasmodic movement of his hand, he seemed to have been pinched on that part of the anatomy usually considered to be unmentionable—apparently be-cause it is situated a little way below the waist.

His place was now taken by a shapely young woman who, holding on to the door jambs, examined me smiling-ly with a pair of blue eyes: "Who are you? A policeman?" she demanded.

"No, it's only my trousers," I replied politely, causing her to burst out laughing.

I was not offended, for her eyes glowed with a smile I had long looked forward to. Her laughter had been obviously provoked by my costume: I was wearing a pair of policeman's blue trousers and, by way of a shirt, a cook's short white tunic. This latter was a very prac-tical article of attire; it served me as a jacket, and when it was hooked up to the throat I could dispense with a shirt. A pair of someone else's hunting boots and the wide-brimmed hat of an Italian bandit completed the splendor of my costume.

Pulling me by the hand into the room and pushing me toward a chair, she confronted me with the question:

"Why are you so funnily dressed?"

"Why is it funny?"

"Don't be angry," she advised in a friendly voice.

A very strange young woman, this—who could be angry with her?

The bearded man, sitting on the bed, was rolling a cig-arette. Eyeing him, I asked her: "Is it your father or your brother?"

"Her husband!" he announced with conviction.

"Why did you ask?" she demanded, laughing.

After reflecting for a moment as I scrutinized her, I merely said: "Excuse me!"

The conversation continued in this laconic tone for about five minutes, but I felt capable of sitting immobilized in that basement for five whole hours, for days and years on end, gazing at the lady's narrow, oval little face and into her affectionate eyes. The lower lip of her small mouth was thicker than her upper lip and looked a trifle swollen; her heavy, chestnut-colored hair had been bobbed and rested on her head like a luxuriant cap, showering in curls about her rosy ears and tenderly blushing girlish cheeks. Her arms were very beautiful: I had seen them bared to the shoulder when she had stood in the doorway, holding on to the door jambs. She was dressed with extreme simplicity in a white blouse with wide lace sleeves and a white, smartly tailored skirt. But her bluish eyes were her most remarkable feature: they beamed joy, affection, and friendly curiosity. And there was no denying that she smiled in a way that was absolutely imperative for the heart of a young man of twenty—a heart wounded by all the crudities of life.

"It's going to rain hard in a minute," her husband announced, curing his beard with cigarette smoke.

I glanced out of the window: the stars were beginning to kindle in a cloudless sky. I understood at once that I was annoying this man, and so I departed in a mood of quiet joy, as though I had just discovered what I had been seeking unconsciously for a long time.

I walked about the fields all night, engrossed in admiring the glow of affection in those bluish eyes, and by dawn I was firmly convinced that this little lady was absolutely unsuited to be a wife to that bearded oaf with the benevolent eyes of a well-fed tomcat. I even felt sorry for her—the poor woman! To have to live with a man whose beard was a refuge for crumbs!

The following day we were out rowing on the turbid waters of the Oka, along the side of a high bank made of broad, variously colored layers of marl. For me, it was the best day since the creation of the world; the sun gleamed with amazing splendor in the bright, festive sky; the scent of ripening wild strawberry was carried above the river; all men remembered they were really good, and this nourished me with joy and love for them. Even the husband of my chosen lady seemed a man out of the ordinary. He climbed into another boat—not the one in which his wife was already sitting and in which I was to handle the oars. For the rest of the day he conducted himself with ideal discretion—first, he related a great many interesting things about Gladstone, and then, after drinking a whole jugful of excellent milk, stretched out under a bush and slept all evening as peacefully as a child.

Needless to say, our boat was the first to arrive at the site of the picnic. When I carried my lady out of the boat, she exclaimed: "How strong you are!"

At that moment I felt capable of toppling over any belfry, and informed my lady that I could carry her in my arms as far as the town—a distance of some seven miles.[1]

She laughed softly, glancing fondly at me. Her eyes glowed before me all day long and, of course, I was convinced that they glowed for me alone.

Very soon I learned that, despite her girlish appearance, she was ten years my senior. She had been educated at the Bialystok Institute for "noble young ladies," had been engaged to the Commandant of the Winter Palace, had lived in Paris, had studied painting, and was also a qualified midwife. Furthermore, it turned out that her mother was the midwife who had delivered me in the hour of my birth. I took this to be predestination, and felt terribly elated.

She had mixed with bohemians and *émigrés,* had an affair with one of the latter, and had led a seminomadic, semihungry life in the basements and garrets of Paris, Petersburg, and Vienna—all this had made of the former Institute girl an amusingly confused and unusually fascinating woman. Light and lively as a titmouse, she viewed people and life with the acute curiosity of an intelligent adolescent, sang provocative French songs, smoked cigarettes very elegantly, drew with skill, acted not at all badly on the stage, and was very clever at sewing dresses and making hats. She did not practice as a midwife.

"I had four cases in practice, but the mortality rate was seventy-five percent," she explained.

This had estranged her forever from the business of

---

[1] *I probably could not have carried her that far.* [Author's note.]

assisting indirectly in the matter of increasing the popula-
tion, but her daughter—a beautiful, darling child of four
—bore witness to her direct participation in this honor-
able pursuit. Of herself she spoke in a tone used about
someone one knows very well and with whom one is
rather bored. But at times she seemed astonished when
speaking of herself; her eyes would grow handsomely
dark, and a slight, embarrassed smile would flash and
twinkle in them. It was the way an embarrassed child
smiles.

I sensed her acute, tenacious mind; grasped that she
was culturally superior to me; and observed her tolerant
yet condescending attitude to people. She was incompa-
rably more interesting than any of the young women and
married ladies I then knew. The casual tone of her stories
amazed me, and it seemed that this woman, knowing
everything that revolutionary inclined acquaintances knew,
yet knew something above this, something of greater
value; but she looked upon everything from a distance,
from the side, as if watching with an adult smile some
endearing but dangerous children's game she had already
tried.

The basement she inhabited was divided into two
rooms: a small kitchen serving also as an entrance hall;
and a large room with three windows giving on the street,
and two facing on a filthy dump of a back yard. The
premises might have suited a cobbler, but not an elegant
lady who had lived in Paris, the holy city of the Great
Revolution, the city of Molière, Beaumarchais, Hugo,
and other such luminaries. There were a great many other
discrepancies between the painting and the frame, and
all of them were a source of cruel irritation to me, evok-
ing—besides other emotions—that of pity for the woman.
But she herself did not seem to notice any of the things
which, in my opinion, should have offended her.

She worked from morning till night: in the morning, as
a maid and cook; and then, seated at a large table under
the windows, she would draw all day long from photographs the portraits of local inhabitants, would sketch
maps, color in cartograms, and help her husband to com-

pile whole volumes of Zemstvo[2] statistics. Through the open window the dust of the street came showering upon her head and on the table, and the feet of passersby cast shifting shadows upon her papers. She sang as she worked and, when tired of sitting, waltzed around with a chair or played with her daughter; and despite plenty of dirty work she was always as tidy as a cat.

Her husband was easy-going and indolent. He loved reading in bed foreign novels in Russian translation, particularly Dumas *père*. "It refreshes the brain cells," he used to say. He liked to examine life "from a strictly scientific standpoint." Dinner he called "the intake of nourishment" and, having dined, he would say: "The conveyance of digested food from the stomach by the cells of the organism demands absolute repose."

And, forgetting to shake out the bread crumbs from his beard, he would go to bed and read Alexandre Dumas or Xavier de Montépin for a few minutes with great concentration, and then whistle lyrically through his nose for a couple of hours, while his fair, soft mustaches stirred as if an invisible something were crawling in them. On awakening, he would stare long and ruminatively at the cracks in the ceiling and then suddenly remember: "But Kuzma went wrong yesterday in his interpretation of Parnell's idea!"

And off he would go to confront Kuzma, saying to his wife: "Will you please complete for me the statistics of those who don't own horses in the Maidansk district. I'll be back soon!"

He would return near midnight, sometimes later, very satisfied with himself.

"Well, you know, I put Kuzma in his place today! That scamp has a highly developed memory for statistics, but I won't yield to him even in this. By the way, it's odd, but he has absolutely no notion of Gladstone's Near Eastern policy!"

He was constantly talking about Binet, Richet, and mental hygiene; and, when staying at home in bad weather, he busied himself with educating his wife's daughter—her chance offspring on the road between two romances.

2 *Zemstvo*—the elective council of a district.

"Lelya, you should chew thoroughly while eating. It helps the digestion and aids the stomach to transform the digested nourishment into an easily absorbed conglomeration of chemical substances."

After the dinner, having put himself "in a state of absolute repose," he made the child lie down, and then began narrating: "Thus, when the bloodthirsty, ambitious Bonaparte had usurped the power . . ."

His wife would go into fits of laughter till the tears came as she listened to these lectures, but he did not have time enough to be offended, for he very quickly dropped off to sleep. After playing a while with his silken beard, the little girl also dozed off, curled up in a ball. I had made great friends with her, and she listened to my stories with much greater interest than to Boleslav's lectures about the bloodthirsty usurper and Josephine Beauharnais's sad infatuation with him. This used to make Boleslav envious in an amusing way.

"I protest, Peshkov! It is first of all essential to inculcate into a child the basic principles of her relation to reality, and only then for her to become acquainted with it. If you knew English and could read *The Hygiene of a Child's Soul* . . ."

His knowledge of English was limited to two words: "good-by."

He was double my age, but was as inquisitive as a young poodle. He loved to gossip and to appear as a man who knew all the secrets, not only of Russian, but also of foreign revolutionary groups. However, he actually may have been well informed. Not infrequently he was visited by mysterious people who, all of them, behaved like tragic actors accidentally obliged to play the role of simpletons. At his apartment I saw Sabunayev, who was engaged in illegal activity, disguised awkwardly in a red wig and a flashy suit that was too short and comically tight.

Calling on Boleslav one day, I caught sight of a squirmy man with a small head, who looked very much like a hairdresser. He wore striped trousers, a little gray jacket, and squeaky boots. Pushing me into the kitchen, Boleslav told me in a whisper: "He's a man from Paris with an important message. He must see Korolenko.[3] Go at once and arrange this. . . ."

I went off to do so, but it turned out that the new arrival had already been pointed out to Korolenko in the street, and the latter had very perceptively declared: "No, please don't introduce me to that fop!"

Bol·· · felt offended on behalf of his "Parisian" and the "· · of the Revolution." He spent the next two days composing a letter to Korolenko, trying every style —ranging from that of indignation and castigation to that of affectionate reproach—and finally burned all the samples of this epistolary literature in the oven. Shortly after arrests began in Moscow, Nizhny, and Vladimir, and the man in the striped trousers turned out to be the subsequently notorious Landesen-Harting, the first *agent provocateur* I had ever seen.

But apart from all this the husband of my beloved was a good little fellow, though somewhat sentimental and comically burdened with "scientific baggage." That indeed was the way he talked:

"The sense of an intellectual's life lies in the uninterrupted accumulation of scientific baggage for the purpose of its disinterested dissemination among the dense mass of the people. . . ."

My love, as it deepened, was transformed into suffering. Sitting in the basement, I watched the lady of my heart working, stooped over the table; and I was sullenly intoxicated with the desire to pick her up in my arms and carry her away somewhere from that accursed basement, cluttered with a wide double bed, a cumbersome ancient sofa on which her daughter slept, and tables piled with dusty books and papers. Anonymous feet flashed insensibly past the windows; sometimes a homeless dog thrust its muzzle at the windowpane; and the smell of sunwarmed garbage poured in from the street. The small girlish figure, humming quietly, worked away with a creaking pencil or pen, her cornflower eyes smiling fondly at me. I loved this woman to the point of delirium and madness, and pitied her to the point of sullen spite.

---

[3] V. G. Korolenko—a noted writer of social conscience, who had also assisted the young Gorky.

"Tell me something about yourself," she would sug-
gest.

I would begin telling her, but she would interrupt me
within a few minutes: "That's not about yourself you're
speaking!"

I realized that what I was speaking about was not yet
my real self, but something in which I had become blind-
ly enmeshed. I had still to find myself in the variegated
tangle of impressions and adventures I had gone through,
but I could not do this yet, and was afraid to do so. Who
was I, and what? This question confused me a great deal.
I was angry at life; it had already prompted me to the
base stupidity of attempted suicide. I did not understand
people: their life to me seemed unjustified, crass, and
dirty. I was egged on by the curiosity of a man who, for
some reason, found it essential to peer into all the dark
corners of existence, into the depths of all the mysteries
of life. There were times when I felt myself capable of
committing a crime just out of sheer curiosity—I was
ready to kill merely for the sake of learning what would
happen to me afterwards.

It seemed to me that, if I discovered my real self then
and there before the woman of my heart, she would be
confronted by a revolting man, a man enmeshed in a
thick, strong net of strange emotions and ideas; a delirious nightmarish man, who would only frighten and disgust
her. I must do something with myself. And I was convinced that this woman, and no other, was alone capable
not only of helping me to feel my real self, but also of
performing some miracle, after which I would immediately free myself from the bonds of my pessimistic impressions of existence, and would then forever cast that something out of my soul, which would at once become ignited
with great power and great joy.

Both the casual tone in which she spoke of herself and
her condescending attitude to people instilled in me the
certainty of her extraordinary knowledge. She possessed
her own key to all the enigmas of life; that was what always made her so joyous, so sure of herself. Perhaps I
loved her most for what I failed to understand about her,
but I loved her with all my youthful ardor and passion.
It was torture for me to restrain that passion—already

physically she consumed and overpowered me. It would have been better for me had I been simpler and cruder, but I believed that man's relationship with a woman was not confined to the act of physiological union, which I knew in all its crudity and bestial simplicity. This act instilled in me almost disgust, despite my being a strong, sensitive enough lad, and one possessed of an easily aroused imagination.

I fail to understand how this romantic dream could have formed itself and persisted in me, but I was unshakably convinced that there existed something unknown beyond my knowledge; that it secreted within it the high, mysterious significance of man's relationship with woman; that something great, joyous, and even terrifying lay hidden beyond the first embrace; and that the experience of this joy constituted man's complete rebirth.

I had not acquired these fantasies, it seems, from reading fiction, but had nurtured and developed them from a feeling of contradiction against reality, for, "I came into the world to disagree."

Besides, I was haunted by a strange and vague remembrance: somewhere beyond the confines of reality, and sometime in early childhood, I had experienced a certain powerful explosion in my soul, a sweet tremulous sensation or, more truly, a premonition of harmony. I had experienced the serenest joy of sunrise or sunset. Perhaps it had occurred in the days when I was still in my mother's womb; and the happy explosion of her nervous energy had been passed on to me in a great charge of heat, which had created my soul and ignited it initially for life. Perhaps, it was this shattering moment of my mother's happiness that was reflected in me for the rest of my life in that tremulous sensation I had of expecting something extraordinary from a woman.

One invents when one does not know. The wisest thing man has yet achieved is his ability to love a woman, worshiping her beauty. Everything beautiful on earth was born of man's love for woman.

While out swimming one day, I jumped into the water from the stern of a barge, hit my chest against the anchor, caught my foot in the cable, and hung head down gulping in the water. A carter pulled me out. They resuscitated me, tearing the skin off me in the process. Then the blood began to gush from my throat, and I was obliged to take to bed and swallow lots of ice.

My lady came to see me, sat down on my bed and, questioning me as to how it had happened, began to stroke my head with her dear, light hand, while her eyes, a shade darker, gazed anxiously at me.

I asked her whether she realized that I loved her.

"Yes," she replied with a discreet smile, "I do realize, and it's very bad, though I have fallen in love with you, too."

Needless to say, the earth quaked after she spoke, and the trees in the garden did a merry dance in a circle. Struck dumb at the very unexpectedness, the surprise, and the delight of it, I thrust my head into her lap; and had I not hugged her closely I would most likely have flown out of the window like a soap bubble.

"Don't move, it's bad for you!" she exclaimed severely, trying to put my head back on the pillow. "And don't excite yourself, or I'll go away! You are, all in all, a very crazy gentleman; I didn't know such men existed. We shall speak of our feelings and relations when you get on your feet again."

All this she said with great calm, an inexpressible look of affection in her dark, smiling eyes. She departed soon after, leaving me in a rainbow glow of expectation, in the happy conviction that now, with her generous assistance, I would soar into a sphere of other feelings and thoughts.

A few days later I was sitting on the edge of a ravine in a field. The wind rustled in the bushes; the gray sky threatened rain. In a businesslike way, using gray words, my lady pointed out the difference in our years, the necessity of my studying, and that it would be premature for me to hang a wife and child around my neck. All this was depressingly true and was spoken in the tone a mother might use, but it only excited me to even greater love and respect for this endearing woman.

It was sad and sweet for me to hear her voice, her tender words—it was the first time anyone had ever talked to me in this way.

I stared into the maw of the ravine where the bushes, stirred by the wind, flowed like a green river, and swore to repay this woman with all the strength of my soul for her affection.

"Before we decide anything, we must think it over," I heard her soft voice say. She was whipping her knee with a broken-off hazel branch as she gazed in the direction of the town hidden behind the green mounds of the gardens.

"And I must, of course, talk it over with Boleslav; he already senses something, and is very on edge. Personally, I don't like domestic dramas."

All this was both very sad and very good, but it was also essential that something trite and comic should occur.

My *sharovary* were very wide at the belt, and I had resorted to fastening the belt with a large brass pin about three inches long—fortunately for poor lovers such pins no longer exist! The sharp point of that damned pin had been delicately pricking my skin all the time; but, when I made an awkward movement, the pin suddenly pierced my side. I managed to pull it out unnoticed, and then was horrified to feel the blood flowing freely from the deep scratch and saturating my *sharovary*. I wore no underclothes, and my waiter's tunic, a short one, reached the waist only. How was I to get up and walk in those blood-soaked *sharovary*, which were now glued to my body?

While understanding the comic aspects of the accident, and yet deeply disgusted by its offensive form, I began, wildly agitated, to speak in the unnatural voice of an actor who has forgotten his role.

After listening for a few minutes to my flow of words, attentively at first and then with obvious perplexity, she said: "What sumptuous words! Of a sudden you no longer resemble yourself."

This finally so astonished me that I relapsed into a crushed silence.

"Time to go, it's about to rain!" she said.

"I'll stay on here."

"Why?"

What could I answer?

"Are you angry with me?" she asked, glancing fondly into my face.

"Oh, no! I'm angry at myself."

"And you mustn't be angry at yourself either," she advised me, standing up.

But I couldn't get up. Sitting in a warm puddle, it seemed to me that the blood, flowing from my side, was gurgling like a stream, and that she would hear the sound within a second and ask me: "What is that?"

"Go away!" I begged her mutely.

Mercifully she made me the gift of a few more fond words, and went off along the edge of the ravine, swaying endearingly on her shapely legs. I watched her small, supple figure withdraw and diminish, and then lay down full length on the ground, prostrated by a sudden aware-ness that my first love would prove unhappy.

Of course, that is what happened. Her husband wept a whole torrent of tears, sentimental slush, abject words, and she could not make up her mind to swim to my side over this sticky torrent.

"He is so helpless, and you're so strong!" she said to me with tears in her eyes. "He says: 'If you leave me, I'll perish like a little flower out of the sun.'"

I burst out laughing, remembering his short legs, his somewhat feminine ribs, and his round melonlike little flower of a stomach. Flies lodged in his beard—there was always food for them there.

"Yes, in a way it is very funny," she admitted, smiling, "but nevertheless it hurts him very much!"

"It hurts me, too!"

"But you are so young and strong. . . ."

Here, for the first time it seems, I felt myself an enemy of weak people. Afterward, in more serious cases, I often had occasion to observe how tragically helpless are the strong in the presence of the weak, how much precious energy of heart and mind is wasted to support the barren existence of those condemned to perish.

Very soon, half-sick and in a state bordering on mad-ness, I left the town and, for almost two years, wandered about the roads of Russia like a rolling stone. I tramped over the lower Volga Lands, the Don, the Ukraine, the Crimea, and the Caucasus; experienced a countless num-

ber of various impressions and adventures; grew tough-
ened, increasingly angry; and yet managed to preserve
uncorrupted in my soul the fond image of this woman,
even though I came across better and more intelligent
women.

And when, after two years and a bit, I was told one
autumn in Tiflis that she had just arrived from Paris and
was glad to hear that I was living in the same town, I, a
virile youth of twenty-three, fainted for the first time in
my life.

I could not make up my mind to see her, but very
soon she herself sent me an invitation through mutual
friends.

She struck me as even more beautiful and desirable,
as youthful in figure, with the same pink, tender cheeks
and the same affectionate light in her cornflower eyes.
Her husband had remained behind in France, and she
was accompanied only by her daughter, who was now as
skittish and graceful as a kid.

A storm with thunder and lightning was raging above
the town when I arrived; heavy rain pelted down and,
along the street from Mount Saint David, a mighty river
rolled impetuously, churning up the paving stones. The
howling of the wind, the angry splashing of the water,
the thud of damage, shook the house and made the panes
rattle. The room was bathed in a blue light, and everything around us seemed to be tumbling into a watery,
bottomless abyss.

The frightened little girl buried herself under the bed-
clothes, while the two of us stood at the window, blinded
by the explosions of the sky, and talked for some reason
in a whisper.

"It's the first time I've seen such a storm," the words
of my beloved rustled near-by. And then she suddenly
asked: "Well, tell me, are you cured of your love for
me?"

"No."

She was evidently surprised and said in the same
whisper: "Heavens, how you have changed! You're a
completely different man!"

She settled slowly into an armchair by the window,

gave a start and shut her eyes, dazzled by an awesome flash of lightning.

"They talk a lot about you here," she whispered. "Why did you come here? Tell me what sort of life you have been leading?"

Oh Lord, how delicate and lovely she was! I spoke to her till midnight as if confessing. The dread phenomena of nature have always had an exciting effect upon me, filling me with stormy joy.

I must have told my story well—her attention and the intent gaze of her widely dilated eyes persuaded me of it. Only occasionally she commented in a whisper: "That is terrible."

Departing, I noticed that she took leave of me without the patronizing smile of maturity that in the past had always nettled me a little. I walked along the wet streets, observing the sharp sickle of the moon slice the ragged clouds, and my head felt giddy from joy. The following day I sent her some verses by mail—she would often declaim them in the days to come, and they became registered in my memory:

My Lady!
    In return for affection and a tender look
    the deft magician surrenders into slavery,
    who well knows the fine shades
    of the amusing art
    of creating small joys
    from trifles, from nothing.
    Take the cheerful slave!
    Perhaps from small joys
    he will create a greater happiness—
    for has not something created the whole world
    from insignificant dust grains of matter?

    O yes! The world is no merry creation:
    Niggardly and wretched are its joys!
    Yet it has a few amusing things to offer:
    for example, your obedient servant,
    and he bears in him a thing of beauty—
    It is of You I speak!
    You!

But—silence!
What are the blunt nails of words
When compared with your heart—
the best of all flowers
of the earth so poor in flowers?

Of course this was hardly poetry but joy and sincerity had gone into its composition.

Once again I sat opposite the person whom I regarded as the best in the world and, for that reason, indispensable. She wore a light-blue dress; without concealing the graceful contours of her figure, it enveloped her in a soft, fragrant cloud. Playing with the tassels of her sash, she addressed me in extraordinary words. I followed the movement of her slender fingers with their pink nails and felt myself to be a violin lovingly tuned by a skilled violinist. I wanted to die, wanted in some way to breathe this woman into my soul, so that she might remain there forever. My body vibrated in song so deeply tense and powerful that it caused me pain, and my heart seemed about to burst.

I read her my first story, which had just been printed,[4] but I forget how she liked it—she was surprised, I think. "So, you've begun to write prose!"

As in a dream, I heard her speak from far away: "I've thought a lot about you during these years. Was it really because of me you had to experience so many hardships?"

I said something to the effect that there was no hardship, no terror, in the world she inhabited.

"What a darling you are. . . ." she said.

I madly wanted to embrace her, but I did not dare to touch her with my idiotically long, awkwardly heavy arms. I was afraid of hurting her. So I stood before her and, swaying to the fierce thrusts of my heart, muttered: "Please come and live with me! Please come and live with me!"

She laughed quietly, embarrassed. Her lovely eyes dazzled me. She stepped into a corner of the room and said from there: "Let's do it this way: you go back to

[4] Presumably *Makar Chudra*, published in 1892.

Nizhny, and I'll remain here, think it over, and write
you. . . ."

I bowed respectfully to her, like the hero of some
novel I had read, and went away walking on air.

In the winter she and her daughter came to stay with
me in Nizhny. "When a poor man weds, even the night's
too short," says the sad, ironic wisdom of the people.
With my personal experience I tested the deep truth of
this proverb.

For two rubles a month we rented a mansion—an old
bathhouse in a priest's garden. I lodged in the bathhouse
entrance, while my wife took over the bathhouse, which
also did duty as our parlor. The little mansion was not
so convenient for family life; it was chilly in all the corners and along the joints. When working at night, I
wrapped myself in every bit of clothing I had, and
capped it all with a rug, and yet for all that I developed
a very serious case of rheumatism. It was an almost
supernatural event considering my robust health and
powers of endurance, of which I was then justly proud.

It was warmer in the bathhouse but whenever I lit the
stove our whole premises were filled with the stifling
smell of decay, soap, and well-steamed birch brooms.
The daughter, an elegant porcelain doll with marvelous
eyes, became nervous and suffered from headaches.

In the springtime a multitude of spiders and wood-lice
began to visit the bathhouse. Both mother and daughter
were frightened to fits by them, and I was obliged to
slaughter the insects with a rubber galosh. The small
windows were soon overgrown with elder bushes and
wild raspberry; it was always dark in the room, and the
drunken, capricious priest would not allow me to pull out
or even to trim the bushes.

Of course one could have found a more comfortable
lodging, but we owed the priest money, and besides, he
had taken a great fancy to me; he would not let us go.

"You'll get used to it!" he would say. "Or pay up your
debts and then you can go to the English if you wish."

He disliked the English, affirming: "They're a lazy nation. They haven't invented anything except politics, and
they don't know how to fight."

He was a huge man with a round red face and a broad

red beard. He drank so much that he could no longer celebrate Mass in church, and was tormented to tears by his fondness for a small, sharp-nosed, black-haired seamstress who resembled a jackdaw.

Recounting her perfidy, he would brush away the tears from his beard with his palm and say: "I realize that she's a good-for-nothing, but she reminds me of the great martyr Saint Thurvia, and for that I love her!"

I carefully went through *The Lives of the Saints,* but could find no such saint there.

Revolted by my disbelief, he shocked my soul with such arguments as these in favor of faith: "Now, you must look at this practically, my son: there are dozens of unbelievers and millions of the faithful! Why is that? Because, just as fish cannot exist without water, the soul cannot live without the Church. Isn't that proof enough! Therefore—let's drink!"

"I don't drink. I have rheumatism."

Spearing a morsel of herring with his fork, he raised it menacingly on high, proclaiming: "That comes of disbelief, too!"

I felt tortured and ashamed before my wife, to the point of insomnia, on account of the bathhouse, the frequent impossibility of my buying any meat for dinner or even a toy for her daughter—for the whole of this damned, ironic poverty. Poverty was a failing that did not embarrass or worry me personally, but this life was degradation and sheer murder for the dainty little Institute lady and especially for her daughter.

At night, sitting at my corner table, copying petitions and appellate and cassation briefs, and also writing my own stories, I used to grit my teeth and curse not only myself, but also people, destiny, and love.

The woman behaved generously, like a mother who does not want her son to notice how difficult it is for her. Not a single complaint against the meanness of this life ever burst from her lips; the harder the conditions, the more cheerfully her voice sounded and the more joyful her laughter. From morning till night she went on drawing portraits of priests and their deceased wives, sketching district maps—at some exhibition the Zemstvo was awarded a gold medal for these. When the commissions for portraits dried up, she made fashionable Parisian hats from various bits of material, straw and wire, for the girls and ladies of our street. I understood nothing about women's hats, but evidently there was something devastatingly comic about those hats, for the master-hatter would choke in fits of laughter when trying on some fantastic headpiece of her own creation in front of the mirror. These hats, I noticed, had a strange effect on her clients: adorning their heads with variegated chicken nests, they strutted about the street with their bellies proudly protruding.

I worked for an attorney, and also wrote stories for the local newspaper at two kopecks a line. In the evenings, over tea, if we had no guests, my wife would give me a most interesting account of how Tsar Alexander II used to visit the Bialystok Institute and treat the noble young ladies to candy, by which certain of them would later become pregnant as if by magic. Not infrequently one or another beautiful girl would disappear, driving off to a hunting party with the Tsar in the virgin forests of Byelobezh: and she would then be married off in Petersburg.

My lady told me many enthralling things about Paris. I already knew something about Paris from books, particularly from the voluminous work of Maxime du Camp. She had studied Paris in the cabarets of Montmartre and the madcap life of the Latin Quarter. These accounts excited me more potently than wine, and I composed hymns of a sort to this woman, feeling that all the beauty of life had been created by the power of my love for her.

What enthralled me more than anything else were her accounts of her own romances. She spoke on this subject in an amazingly fascinating way and with a candor that, at times, greatly embarrassed me. With deft words like the strokes of a finely sharpened pencil, she laughingly delineated the comic figure of her former fiancé, the General, who, having shot an aurochs before the Tsar had time to pull the trigger, had shouted after the wounded beast: "Forgive me, Your Imperial Majesty!"

She told me about the Russian *émigrés* abroad, and I always sensed a hidden smile of condescension in her words. At times her sincerity descended to naïve cynicism. With her sharp, pink tongue she would lick her lips appreciatively, like a cat, while her eyes glittered in a peculiar manner. Sometimes they seemed to flash with a fastidious light, but more often I saw her as a young girl absorbed in playing with dolls. Once she said to me: "A Russian in love is always rather wordy and ponderous, and not infrequently repulsive in his eloquence. Only Frenchmen know how to love beautifully; love for them is almost a religion."

After this I involuntarily treated her with even greater restraint and care.

About French women she said: "You won't always find them passionately tender, but they replace it wonderfully by their joyous, subtly developed sensibility. Love for them is an art."

She said all this very seriously, in a didactic tone. Those were not the aspects of knowledge I most needed, but it was information all the same, and I avidly absorbed it.

"There is probably as much difference between the Russians and the French as between fresh fruit and fruit candy," she said one moonlit night, sitting in the garden arbor.

She herself was a fruit candy. She had been terribly astonished when, in the early days of our marital life, I, it goes without saying in an inspired mood, exposed to her my romantic views on the relations between man and woman.

"Are you serious? You really think so?" she had asked, resting in my arms under the bluish light of the moon.

Her rosy body, exuding the bitter, intoxicating scent of almonds, looked transparent. Her slender little fingers toyed thoughtfully with the mane of my hair. She gazed into my face with her wide open, tremulous eyes, and smiled suspiciously.

"Ah, good heavens!" she exclaimed, jumping down to the floor. Pensively she began to pace about the room, passing from light to shadow, her satin skin gleaming in the moonlight, her bare feet noiselessly touching the floor. Approaching me then once more, and stroking my cheeks with her palms, she said in a mother's voice:

"You should have started your life with a younger woman—yes, yes! Not with me. . . ."

When I took her in my arms, she began to cry. Then, speaking softly, she said: "You feel how much I love you, don't you? I've never succeeded in experiencing so much joy as with you—that is true, believe me! I've never loved with so much tenderness and affection, with such a light heart. I feel wonderfully well with you but, all the same, I must say: we have made a mistake. I'm not the woman you need. I'm not! It was my mistake."

Failing to understand her, frightened by her words, I hastened to extinguish this mood of hers with the joy of caresses. But, nevertheless, her strange words stuck in my memory. And several days later she, in tears of rapture, was again sadly repeating these words: "Ah, if I were only a young woman! . . ."

That night, I remember, a blizzard was sweeping the garden: branches of elder thrashed against the window-panes, the wind howled in the chimney like a wolf, it was dark and cold in our room, and strips of unglued wallpaper made rustling sounds.

Having earned a few rubles, we used to invite acquaintances and prepare splendiferous suppers: we ate meat, drank vodka and beer, swallowed pastries, and, in general, indulged ourselves. My Parisian lady was possessed of a fine appetite and adored Russian cooking: *zichug*—beef tripe stuffed with buckwheat and goose fat; pies with fish fats and *somina*—catfish; and potato soup with mutton.

She organized the order of "The Greedy Little Bellies" —a dozen or so people who, fond of solid fare and steady drink, were subtly and esthetically aware, and eloquently, inexhaustibly discussed the taste mysteries of the kitchen, whereas I, interested in mysteries of another kind, ate sparingly and was unattracted by the mere process of stuffing myself, a process that has remained outside the sphere of my esthetic needs.

"Those are hollow people!" I judged, referring to "The Greedy Little Bellies."

"Like everyone else, when properly shaken up," she

replied. "Heine has said, 'We all walk naked beneath our clothes!' "

She knew a good many such skeptical quotations, but she did not always use them appropriately or to the best advantage.

She was very fond of "shaking up" the males in her entourage, and this she accomplished very easily. Inexhaustibly gay, witty, supple as a snake, she could quickly kindle a noisy commotion around her, rousing emotions of no very high order. It was enough for a man to chat with her for a few minutes for his ears to turn red; they would then turn purple, and his eyes, growing moist, would stare at her with the glint of a he-goat eyeing a cabbage.

"A magnetic woman!" exclaimed a certain deputy notary, a failed gentleman with warts like the False Dimitry's, and a belly the size of a bishop's.

The fair-browed ex-high-school senior from Yaroslav composed poems for her—always in dactyls. I thought them revolting, but she laughed over them till she cried.

"Why do you excite the men?"

"It's as interesting as fishing for perch. This is what is called coquetting. There isn't a woman with any respect for herself who does not love to play the coquette."

Looking into my eyes with a smile, she would sometimes ask: "Are you jealous?"

No, I was not jealous, but all this interfered a little with my life. I disliked worthless people. A cheerful person myself, I knew that laughter was man's most beautiful quality. But I personally regarded circus clowns, music hall humorists, and comedians as people of little talent, feeling certain that I myself could make people laugh much better than they could. Often enough I succeeded in obliging our guests to laugh till their sides split.

"Heavens!" she would exclaim admiringly. "What a wonderful comic you would make! You must go on the stage, you must!"

She herself had acted with success on the amateur stage, and established theatrical producers kept inviting her to turn professional.

"I love being on stage, but am frightened of what goes on backstage," she used to say.

She was sincere in her desires, thoughts, and words.

"You philosophize too much," she admonished. "Life is in essence simple and crude. There's no need to complicate it by trying to find some special meaning in it; one has only to learn how to smooth out the rough edges. More than that—you will achieve nothing more than that."

In her philosophy I sensed an excessive amount of gynecology. A textbook on *How to Be a Midwife* might well have been her gospel. She herself had told me how shocked she had been by some scientific book, the very first she had read after leaving the Institute.

"A naïve girl, I felt as if I'd been hit on the head with a brick; I seemed to have been thrown out of the clouds into the mud; I wept out of pity for what I could no longer believe in, but very quickly I began to feel firm, if harsh, soil under my feet. It was God I pitied most, for I had felt Him so closely; and now of a sudden He was dissipated like cigarette smoke, and with Him vanished the dream of love and heavenly bliss. And all of us at the Institute had thought so much, had talked so well about love!"

Her Parisian-Institute nihilism had a bad effect on me. Sometimes at night I would rise from my working table and go in to gaze upon her—in bed she always looked smaller, more graceful, and more beautiful. I would gaze at her and reflect most bitterly upon her twisted soul and muddled life. Pity for her only fortified my love.

Our literary tastes were irreconcilably divergent. I used to read Balzac and Flaubert with enthusiasm; she preferred Paul Féval, Octave Feuillet, and Paul de Kock, especially the latter's *La Fille Girot, Ma Femme*. This book she considered extremely clever, while I found it as dreary as *The Code of Penalties*. In spite of all this, our relations were very good; we did not lose interest in each other, and our passion did not die. But in the third year of our life together, I began to notice a certain sinister creaking in my soul—ever louder and more obvious. I was studying avidly, without interruption; I read a great deal, and had begun to be seriously involved in literary work. But our guests increasingly got in my way; people of little interest, they multiplied in quantity, for both my wife and I were now earning more, and were therefore able to entertain more frequently at dinner and supper.

Life for her was something like a panopticon; and, since the men wore no labels warning: "Hands off!" she sometimes approached them with too little care; they valued her curiosity for their own profit, and this gave rise to misunderstandings that I was forced to correct. At times I did so with too little restraint and, probably, always very awkwardly. The man whose ears I once pulled gave vent to this complaint: "Well, all right, I admit I was to blame! But to pull me by the ears—am I a boy or what? I'm almost twice as old as that savage, and he tweaks my ears! Well, he might have hit me, that would have been more decent!"

Apparently I lacked the art of punishing my neighbor in keeping with his scale of self-respect.

My wife's attitude to my stories was indifferent enough, but this caused me no annoyance until a certain moment; I did not believe as yet that I could become a serious writer, and I regarded my publications in the local newspaper as only a livelihood, even though I had not infrequently experienced the onrush of a warm wave of a peculiar self-denial. But early one morning she fell sound asleep while I was reading her my new story *Old Woman Izergil,* which I had just written the previous night. For the first minute or so I did not feel hurt; I merely stopped reading and began to reflect as I gazed at her.

Propping her small head, so precious to me, against the back of the old sofa, her mouth open, she breathed equably and peacefully as a child. Through the elder branches the morning sun peeped in at the window, and golden patches, like some sort of aerial flowers, rested upon this woman's breast and knees.

I rose and stepped quietly into the garden, suffering the pain of a deep hurt, overcome by doubt in my own powers.

In all the days of my life till then, I had seen women only in conditions of heavy, slavelike labor, filth and debauchery, and beggary, or semimoribund, self-satisfied, and low satiety. Only one beautiful childhood impression remained—that of Queen Margot [5]—but a whole mountain range of other impressions now separated me from it. I thought that the story of Izergil's life would please women and excite in them the thirst for freedom and beauty. But here was the woman I cared for most, asleep, unaffected by my story!

Why? Was the bell that life had cast in my breast not sufficiently sonorous?

In my heart I had accepted this woman like a mother. I believed her capable of nourishing me on the intoxicating honey that would stimulate my creative powers; I expected her influence to soften the rough edges I had put on in the course of my journey through life.

That was thirty years ago, and now I recall it all with a smile in the depth of my soul. But at the time, man's indisputable right to sleep whenever he feels so inclined grieved me a great deal.

I believed that sorrow would disappear if we spoke cheerfully about sad things.

I suspected, too, that in the world a certain somebody was cunningly active, who took pleasure in gloating over the suffering of people; it seemed a certain spirit did exist—the author of domestic dramas—who very cleverly spoilt life. I regarded this invisible dramatist as my personal enemy, and did my best not to fall into his traps.

I remember my deep disgust on reading in Oldenburg's book, *Buddha, His Life, Teaching, and Community,* that "every existence is essentially suffering." I had not experienced very many joys in life, but life's bitter torments had seemed to me the result of chance, not of law. Having read attentively that solid work, *The Religion of the Orient* by Archbishop Chrysanphemus, I felt with even greater indignation that the doctrine of a world founded on fear, depression, and suffering was utterly unacceptable to me. And, having once lived painfully through a mood of religious ecstasy, I felt insulted by the fruitless nature of that mood. Disgust with suffering has roused in me an organic hatred for every sort of

5 A character referred to in Gorky's autobiographical work, *In the World.*

drama, and I have learned, not too badly, to convert such drama into comic vaudeville acts.

Of course, I might have avoided saying all this for the sole purpose of stating that a domestic drama was brewing between a woman and myself; but we were both united in resisting it. If I have philosophized a little, it is because I wanted to recall some of the amusing twists and turns on the path I was walking in search of my own self.

My woman, by virtue of her joyous nature, was likewise incapable of dramatic scenes at home—those scenes in which extremely "psychological" Russians of both sexes are so fond of indulging.

But the dreary dactyls of the fair-browed ex-high-school senior did nevertheless affect her like the autumn rain. In a handsome, rounded hand he scribbled whole pages of verse and left them secretly in every nook he could find—in books, in a hat, in the sugar bowl. Finding these accurately folded pages, I handed them over to my wife, saying: "Please accept this current attempt to touch your heart!"

At first these paper arrows from Cupid made no impact upon her; she would read me the lengthy verses, and we laughed in unison on coming across the memorable lines:

> I am with you alone by day and night;
> All is reflected in my heart:
> The gesture of your hand, your nodding head.
> You're cooing like a tender dove,
> And I, a hawk in thought, above you soar.

But having read one day a similar epistle in the same hand, she musingly exclaimed: "I'm sorry for him!"

I remember—it was not him I pitied; but, from that minute, she stopped reading the dactyls aloud.

The poet, a sturdy lad, some four years my senior, was taciturn, very partial to alcoholic beverages, and remarkably fond of just sitting on in his chair. Arriving at two o'clock in the afternoon on a holiday, he could sit there, dumb and immobile, till two o'clock in the morning. He was, like myself, a law clerk, and greatly amazed his good-natured employer by his absent-mindedness, performed his work carelessly, and often repeated in a hoarse bass voice: "In general, all this is nonsense!"

"And what is not nonsense?"

"What is there to say?" he asked thoughtfully, raising his gray, dreary eyes to the ceiling, and said no more.

He was somehow boring in a very ponderous and almost exhibitionist way. This irritated me most of all. He got drunk slowly; once drunk, he snorted ironically. Except for that, I noted nothing special about him; for there is a law by virtue of which, from a husband's standpoint, any man courting his wife is always a bad man.

A rich Ukrainian relative used to send him fifty rubles a month—a large sum of money in those days. On holidays this young man used to bring candy for my wife and, on her name day, made her a present of an alarm clock in the shape of a bronze tree stump, with an owl upon it worrying a hedgehog.

This revolting machine always woke me an hour and seven minutes earlier than it should have.

My wife, desisting from the flirtation, began to treat this youth with all the tenderness of a woman who feels guilty of having upset a man's spiritual balance. I asked her how, in her opinion, this sad affair would end.

"I don't know," she replied. "I have no defined feeling for him, but I want to shake him up. Something in him has fallen asleep, and I might be able to wake him up."

I knew she was speaking the truth. She wanted to wake up each and every one, and in this she easily succeeded: wake up the man next to you, and the beast in him will raise his head. I reminded her of Circe, but this is no way restrained her urge to "shake up" men; and I perceived gradually multiplying around me a herd of rams, bulls, and swine.

Acquaintances very generously told me horrendously depressing legends about my family life, but I, blunt and coarse, warned the authors of these legends: "I'll beat you up!"

Some of them falsely tried to justify themselves; a few, not very many, took offense; a certain woman said: "Believe me, coarseness won't get you anywhere; they'll only say worse things about you! You're not being jealous, are you?"

Indeed, I was too young and sure of myself to be jealous. But there are feelings, thoughts, and surmises, that one shares with one's beloved and with no one else. There is an hour of communion with a woman when a man becomes detached from his self and reveals himself to her as a believer does to his God. Whenever I imagined that all this—so very much and uniquely mine—might be communicated by her in a moment of intimacy to some other man, I became depressed, and sensed the possibility of something very like a betrayal. Perhaps it is this apprehension that lies at the root of jealousy?

I felt that this sort of life might turn me from the path I was following. I had already begun to think that literature was the only place I had in life. But it was impossible to work in these conditions.

I held back from serious quarrels, because I had learned in the course of my life to tolerate people, without, however, losing my spiritual interest in or respect for them. Even then I had already perceived that all people were more or less sinful before the unknown God of perfect truth, and that the admittedly righteous sin more especially before man. The righteous are the hybrid offspring of the union of iniquity and virtue, and this union represents no violence done by iniquity to virtue or vice versa, but is the natural result of their legal marriage, in which ironical necessity plays the role of priest. Marriage is a mystery by virtue of which two very distinct opposites, joining together, almost always give birth to a drab mediocrity. At that time I liked paradoxes as a boy loves ice cream; their wit stimulated me like good wine, and the paradoxicality of words always smoothed away the coarse, hurtful paradoxes of facts.

"It seems I'd better go away," I said to my wife.

After thinking it over, she agreed: "Yes, you're right! This life doesn't suit you. I understand!"

Embracing each other closely, we grieved for a while in silence. Then I left town; soon she departed, too, embarking upon a stage career. Thus ended the story of my first love—a good story in spite of the bad ending.

Not long ago my first woman died.

In praise of her let me say: she was a real woman! She knew how to make do with what there was, but every day was for her the eve of a holiday; she always expected the next day to bring to bloom new, extraordinary flowers; people of unusual interest to appear from somewhere; and wonderful events to unfurl.

Treating the discomforts of life with irony and a touch of contempt, she waved them away as she might a swarm of mosquitoes, and she was ever ready in her soul to quiver with the joy of surprise. But hers was no longer the naïve exultation of a young Institute lady, but the healthy joy of a human being who liked the varied bustle of life, the tangled, tragicomic relations between people, the torrent of minor events that flash like grains of dust in a sunbeam.

I would not say that she loved her neighbors, no, but she liked studying them. Sometimes she speeded or complicated the course of domestic dramas between married couples or lovers, artificially stimulating the jealousy of some, helping the reconciliation of others. This game not without peril fascinated her.

" 'Love and hunger rule the world,' but philosophy is its misfortune," she used to say. "To live for love, that's the main business of life."

Among our acquaintances was an employee of the State Bank. Long-legged and gaunt, he walked about with the slow, pompous gait of a stork, always meticulously dressed and anxious about his appearance, snapping his yellow fingers and flicking off with them from his suit the flecks of dust that were invisible to anyone but himself. He was hostile to any original thought, any vivid expression, interpreting them as an attack against his own ponderous, precise speech. His speech was solid and impressive and, before delivering himself of some invariably indisputable statement, he stroked his thinning, reddish mustaches with his chilly fingers.

"In the course of time chemistry has been assuming an ever greater significance in the sphere of industry and raw materials. . . . It has been said with perfect justice that women are capricious. . . . There is merely a legal, rather than a physiological, difference between a wife and a mistress."

With a serious air I asked my wife: "Could you really maintain that all lawyers have wings?"

She replied sadly and apologetically:

"Oh, no, I wouldn't have the strength to do that, but I can affirm that it's comic to feed elephants on soft-boiled eggs!"

After listening to this mock dialogue for a couple of minutes, our friend declared: "It seems to me that you are not serious in saying all this."

Having bumped his knee painfully against the leg of a table, he pronounced with absolute conviction: "Solidity is the indisputable quality of matter. . . ."

On occasions, my wife, after seeing him to the door, would return pleasantly excited, glowing, and light-hearted. Half-reclining on my knees, she would comment: "Just look, how completely, how perfectly stupid he is! Stupid in everything, even in his walk, his gestures —stupid in everything! He appeals to me as a sort of model. . . . Stroke my cheeks now!"

She loved me to smooth, with fingers scarcely touching the skin of her face, the barely noticeable wrinkles under her adorable eyes. Closing her eyes and curling up, she purred: "How wonderfully interesting people are! Men excite me even when they do not interest others. I want to peer into a man as into a little box. What if it contains something no one else has noticed, something never seen before, and I alone am the first to perceive it!" In her quest of "something no one else has noticed," she pursued her search with all the pleasure and curiosity of a child who has penetrated for the first time into a previously unfamiliar room. At times she did succeed in kindling a sharp glint of intense thought in the eyes of some dull, hopeless, boring man, but more often she merely provoked a man's stubborn desire to possess her.

She loved her own body and, standing naked in front of a looking glass, exulted: "How beautifully shaped is woman! How harmonious everything about her!"

She would also say: "When I'm well dressed, I feel healthier, stronger, and cleverer!"

And so she was. Dressed up, she grew gayer and wittier, and her eyes sparkled victory. She could sew satin dresses very beautifully for herself, and wore them as if they were silk or velvet; and, always dressing very simply, she gave the impression of being splendidly apparelled. Women admired her costumes—not always sincerely of course, but always very vociferously; they envied her, and I remember one of them saying glumly to her:

"My dress is three times as expensive as yours and ten times inferior. It even pains and hurts me to look at you!"

Of course women did not like her and, understandably, fabricated slanders about us. A woman medical assistant of our acquaintance, a very beautiful but hardly an intelligent woman, used to warn me rather grandiloquently: "This woman will suck all the blood out of you!"

I learned a great deal in the company of my first lady. Nevertheless I was being painfully consumed with despair at the irreconcilable differences between us.

Life was for me a serious problem: I saw too much, thought hard, and lived in a state of ceaseless perturbation. Problems alien to the spirit of this fine woman shouted in discordant choir within my soul.

In the marketplace one day, a policeman had beat up a decent old man, a one-eyed Jew, because the Jew had supposedly stolen a bunch of horse-radishes from a vendor. I came across the old man in the street. He was all covered with dust and walked alone slowly with a sort of picturesque solemnity, his large black eye staring austerely at the vacant sultry sky, while thin rivulets of blood flowed from his smashed mouth down his long white beard, coloring in bright purple the silver of his hair.

That was thirty years ago, and even now I can still see before me the old man's gaze directed in mute reproach at the sky; I can still see the silver needles of his eyebrows quivering on the old man's face. The insults to which a man is subjected are not forgotten; nor shall they ever be forgotten!

I came home utterly crushed, twisted with rage and spite. Such impressions threw me out of life, estranging me from it and making of me a man to whom—in order to test him—they show all the most filthy, stupid, and terrifying things on earth—everything that insults the soul. And thus, in those hours, on those days, I perceived with particular clarity how remote my neighbor was from me.

When I told my wife about the beaten-up old Jew, she evinced great surprise.

"And is that why you're going off your head? Oh, what bad nerves you have!"

Then she asked me:

"You say he was a handsome old man? But how could he be handsome if he was bent?"

She was hostile to all suffering. She disliked hearing stories of misfortune; lyrical verse hardly moved her; and compassion rarely stirred in her small, sprightly heart.

In her attitude to life there was something akin to a child's faith in a magician's infinite sleight of hand: interesting as were all the tricks so far performed, the most fascinating trick was still to come. It would be performed within an hour, or tomorrow perhaps, but it would certainly be performed!

I think that, even in the hour of her death, she still had hoped to behold this ultimate, utterly baffling, wonderful sleight of hand.

A SKY-BLUE LIFE

Konstantin Mironov sat at a window and tried not to think as he gazed at the street.

The wind had swept the sky clean, scattering tufts of smoky cloud very like wool and forming amusing festoons of dust upon the unpaved streets before dying down as if wrapped in a pall of dust. The sparrows flocked together and, bouncing like balls, began to quarrel shrilly while picking at the feathers of a severed cockerel's head. From under the Rozanovs' gate a black, one-eyed tomcat crept out into the open, crouched, measured the distance, sprang at a sparrow, and, missing it, pawed tentatively at the cockerel's head, picked it up in its teeth, shook it and, with tail erect, carried its prey without haste back under the gate.

The venerable Ivan Ivanovich Rozanov came striding purposefully along, driving before him with a stick a red-haired goat. The church bells sounded evensong. Rozanov doffed his cap, baring the bald skull of a devout servant of the Lord, and glanced approvingly at the cool blue sky. The goat likewise halted and, tossing its beard, dug its hooves sturdily in the dust.

"This couldn't possibly happen in Paris," Mironov thought. "They wouldn't allow goats to be driven through the streets of Paris. Nor would they throw cockerels' heads under the windows. . . ."

Below him in the distance—beyond the leaden band of the river, beyond the reddish pile of the vodka distillery buildings, and the gray blotches of the houses belonging to the local *zemstvo* clinic for psychiatric patients —a swollen, rayless, orange sun dropped down toward the sand hills, into the black tousled bushes of juniper; and that smoothly shaven sun looked like an inmate from the psychiatric colony who had just escaped and was trying to hide. This event was repeated every evening, and had become as tiresome as a page of a frequently read book.

To avoid thinking, Mironov was engaged in plotting small black circles in the pearly sky to denote various railway terminals: Moscow-Riga-Berlin-Cologne-Paris. But this day there was not enough clear space left in the sky for all of these dots, and so he had no alternative but to place the last of the five circles either too near the sun or right in the center of it. This, to his regret, would render invisible the dot representing Paris. But it was absolutely essential for Mironov to place this dot in the sky. Based upon it, his imagination could, as always, immediately create a sky-blue city full of solemn organ music, a city of light-hearted people and startling adventure, where life flowed easily and where even so evil a man as Rocambole was unable to pursue an evil course to the end of his life. In Paris even Quasimodo proved inhumanly attractive. The Three Musketeers had lived there. The mysterious Knight of the Hen-House, and the fearless d'Arville, one of the three favorites of the Empress of Austria, had all performed their deeds there. But here, in this place . . .

On the banks of the river two voices accompanied the setting sun with a long-drawn-out song, which blended happily with the brassy sonority of the pious churches; softened by distance, even the howling bass voice of Artamon, the carter, droned as softly as the brazen bells. All day long, ever since early morning, the dry whistling wind had scattered dust, while the church bells and the song, having nourished the air with a flood of tender sounds, seemed now to be trying finally to establish a quiet musical order on earth and in men's hearts.

But the singing silence of a Saturday evening could not calm Mironov. Inside, he was utterly torn and confused; and his agitated memory kept projecting images of his past experiences and plunging him into an oppressive, multicolored chaos.

It was the first time he had experienced so great an agitation in his memory and such a compelling necessity to think. He was even frightened by this. Several times already he had examined every corner of his room, as if expecting to discover in the bluish evening twilight someone who had forced him to remember and reflect.

It was strange: whenever he shut his eyes, the darkness moved; in it, in every point of it, small whorls were generated; they either rested their circles horizontally on the water or, spinning in little columns of black dust, stirred an infinity of darkness into a soundless commotion, so that the whole darkness was saturated and perspiring with thought; and they finally assumed the tedious outlines of those tiresome words: "How shall I live?"

When his father had referred to meat, fish, or milk, and had suggested they were "reflecting," he meant that the meat and the fish had gone putrid, and the milk sour.

Shortly before his father's death, his mother had shouted: "You'd better start thinking a little before you drop dead!"

Father had replied with a laugh: "Do you know what it means 'to think'? It means to wipe off the dust. You may now have a towel in your hand and may use it for dusting; the towel was clean, but now it's dirty. The same applies to you and me, Lydia, we've done enough thinking. . . ."

Mother, who jealously watched over the cleanliness of the house, was infuriated.

"So—I'm a dirty rag, am I?" she said, attacking Father. "And my house is dirty, is it?"

Slowly, thirteen days had passed since the morning when Mironov, on entering the kitchen to wash himself, caught sight of his mother's enormous body on the floor: she sat there with one shoulder propped sideways against the stove, a hand pressed against the floor, moaning, and with horribly protruding eyes staring at a corner. When he stooped to raise her, thinking she might be drunk, his mother pulled her hand with difficulty away from the floor, waved it, and fell at his feet snorting like a horse. For another four days and nights she gasped and moaned and continued to wave her hand as if pushing someone away. On the fifth day she fell with a thud from the bed, crawled toward the trunk in a corner of the bedroom, and uttering a great gasp, died.

For a whole week, strange people bustled about the house from morning till night. An irritable nurse, small and hunchbacked, darted through all the rooms; a stout doctor, chain-smoking, shouted commands; and the red-bearded, lavender-robed priest, Boris, sat in one place with his feet wide apart. All of these people kept questioning Mironov; and Kallistrat, the carpenter, whom everyone in the street detested, pestered him and probed: "And what are you thinking of doing now, you orphan?"

In Paris, a man's death and all that followed was a far more simple, comprehensible, and interesting occurrence, neither so unnecessary nor so terrifying. There, no strangers came to gape at a dead woman and there, of course, a character such as Kallistrat the carpenter was quite impossible.

On the day of his mother's funeral Kallistrat carried a pot of sour cream into the street and, dipping a paint brush into it, began to smear the garden fence. What for? He was not drunk, and yet he applied himself quite seriously to this stupid business. When they asked him what he was doing, he calmly replied: "I'm painting the fence."

"With sour cream?"

"I didn't have any paint."

For about ten minutes, assiduously and in silence, he dabbed the gray, sun-bleached planks, while some three dozen grownups and a multitude of boys watched him at work. Then the venerable Ivan Ivanovich Rozanov walked up to him, kicked the pot of sour cream and shattered it to smithereens.

The doctor, scrutinizing his mother's bulky body, had most indecently and rudely remarked: "If she hadn't drunk so much, she'd have lived another forty years."

Mironov remembered that, though these coarse words had shocked him, he had at once calculated: if his mother had lived another forty years, he would have been fifty-nine the year she died. And most likely she would have screamed at him the rest of her life: "Fool! You've taken after your father."

His mother was a large-eyed, nagging woman, who, already tipsy in the morning, would tramp heavily about the rooms and, rag in hand, exterminate flies and wipe off the dust, saturating the air with the smell of marinated onion and soaked apples, her favorite appetizers. And she was always angry at his father.

She was always scolding him, particularly on holidays when, hanging a topographer's uniform upon his long angular bones, he set off to play billiards in town. He was reputed an expert at this game and, in general, he was a remarkable man—both in word and deed.

His gaunt figure, long sparse mustaches and a dark tuft of hair under the lower lip, rose before Mironov. His father would cough and, when he did, his spittle showed pink and red. With a wink of his dark, gleefully burning eye, he would then relate wonderful stories about General Skobelev and the Turkmen, about the campaigns in the Caucasus, Khiva, and Bukhara. These stories revealed him to be a man as restless as a bird, a lighthearted wanderer over the earth. He had a red, wrinkled hollow under his left eye; it pulled down the eyelid, and as a result the eye seemed to stare intently into this hollow. Father used to explain that it was the scar of a wound inflicted by a Turkman.

Father never berated Mother; he quarreled with her very seldom, but he always infuriated her when he uttered certain sarcasms.

"Stop it, Mitka! Take care or God will punish you for being stupid," Mother would often shout.

"God doesn't punish one for being stupid; God loves fools," Father would protest.

His father's words also disturbed Kostya, sticking to his memory as imperceptibly and firmly as the scales of a fish cling to the skin of a man's hand. One day his father, gluing together a broken violin, picked out of it a short, round piece of wood and said: "This thing is called 'the soul.' And as for you, Lydia, the devil has inserted a like piece of wood inside you. . . ."

"You're lying," Mother shouted back. "My soul comes from God. . . ."

When she returned from church on her saint's day, dressed in all her finery and looking very impressive, Father presented her with a length of cashmere for a dress. But she found wrapped inside this gift a nasty green painting, *A Sinner's Death*, depicting a green devil with bared teeth and a tongue of flame standing at the feet of a dying man.

At first Mother was amused. Then she took offense and, after drinking a great deal at lunch, suddenly burst out weeping.

"You're my sorrow, my misfortune!" she blubbered, addressing Father.

In the rare moments of her more peaceful moods she used to call Father a "magician," because he had constructed a musical box that played the quadrille "Dampers," the song "Mother, Darling," and the hymn "Glory Be to God." In one of her drunken bouts Mother smashed and trampled this box to pieces. Kostya gathered the fragments, hid them in the attic, and for a long time implored his father to mend this amazing contraption of wood and metal that Father had induced by some magic means to sing with joy, sorrow, and solemnity.

"Stop annoying me. It's just a bit of nonsense, a box!" Father had replied.

And then, toying thoughtfully with Kostya's ear, he added with a sigh: "But if one day she burst from all that drink, I'd really invent something!"

He loved minute, detailed work, such as sawing frames for photographs, mending accordions, and gluing together broken violins. And while working he always hummed:

> Seven sous,
> Seven sous,
> What shall we do with seven sous?

The best thing his father had ever made was a terrestrial globe, which Kostya had preserved with the greatest care. His father had given it to Kostya on the day he graduated into the second class of his gymnasium. It was an ordinary globe, but his father had fixed the lower half of the sphere in a copper bowl used for washing china. On the copper he had engraved the oceans, continents, and islands, and had artfully colored them; he had also hammered steel pins to the bottom of the copper bowl and had welded a steel comb onto the base, so that the comb was bent around the lower part of the globe.

When Kostya turned the globe on its axis, the comb tinkled out a gay little ditty:

Siskin, siskin, where have you been?

Even his mother liked it, and for a long time she turned the globe about on its pivot, laughing in her hoarse drunken voice. But the cat, taking a dislike to the sky-blue, tinkling sphere, ran away spitting. Kostya, when he had nothing else to do, loved to tease the cat with the amusing, metallic music of the globe.

His father, a very cheerful man, loved joking, but it was depressing rather than cheering to remember his jokes.

The year she died Mother had gone to pray in a monastery. In her absence, Father had attached some wooden pipes with rubber balls to the handles of all the doors; the pipes emitted a shrill whistle whenever a door was opened or shut. This made Mother furious on her return.

"What are you mocking me for, you devil?" she screamed, turning purple. Then, after striking Father repeatedly across the face with the damp, dirty rag, she broke all the pipes.

Father ran off into the garden, hopping in an odd manner, and, lying down there on the grass under the maple tree, laughed to himself for a while before falling into a restless sleep. Mironov remembered how frightened he was to hear his father's delirious whispers, and how sorry he felt looking at the gray, gaunt face of a man so dear and yet so incomprehensible to him. In that hour a sad shadow fell upon the affection he felt for his father and he developed a feeling of distrust for all the cheerful things his father had told him.

And then he also had one of those lasting experiences that help to form a man's soul: there was a buzzing of bees in the thick foliage of a richly flowering linden tree; and this continuous, stringed sound, absorbing all the other less rich sounds of the sultry day, ascended into the azure void of the skies, there to be transformed into a miraculous song.

Mironov, astonished, gazed a long time with straining eyes at the sky, and finally spotted a trembling speck there, a sort of dark, rayless star, which he suddenly guessed must be a lark. From that day on, he felt the need to think in sounds, to hum a wordless accompaniment to every thought.

But for the last thirteen days he had lost the capacity to drown his thoughts in imageless sounds; the variegated dust of memories kept intruding into his brain; his father's muffled voice and the senseless exclamations of his mother always drunk or nagging, rang in his memory. His mother's reproaches and complaints forced him to realize that she had married a second time, and that her first husband had been not only his father's chief, but also the man who had tried to kill him with a pistol.

"It was my misfortune that he didn't kill you!" she would shout at Father.

Kostya sensed something obscure and perilous about their life, something criminal perhaps, which he had no wish to know and of which he was afraid to think, but it was precisely this that disturbed his imagination most. This continued until he began to read books, which disclosed to him the existence of other more interesting and more soluble mysteries, a sort of lighter and more festive life. He was a shy, awkward young man, and had no friends; he easily caught cold, and was often sick. This circumstance allowed him to read a great deal, and in the pale blue mist of his excitement he used to evoke the image of the miraculous city of Paris.

His father died in the spring, when digging around the apple trees in the garden. Mironov remembered with anguish his mother muttering as she bent over her dead husband: "There, Mitya, there . . . I told you . . ."

Four years of a difficult, shameful life with his drunken mother had made of Mironov a still more isolated individual. He was fond of fishing and wandering alone in the fields and the forests, of listening to the birds singing, the grass and the foliage rustling, the strange whispering of the breeze. On holidays it was especially good to hear the distant music of a military band; at close quarters, when you saw the soldiers blowing out their cheeks, the music did not please or console as much. Sometimes he would take with him a French grammar and study it, trying to memorize the precise words, but his memory would not retain them and, failing to make coherent sense, they melted away and were transformed into extraordinary combinations of beautiful sounds—into azure music.

When Mironov saw Lisa Rozanova in a sky-blue dress on Easter Sunday, she pleased him very much; to the solemn pealing of bells she was walking home from church, all glowing in the generous light of the festive sun. Small, shapely, and at the same time luxuriant like an exotic flower, she was all in sky-blue—even her stockings were sky-blue.

Lisa lived in the house opposite. Mironov had seen her often before, but her slender flat figure, her sharp-nosed birdlike face with rounded eyes, and the capricious or morbid curve of her bloodless lips—nothing about her had previously stirred his heart or imagination. This girl even seemed to him as ugly as himself. He knew, besides, that Lisa was taking a cure of goat's milk, the odor of which he found repugnant. But on that particular Easter Sunday he was agreeably surprised. How had he missed noticing that Lisa was so beautiful? And ever since that day he made Lisa the partner of his dream world of a lyrical, sky-blue life; she became the straw at which he clutched in the midst of the noisy torrent of incomprehensible, frightening things.

He could not make up his mind to become acquainted, but, returning from work, always slowed his steps when passing her house. After his meal, he would sit down with a book at the window and watch for her to come out into the street. Sometimes she would emerge and, rapidly striding on her thin legs, proceed in the direction of the river to find her father in his lumber yard; she hugged the fences as she walked, as if bearing in mind the possibility of taking refuge in the nearest gateway. A short plait of dark hair tied with a blue ribbon at the end quivered on her narrow back. Mironov fancied that this girl, like himself, disliked people and was frightened of them; and this made him feel still closer to her.

When she was out of sight, he would walk up to a mirror and, feeling sad and hurt, examine the reflection of his face: his dark, immobile eyes were separated by a wide bridge; his left eye squinted slightly as if peeping at a protruding, waxen ear; a yellow nose dropped in a formless lump above his upper lip covered with black down; and his dark wiry hair bristled in rebellious tufts. Everything about him seemed to grow in opposite directions, to crawl apart like the roots of a tree in barren ground; his hands were too long and their fingers unpleasantly slender; his mouth was too large, and his teeth so uneven he hated to smile.

In general he disliked facing himself in a mirror. He had observed that if he looked too long his eyes grew dark and his image began to disappear. He feared he himself might disappear.

Several days before his mother's death, he made an unexpected suggestion: "You might arrange a marriage for me with Lisa Rozanova. . . ."

Having suggested this, he became frightened, and blushed, ashamed and alarmed at revealing his secret to no purpose.

But that day his mother was sober and morose, as she usually was when she did not drink. Pouring cream into her tea, she replied without looking at her son: "Fool."

Then, wiping the perspiration from her purple face, she added three minutes later: "What sort of a husband would you make? A husband should be like this!"

And she clenched her swollen fingers tightly into a large red fist, and shook it in the air.

It was painful to remember her. The more Mironov thought about his mother, the more frightening and alien she seemed—this coarse woman, suffocating in fat, with enormous clouded eyes. By thinking about her he seemed to be removing layers of dust, and thus making her look stranger and more terrifying. Everything else he tried to think about and understand was bared as unpleasantly before him.

Mironov shook his head and looked round—the blue twilight in the room had grown thicker and warmer. An evening star gleamed in the roselit sky beyond the river.

A cart, loaded with furniture, mattresses, and potted

plants, lumbered along the street; under a palm tree upon gray bundles sat a girl in a red blouse and a white kerchief; on her knees she held a cage with a species of black bird—probably a thrush. Some brightly colored children's wooden blocks fell into the dust under the cart; an old man walked alongside the heavy, thick-legged cart horse; waving the reins and jerking his head up, he shouted in a hoarse voice to the girl: "And where will you go now? Whom will you tell?"

"The old fool," Mironov scolded him in thought.

And there came Artamon, the carter of the lumber yard, sturdy and massive as a bear; his shaggy, eyeless face was disfigured by a harelip, which formed his mouth like a triangle and revealed in a revolting way the broad yellow crags of his fierce teeth. Beside him lightly walked the slender, well-built carpenter Kallistrat, barefoot, in an apron soiled with ochre and glue, and with a leather strap around his fair, curly hair; a golden mustache gleamed under his hawklike nose. Twisting a pointed beard of copper hue around his finger, Kallistrat glanced in Mironov's direction and exclaimed in a ringing voice: "Boredom!"

"Leave him alone, let him be bored," Artamon said in his coarse, bellowing voice. They walked on slowly, their feet lazily kicking up the dust, and the dust rose behind them in a reddish cloud. The whole of the street admired the carter's inhuman strength and was afraid of him, just as it was frightened of the carpenter and his strange pranks.

Mironov shut his eyes tight; he sometimes imagined that a man became invisible when he shut his eyes.

The days rolled by rapidly, leaping over the dark chasms of the nights; the nights were hot and sleepless, and whenever he drowsed off for a while Mironov had strange dreams: along a wide highway, illuminated by a multitude of bonfires, walked a countless crowd of copper coffeepots all of the same shape; they all had long legs and had something in common with spiders; a small hunchback was paving the street by hammering nails into the ground so close to one another that the earth looked covered with iron scales; a huge fish swam down a river, swallowing the reflection of the moon; and in a very dark sky the moon swung and swayed like the pendulum of a clock. He dreamed a great deal more that was very disturbing because it made no sense.

Mironov now lived without hearing his mother's heavy footsteps and coarse shouts; the sickening smell of vodka, soaked apples, and marinated onions had been aired out; Pavlovna, the cook, a withered old woman, moved about as softly as a cat, said nothing, and only sighed in a whistling way. Nevertheless, he felt uneasy living in this silence; it seemed to him that all his possessions—the photographs and the icons—seemed to ask him a mute, stringent question: "Well, what are you going to do?"

Mironov noticed the people in the street looking demandingly at him; they all seemed to expect something; and their sticky stares oppressed him.

On Sunday, at sunset, he sat fishing for perch on the edge of a barge, which had been partly submerged by the ice floe, and listening to the distant brass blare of a military band; the music and the slow motion of the pale blue water induced in him a desirable state of vacuity; and the warm waves of sound raised him gently above the earth. If you paid attention, the river current also seemed to emit a soft deep sound that almost blotted out all the other sounds; as through frosted glass, these sounds were visible to the ear. Mironov failed to notice a boat drawing up: "Biting well?"

Starting, he plucked the line out of the water. A small, plump perch dangled from the hook.

"We bring you luck!"

"Yes."

"Have you caught many more?"

"Three. This is the third."

Lisa Rosanova, in a lavender dress with a pale blue ribbon in her plait, sat at the stern, while her plump, black-haired friend Klavdia, in a pink blouse and blue skirt, held the oars; she maneuvered the oars gently to prevent the boat from being swept away by the current. Lisa was smiling. Mironov also longed to smile but, remembering his ugly teeth, suddenly compressed his lips.

"Let's go on," Lisa suggested.

Her friend dipped the oars in deeper and threw her

body back; one of the oars slipped out, splashing the fisherman's feet.

"Oh, excuse me!"

Lisa laughed like tinkling glass. Mironov, embarrassed, moved his legs, shaking the water off his boots and trousers. As he did so, he thought: "Another man would have started a conversation, but I . . . Maybe they splashed me on purpose, as a joke, to become acquainted. . . ."

The boat descended the current, impelled by strong thrusts, the oars creaking derisively. Mironov tossed the water and the perch out of his little pail, picked up his fishing rods and went home, stopping now and again to stare at the ground, and feeling sorry for himself. When he reached his house he noticed that the brown paint of the façade and the gateway had turned a greenish hue, that the paint of the window frame had faded, swollen, and cracked.

"I must have it repainted," he decided.

Early on Wednesday morning a bald little old man, insolent as he was caustic, began to scrape the house with an iron scraper; he was assisted by a snub-nosed boy all stained in bright paint. While working, the old man sang in a good mellow voice:

"He departed without bidding good-by . . .
"He's fallen in love with another . . ."

The boy joined in, singing in a fine treble. Mironov, awakened by the scraping and the singing, lay in bed thinking: "How stupid. For the one, it's too late to be singing of love; for the other, too early. And why do house painters always sing when working?"

Several days later, when the house painter began to daub with sky-blue paint the motley, patched façade of the house, which looked as if it had smallpox, the venerable Ivan Ivanovich Rozanov suddenly materialized before it like a statue. In a harsh voice he cried out: "Hey, how are you painting this?"

"As ordered," the house painter replied with scant respect.

"Why sky-blue?"

"That's the order!"

"It spoils the street!"

"That's none of my business."

"What stupidity."

"The stupidity isn't mine either."

Mironov overheard this dialogue as he watered the flowers and plants on the window sills; he felt hurt and alarmed.

"Why should a sky-blue house be so monstrous and stupid?" he asked. "Rozanov's likely to turn me down now if I ask for his daughter's hand."

He hurried out into the street and stared at the faded, weather-beaten little houses interconnected with gray fences and shaded with the dusty foliage of white willows; like beggars, they descended toward the river in two rows of seven and ten houses respectively. Rozanov's single-storey brick house stood out in the row of seven, and four of his windows stared glumly at the street. The triangle under the roof of Mironov's house had already been painted; as if hung with silk, the shiny oil paint glowed in the sun and caressed the eyes with cool blue.

Solemnly touching the peak of his cap with his index finger, Rozanov commented: "An impractical color."

"But beautiful."

"And expensive."

"Durable."

"I don't know about that."

"The house painter says it's durable."

"All house painters are liars," Rozanov declared with finality and walked away—solid, upright, his serious face and broad silvery beard offered generously to the sun. Mironov didn't have time to inquire why house painters were liars. He went home, picked up a book, and sat down by the window. Almost at once Rozanov reappeared in the street with a broom and began to sweep the dirt and dust from under his windows into the middle of the street.

"Hey, venerable!" the house painter cried out. "A pity you've started raising the dust—it's spoiling my work."

Rozanov made no reply and went on sweeping. Mironov grasped that he was doing it on purpose, out of spite; upset, he retired into the garden and sat down under an old apple tree.

"He won't let me marry his daughter now. Why did I start painting the house?"

He heard the painter exchanging words with Rozanov in the street. He should have told the painter to hold his tongue, but he was rendered powerless to do so by the gray, dreary reflections he had been indulging in about people who so very strangely prevent each other from enjoying a free life. Mironov sat on in the garden until supper time.

He could not fall asleep during that still, stifling night. The moon shone bright and irritating, and the dogs barked and howled. There was a yellowish square of light on the floor, and the cross sections of the window frame were shadowed with precision upon it. Suddenly three other dark stripes appeared in the patch of light, and then a man's shadow covered it—suggesting a street lamp-lighter with a ladder on his shoulder. Then he heard a rustling sound and the creaking of wood. Mironov threw off the sheet and sat up in bed, staring at the window: before the window stood a ladder, which the house painter had evidently forgotten there, and apparently someone was now trying to remove it. Mironov jumped up, cautiously opened the window, and looked up; someone was stuck at the top of the ladder, and he could see bare feet. Mironov, more surprised than alarmed, climbed silently out of the window into the street.

A man was on the ladder, brightly lit by the moon. Dipping a stubby paint brush into a small wooden pail hanging at his waist, he was hurriedly daubing around the dormer window.

"Who's that?" Mironov asked in a low voice.

With inexplicable ease the man slipped down the ladder, splashing the wall of the house with some dark liquid out of his pail; a pungent smell of tar spread through the air. Snatching the ladder, the man ran off. But Mironov recognized him—it was Kallistrat, the carpenter.

Mironov walked into the middle of the street and made out, through the silvery dust of the moonlight, the large though blurred letters above the dormer window. They spelled out the word "HOUSE."

From each letter dark rivulets of tar flowed down, and one could distinctly hear the heavy drops of tar striking the ground. The carpenter, shouldering the ladder, stood some twenty paces away by the gate of his own house. Mironov could clearly distinguish the copper wedge of his beard and the black strap circling his fair head and forehead.

"Listen! Why did you do that?" Mironov asked.

The carpenter gave no answer, did not stir.

"It's amazing! You mess things up either with cream or tar."

The carpenter laughed. It seemed to Mironov that his laughter was astonishingly strange, something between the clucking of a hen and the yelping of a puppy. It wasn't good laughter, and it made everything seem even more senseless and offensive. The dim windowpanes gleamed like ice, and the air was so hot it seemed to glow. It all resembled an unpleasant dream.

"Don't try and fight me—I'll thrash you," the carpenter suddenly declared in a shrill voice.

"I've no intention of fighting," Mironov muttered, walking toward his own gate. The carpenter, setting the ladder against the fence, slowly followed.

"So you've taken offense?"

The carpenter's ringing voice sounded both fresh and familiar. At times Mironov's father had spoken like that, mingling kind and severe words.

"No, I'm not offended, but all the same . . . Why spoil things?"

The carpenter came up close and slapped Mironov on the shoulder with the palm of his hand; his hand was light as a bird's wing.

"Don't take it badly! I'll set it right. The tar isn't sticking to the oil paint, it's flowing. I didn't put it on right. I should have mixed some soot and kerosene—then it would have . . ."

"But why do it at all?"

"As a joke, of course. A funny thing one thinks up —no one paints his house that color."

The carpenter suddenly bit his lower lip, jerked his head back and, concentrating his gaze, began to examine the sky as if pondering. From his pocket he pulled out a wooden cigarette case, lighted a match, puffed at a cigarette and threw the match up so deftly that the flame described a quivering arc in the air before going out. Then he pressed his hand down on Mironov's shoulder, forcing him to sit on the bench by the gate, and sat beside him, speaking with instructive irony:

"I understand your calculation—you want to stand out from other people. You think that, being a free orphan, you can play pranks? Stop it, Mironov! There are only two people who can play strange pranks: the devil and I. But you're just a naughty child in the sight of our God!"

"What God?" Mironov asked.

"Just the ordinary God, you old boredom; God is one, or have you forgotten it?" the carpenter said with irony. "You'd better get this into your head: there was your mother—a human being—dying; all the neighbors, showing interest in this event, crowded around you, but when I began to daub my fence with cream they all ran over to gape at me—do you understand?"

"I understand nothing," Mironov replied with a puzzled shake of his head. "It's some sort of nonsense . . ."

"You're no good if you don't understand. But you're crawling to take first place. Nonsense also must be understood, you orphan. Can you think up anything like that sour cream? No, you can't, you see. But I'm an old hand at it. I was even tried in court for my fancies. I used to pour kerosene in the mailbox and throw in a lighted match—the letters would catch fire and no one could understand a thing. They even wrote about it in the papers: 'Why are the letters burning?' they asked. 'From the heat of passion; write calmly.' It was a stupid thing to do, of course, but youth's to blame. You don't sleep at night; you keep thinking how to do something out of the ordinary. Even now I like to astonish people. It's funny to see them trip as they walk. Everything seems simple, but suddenly something you don't understand happens . . ."

The carpenter twirled the points of his mustaches, licked his lips, narrowed his right eye, stared at the moon with his left, and sighed:

"A luminary, but the dogs don't like it."

Observing out of the corner of his eye the carpenter's sharp, changing face, and listening closely to his talk, Mironov felt two contradictory desires: to go on questioning this man, and also to be rude and then leave him.

"Maybe the dogs fancy the moon is a fox," was all he said.

"It's not known what dogs fancy," the carpenter replied with a sneer, and then resumed his didactic tone, warning him about something and becoming ever more difficult to understand. His boastful talk depressed Mironov; he felt it had something sadly in common with French grammar—the words seemed familiar, but their sense was obscure and elusive. The moonlight fused the twilight with the foliage of the white willows; the leaves gleamed silver; the carpenter's curled hair glowed golden; and the strap around his forehead showed black. His greenish eyes had an extraordinary look; shifting and sneering, they glittered sharply like needles. You could put no trust in a man with such eyes. And he was also mocking him, so obviously false did his clear voice sound. With a sigh, Mironov unexpectedly declared: "You're sort of mad. You're like a madman."

"You don't say!" the carpenter exclaimed.

"What did you write up there?"

"You frightened me off, but I wanted to write a sign: THE HOUSE OF A MADMAN. The whole street would have laughed the next day."

And suddenly slapping Mironov on the knee with his palm, he suggested in a serious, businesslike way: "Look here, Mironov, give me ten rubles. . . ."

Mironov angrily backed away from him.

"Wait, wait! Don't jump away, I've thought of something! Just listen: I like you. Another man in your place would have yelled and made a row, but you did nothing of the sort. That's quite a thing, you orphan, quite a thing, brother. . . . Well, all right! For this I'd like to do you a service in this way: the prank failed, and now I'd like to please you—do you understand?"

The carpenter now spoke in a lower voice, without any mockery in his eyes, while Mironov kept repeating to himself with growing confidence: "Of course he's a madman, being a prankster."

This reassured him very much, resolving his deep perplexity; he smiled as he stared at the sky and listened to the carpenter's words: "I'll get the paint and paint this

very house for you in a way that will make everybody
gape!"

"What for?" Mironov asked, but the carpenter seemed
not to hear his question. Twisting his copper-colored
beard around his finger, he tugged at it, saying, "I'll tell
you straight: I'm handy at everything, but I don't like
work because I get no chance of working according to
my taste. People don't like my taste—do you understand? So give me a chance to show myself."

"All right," Mironov agreed, grasping that to reject the
carpenter now would be to invite him to do more damage.

He noticed that his promise of money had surprised
the carpenter; starting back, Kallistrat measured him with
strangely glowing eyes. Then, adjusting the strap around
his head, he muttered: "Well, Mironov, that's . . . All
right! You won't regret it. I'll come around in the morning."

He jumped up and walked rapidly away; but, halting
as if his foot had caught against something, he said, holding up his arm in the air: "I'll do a job! A work of the
soul—they'll gape!"

With amazing precision his figure was silhouetted
against the sky-blue background of the river and then—
suddenly—it vanished. Mironov strode into the middle of
the street, stared at the window frame splashed with dirty
reddish liquid, read once more the inscription "HOUSE"
and, wearily dropping his head, went home to bed, repeating: "A madman . . . And a swindler, most likely . . ."

Early next morning the cook wakened Mironov: "The
carpenter's come, he's asking for the money."

"It wasn't a dream then," Mironov thought.

He gave the money to the old woman and, before
drowsing off again, thought: "One ought to lodge a complaint against him . . ."

This thought recurred again when, setting out to work,
he saw the reddish oily streaks on the bright paint; the
inscription "HOUSE" had completely run and was now
indecipherable. After staring at it, he lowered his head
and quickly walked down the street, conscious of the
ironic smiles of the townsmen fixed upon him.

"Lisa must be laughing at me too. . . . In Paris there are no wooden houses. . . ."

Returning from work at about five in the afternoon, he noticed at a distance a group of boys standing opposite his house, a ladder set against the façade, a sort of can shining dazzlingly at the upper rung, and then the carpenter, his leg thrust into the dormer window, swaying and twisting in the air. Waving his cane, Mironov ran up to his house.

"I forbid it! Go to the devil!" he shouted.

The boys, who greeted him with a joyful squeal, fell silent and jumped away from the fence. Rage made Mironov hear noises in his head. Dimly he perceived the carpenter's bony face looking down at him, his wide-open sinister eyes; and with shame he felt that he might burst out crying. Only too easily the carpenter slid down the ladder, bumped into him with his shoulder, and pointed above with his paint brush, the handle of which was red at the tip and very like a lighted candle.

"What are you yelling for? Is it so bad?" the carpenter asked.

The semicircular hole of the dormer window stood out in sharp outline against the blue triangle; the frame had been removed; from the side there peered into the window a checkered, white-and-yellow monster with red gills but no tail, and with a large protruding red eye ringed with white. The snout of the monster had something in common with a sheep's head, though it reminded one more of a fish. Stamping his foot, the carpenter explained in a low voice:

"There'll be three of them: a second one on the right; and a third one at the top. And I shall paint the window to resemble a fish pond, and all three of them will look as if they were crawling in . . ."

The carpenter's hand trembled; he seemed drunk, but did not smell of vodka; it must have been drowned in the smell of the paint. The carpenter was liberally stained with paint—even one of his cheeks had a bright red oily daub very like a comma. His green eyes had a strange glitter.

"Smart, isn't it?" he demanded. "Beautiful, isn't it?"

The boys kept laughing and squealing behind Mironov's back. Then a gray-haired beggar approached and set up a whine, bowing low and stretching forward his cast-iron hand; a shaggy dog with tongue lolling and head tilted sat at his feet. The dog looked dumfounded at the sight of the carpenter's gaudy painting. Then Rozanov could be heard saying in a harsh voice: "What's this? A show booth?"

Mironov turned around, and Rozanov poured out his indignation into his face: "You should be ashamed of yourself, young man. You must stop this nonsense."

Mironov felt himself as numb and powerless as he always did when he failed to understand. His irritation, flaring up for a moment, died away; Rozanov's reproach crushed him even more. In a quiet, plaintive tone he asked the carpenter: "Did you hear that?"

The carpenter waved his hand with contempt and stated with ringing conviction: "Every man can paint his house any color he likes!"

He walked toward the ladder, but Mironov stopped him: "Please leave it alone! Or you'll make people laugh at me."

"They won't laugh at me," the carpenter said, tearing free. There was something desperate and frightening about him.

"This house is mine!" Mironov exclaimed by way of reminding both the carpenter and himself of the fact.

"Tell them to go to hell and the devil!" the carpenter shot back.

He quickly mounted the ladder and shouted from above: "I'll make them gape!"

Dumfounded, crushed by a sense of physical exhaustion, ashamed and numb, Mironov went into the house, resolved to lodge a complaint with the police against the carpenter's arbitrary conduct. Without undressing, he sat down at a table and, after thinking for a while with eyes shut, began to write. But the ink clogged, the pen was messy and, instead of "loss," he scribbled "last," threw down the pen, and then suddenly decided to call on Rozanov and ask his advice about what he should do. He immediately put on a formal suit, tidied his hair with a hairbrush dipped in water, walked out of the house, and

is always a bit of a fool."

This statement offended Mironov, who wished to give a sharp reply, but could only repeat in a challenging tone his father's words: "God loves fools!"

The carpenter nodded affirmatively. "That's so, orphan. God's not without cunning, that's true! I know. I've thought it all over. You must believe me. You don't understand what sort of a fish you've hooked, but I'm your friend—for eternity! And what you've done! By your humility you've shamed my soul's conscience. . . ."

Again, as earlier that day, the carpenter's face had a look of desperation, and his greenish eyes grew moist. Prodding sideways at the bridge of his nose, he squeezed out a couple of tough teardrops.

When the carpenter had begun his explanation, Mironov felt merely bored and sad, but these incomprehensible, forced tears amazed him. With a handkerchief he wiped his fingers wet with vodka and watched those strange blinking eyes, those quivering twisted copper mustaches; watched the perspiration start on the carpenter's temples. Then, without realizing what he was doing, he wiped the carpenter's white perspiring forehead. It was the carpenter's turn to be amazed. For a whole minute he stared at Mironov in silence and then, with a smirk, asked, "Why did you do that? What for?"

"Perspiration."

The carpenter laughed softly, his body shook and, stamping his feet, he mumbled through his laughter: "Yes, but am I a child to have my little face wiped?"

"It was an accident," Mironov explained.

"No, you . . . We . . . all right, enough of that! Tomorrow I'll repaint everything, you can rest assured."

"No, please, don't do any painting at all!"

"You don't want me to?"

"No, I don't!"

The carpenter sighed deeply, staring at the ground. Then he stood up and held out his hand: "Forgive me. . . ."

And he went off, hopping as if he had just gone lame; one of his legs had apparently become numb. Stopping at the gate, he glanced around the yard, thick with weeds, and finally departed, banging the gate loudly behind him.

Mironov remained sitting motionless in the yard, feeling emptied, and longing for only one thing—to forget all this. He was not even pleased that all this fuss with the painting of the house had come to such an unexpected, favorable end.

In the late evening, when the foliage of the trees had already grown dark and the birds had fallen asleep in their nests, Mironov came out into the garden, lay down on the grass under an apple tree, and gazed at the sky through the dusty mesh of leaves. It was hard to understand why such heavy, stifling air poured down out of the bluish, icy cup of the sky. A wan fragment of the moon was melting above the apple tree. In the dusty air floated the voices of people exhausted by their day's work and the stifling heat. These voices disturbed Mironov. He loved to immerse himself in silence as in water, and to achieve this, it was essential for the silence to be absolute. Then he would feel himself free and light, swaying and swimming, and within him would rise, pleasantly chanting, an endless train of thought devoid of word, form, or image.

Then the sky and the earth with everything upon it seemed to fuse and melt, flowing somewhere in slow waves and rising boundlessly in circles. He himself was resonant and at the same time nonexistent; all he felt was a sensation of smooth flight.

He had known and experienced nothing better, nothing more mysterious, than this thoughtless, songlike soaring from the earth to the stars and, with them, into ever higher regions where in all probability lived a certain majestic, extraordinarily affectionate creature—the inexhaustible source of this intoxicating music. The image of Sabaoth on a golden throne, surrounded by cherubim and seraphim chanting hosannas, did not satisfy him; for a long time he had been indifferent to the God worshiped in the temples of this earth, Whose name is daily invoked for aid by millions of people, but Whose power is not very noticeable in this life. For some time he had entertained a vague, recurrent suspicion that the Deity so familiar to all had rejected men, and that another God, a prankster both taunting and testing, a sort of malevolent fancy like the Devil, was acting in His place.

But when he attempted to picture to himself the creator of the music of the world, his as yet virginal mind evoked from the azure mist the image of a naked woman. Her body excited in him a tremulous desire, the force of which made his heart so faint that he felt himself falling headlong to the earth. Then the sensation of flight and song was abruptly interrupted, and his memory then showed him at once all the girls and women who, one after another, had ever attracted his attention. These ups and downs were as unpleasant as they were inevitable; they always produced in him a burdensome feeling of dependence, shame, fear, and acute curiosity. For that reason, Mironov tried not to summon the image of the woman of the starry spheres—an image the beauty of which invariably tossed him back to earth.

That evening he could not evoke the sensation of flight, which he had always succeeded in doing with ease. Against his will, he was assailed by other thoughts demanding an answer. Had Lisa heard his stupid suspenders creaking? Her father disliked people, judged them severely, interfered tyrannically in their lives—and was respected for that very reason. . . . How was one to live without anyone interfering? And he kept thinking with particular persistence of the carpenter. His strange figure intruded before his eyes and demanded an explanation.

"Stupid, everything is stupid," Mironov said aloud. In order to banish his disquiet, he closed his eyes, lay down more comfortably and, in a soft voice, began reciting the dialogue of a play he'd read an hour ago.

> "O yes, in certain respects
>   A bull can be more pleasant than an eagle."
> "A bull—is that me?"
> "Yes, sir, if you will."
> "I'm insulted!"
> "And what then?"
> "I'm insulted!"
> "It seems to me that nature has
>   Insulted you worse than anyone else, my dear sir."

"I am by nature a nobleman!"

"Then it's the nobility who are insulted . . ."

"Your yard is full of weeds, your garden's neglected," the carpenter's resonant voice rang out. He stood over Mironov's head, dressed in a pink unbelted shirt with collar open, in striped underpants, barefoot; his hair was tousled, as if he'd just woken up, and the black leather strap had slipped over his ear.

Mironov raised himself and sat up, his hands pressed against the ground.

"How did you get in?"

"I climbed over the fence. We must tell Artamon to put the garden and the yard in order, to clean them up; he loves doing it. Let him have some fun in the evening."

The carpenter dropped to his knees and held out his hand.

"Take it—it's the change. For six rubles I bought paint and two brushes. You can have them too; they'll come in useful."

"I don't want the change," Mironov replied softly with a tinge of sadness.

"I don't want it either."

The carpenter placed the money on the grass at the foot of the apple tree, sat down beside Mironov, and looked him in the face.

"What are you thinking about?" he asked.

"About nothing."

"About girls?"

"No."

Tearing off a blade of grass and scratching his bulging forehead with it, the carpenter said in a worried, didactic tone, "Be careful with the girls. A lively one will muzzle you; with a quiet one—both of you will come to a bad end."

Mironov was silent, thinking as he rocked: "If I don't reply, he'll go away."

"I keep thinking about you. You've got under my skin, Mironov!" the carpenter resumed. "You've shaken me up. What were you muttering here? What sort of spell were you casting?"

"Just verse."

"You surprise me, Mironov."

"I don't want to surprise anyone."

"You do surprise."

There was a note of disapproval, even of menace, in the carpenter's words. Mironov gathered his legs under him. What should he say to this man? What was there, after all, to discuss with him?

"It's hot," he said.

"Very true. But what are you thinking about, all the same?"

"I dislike thinking—I like calm."

He had wished to say this in an angry tone, but felt he'd spoken apologetically. Then he added: "Now the sky is bright and calm, but when the clouds . . ."

He did not finish the sentence, aware of his plaintive but loud tone. But the carpenter, casting a sidelong look at the sky, declared: "The sky's empty, Mironov. That's why it's so calm."

"But the sun? The moon? And the stars? And there may be many other things yonder we don't see."

Dubiously, the carpenter shook his head.

"Doesn't look as if you believed in God. You don't go to church. . . ."

These words helped to anger Mironov, to provoke his desire to utter insulting words, but his memory prompted no insulting words and all he did was to mutter grimly: "My father did not believe in God. . . ."

"Many people will admit that. . . ."

"And he said that thoughts were mere dust, that they only obscure everything. . . ."

"Well?" the carpenter asked, surprised. "And is that the way he spoke?"

"Yes. I can now see it myself: thoughts are like worms. You dig up a lot of worms, and they just crawl and twist. . . ."

With his head bent over his shoulder, the carpenter pinched off the tips of grass blades with his nails, listened and, smiling, twitched his mustaches.

"When you begin thinking, there seem to be two people inside you: one of them knows; the other is confused. But I don't want to think. The soul doesn't like thinking."

"As for that, Mironov, you're not talking very reasonably, perhaps . . ."

"And what is there to know?" Mironov continued, hoping to crush the carpenter, to frighten, hurt him, and, in general, to alienate him and make him go away. "We already know everything: people are born, get married, give birth, die. They set houses on fire, thieve, murder. A circus opens. A religious procession goes by, a wife runs away. Drunkards fight. Cabbage is made into sauerkraut, cucumbers get pickled. People play cards. . . . Why do I need all that? I don't want any of it!"

"What do you need then?" the carpenter asked calmly, and his calm immediately cooled Mironov.

"I love silence," he mumbled.

"Then you should have been born deaf. It's hard to understand you, Mironov!"

"I haven't asked you to . . ."

Mironov, having said this, glanced sideways at the carpenter with alarm and hope. Would he take offense and go away?

The carpenter gestured with his hand in the air; the shadows of apple-tree leaves touched his hand and, after stroking it, fell on the grass; the grass grew darker, more velvety; gazing at it, the carpenter said nothing. With a sigh Mironov also held out the palm of his hand under the moonbeams and the shadows; for a minute or so, both of them sat like blind beggars with their hands stretched out in the void. Then the carpenter said in a ringing, boisterous voice, "No, Mironov, you can't astonish me! You can't surprise me with words. And as for your blue house—it's a laughing matter rather than a cause for astonishment. . . ."

"Ah, go to the devil! Why do you keep pestering me?"

The carpenter gave a laugh, shook his head, and winked. "Showing your temper, eh?"

His eyes smiled affectionately as he adjusted the leather strap round his head; without haste he lit a very strong cigarette, and a ribbon of gray smoke unfurled in the air.

"I understand, Mironov. Boredom has got you down. It's your age. You haven't got used to life yet, and your age demands enjoyment. There are girls to provide enjoyment; well, that doesn't last long if a man is serious. In general, there isn't much cause for joy. . . ."

The carpenter's didactic tone once more irritated Mironov. There he was—a semiliterate craftsman who read no books, and yet he kept on talking, talking . . .

"Everything has got to be changed, altered," he declared in the same didactic tone.

"Are you referring to politics?" the carpenter asked, blowing the ash off his cigarette. "No, I don't meddle in politics. I want to construct a thing, a work of the soul, something full of excellence, and then let people gasp . . ."

"Bite the governor," Mironov angrily suggested.

"What did you say?" the carpenter asked with a wink.

"Bite the governor. In church, during the service—then everyone will gasp . . ."

The carpenter laughed, slapping one of his knees. "Don't be angry, you eccentric. You're an interesting man all the same. You've got muddled, but you're interesting. Yes, brother Mironov, everybody's bored, everybody wants to astonish himself and someone else besides, but there's nothing to astonish with. . . . Nobody's got the capacity to astonish. It isn't worth your while to think—you have an unfortunate little mind. You're wordless, sort of dumb. Better go and sleep! He who sleeps is well satisfied."

The carpenter stuck the butt of his cigarette into the ground, rose to his feet with one easy, springy motion, and, without a word of farewell, walked off toward the fence, repeating with manifest sarcasm: "He who sleeps is well satisfied. . . ."

Hearing the fence crack under the weight of his body, Mironov thought with satisfaction: "He won't come back any more, he's offended. The thing I said about the governor was just to the point. . . ."

At once he pictured the pale blue smoke of incense and, in front of a mass of dark and fair heads, the big, large-eared, bald head of His Excellency, the governor of the province; and then came the carpenter stealthily creeping up to him; in a moment, his small insolent teeth had bitten into the general's red ear; the congregation gave a resounding gasp, so resounding a gasp that the flame of all the candles wavered; the carpenter was promptly seized, dragged away, and beaten. . . .

Mironov laughed, but then heard a creaking sound somewhere near-by; convinced it was the carpenter spying on him over the fence, he forced a cough and, stooping, abandoned the garden without looking back.

The next morning he noticed that the monster under the roof had been painted over with dark blue paint. This solid color gave added weight to the triangle above the windows and had the effect of squashing the sky-blue house to the ground. The reddish stains and the blotches of tar on the wall and the window frame had also been painted over, though not in keeping with the general light, silky tone of the paint.

"So that's it—he kept his word!"

Mironov, as he gazed upward, tried to picture how the carpenter had kept his word; it must have been a hard thing to do—each word contained a tendency to evoke in the memory words of like sound and, catching at these words, to make them expand and merge in vague, disconnected thoughts. Take the word "scan," for example, a simple word, but it immediately suggested "descant." Or take "cropper"—"crop her."

Mironov shook his head and went into the house to eat.

The gate banged as soon as he sat down at table. Artamon, the carter, staggered clumsily into the yard carrying a scythe and an iron spade over his shoulder. Halting by the porch, he set the scythe and the spade against the wall, crossed himself, spat on the palms of his hands, heaved a sigh, picked up the scythe, and began to swing it as lightly as a whip, cutting down with a whistling sound the burdocks, dog grass, and wormwood.

Mironov stood up and, hiding behind the window, watched him work.

"They're acting as if they owned the place. . . ." he thought.

On Artamon's hairy face a row of teeth glittered fiercely in the gaping red hole of his triangular mouth; his small, bearlike eyes were cunningly concealed beneath his eyebrows; his broad nose was also hidden in his mustache and wild beard. It all looked unnatural, and made it seem as if Artamon had no face at all. He moved with such effort he seemed to be pushing through invisible but extremely thick-set bushes.

"The carpenter invented Artamon to make people gape. . . ."

In a few minutes the carter had scythed the whole of the high grass. He stopped in a corner of the yard, holding the scythe like a spear, glanced at the sky, and began to cross himself once more, prodding his broad shoulders and his bulging canine brow with his fingers. Mironov carried out and handed him a tumbler of vodka and some fried chopped meat on a piece of bread.

"Thanks," he said.

"Thanks," Artamon repeated, missing his labials. Throwing back his head and tossing the vodka down his torn mouth, he thrust half of the portion of meat and bread inside, glanced at the remainder, thrust it in likewise, swallowed it, and then said in a thick, inarticulate voice: "I'll do the garden now."

"How much will you charge?"

"Well, I'll do it for fun."

And off he went, plodding on his short legs in their forty-pound boots whitened with lime or flour.

In an hour's time Mironov, looking into the garden, saw that all the grass had been cut. Artamon stood under an apple tree, stroking its branches with his hand. Catching sight of Mironov, he cried out: "Hey!"

Mironov came up and cautiously stopped, prevented from advancing further by an angry growl.

"Look, master! Look at all the lichen! And the caterpillars! The branches should be smeared—there's an ointment for that! The ground around the trees should have been dug up and manured long ago. You're the devil of a gardener, master!"

Growling, Artamon held out his hand with fingers extended; they were soiled with the revolting slime of crushed caterpillars. Mironov squeamishly shuddered and started back.

"Don't be frightened of me. I'm well disposed toward you. Kallistrat sent me here. Why are you trembling? Akh, what kind of people are you all. . . ."

The carter's deafening speech sounded even more unpleasant without the labials, while it recalled at the same time the babbling of an infant.

"I'll fix it all for you, I like doing it," he said, wiping his hand on the uppers of his boots. He apparently had difficulty bending his broad back, for he groaned as he stooped. Mironov, not knowing what to say, stared apprehensively at him.

"Where's Kryukov?" he asked in order to say something.

"Kallistrat you mean? Don't go near him. He's angry with you, the monster, because you didn't let him decorate the house."

And the carter, opening his terrifying mouth, groaned three times: "O-ho-ho!"

The sound was somewhere between an *o* and *ou*, reminiscent of a howling winter blizzard in a chimney. It made Mironov cringe, draw his head in between his shoulders, and say in a low voice, "You're stronger than he."

"Stronger? Of course I am. I've been on show in a circus, wrestled there. They broke all my fingers, otherwise I'd have fixed them all . . . Those people live by cunning, not strength. . . ."

He dug his spade into the dry soil at the foot of the apple tree as easily as if it were butter, turning up dark reddish sods full of uncoiling worms.

"They're all frightened of me here because of my strength, but I'm well disposed to people and like to talk to them. It's my voice frightens people, otherwise . . . Last year I drove over a man and they started judging me. The judge, he shouts at me: 'Quieter there!' but I couldn't manage it, so he acquitted me . . ."

"Are you married?"

"Well, well! What woman would be fool enough to marry me? Just look—see the lip I have."

Mironov was aware that the townsmen treated the muzhiks with a mixed feeling of contempt and hostility. Both his father and mother had treated them thus, and this feeling had been grafted on him since childhood. But Artamon excited in him only amazement, fear, and a certain vague hope.

"If I treat him nicely, then the carpenter . . ." he thought.

"Is he working?" the carpenter's ringing voice demanded from somewhere above. With a cigarette stuck between his teeth Kallistrat was sitting on a post of the fence, his bare feet dangling into the garden; a cloud of smoke wavered above his fair head, and the strap stood out clearly on the white skin of his forehead.

"Oh!" Mironov inwardly exclaimed. "He'll be sucking the blood out of me again. . . ."

"Listen, Kryukov," he began, straightening his stooping back and waving his hand. "What are you after? I don't want all . . ."

His irritation, gripping him nervously by the throat, impeded his speech; he began to choke, while a question once more fell from above: "What is it you don't want?"

"Don't you dare . . . I shall complain!"

"Against me? What for?"

The quiet questions irritated him even more; stamping his foot, Mironov screamed: "I don't want all this scything and digging here. . . ."

As lightly as a bird the carpenter dropped down into the garden, gripped Mironov by the shoulder and, shaking him, suggested, "You'd better pull yourself together! Have you gone out of your mind? People are working for you free and you should thank them, you dolt, instead of . . ."

But Mironov was already embarrassed by his outburst of indignation. The carpenter's hand had fixed him to the spot and squeezed the rage out of him. He saw Artamon, leaning on his spade, open his mouth still wider, as if expecting something else to happen.

"I understand," he muttered.

"You understand, but you're yelling?"

"I'm very grateful, of course . . ."

"That's more like it!"

The carpenter prodded him in the chest with his finger, walked away toward Artamon, and began giving him strict instructions: "Tie up the twigs, you understand? Dispose of the dried-up raspberry!"

"They're really working free," Mironov gasped and,

in gratitude for this free labor, resolved to give these people a treat.

Within half an hour he was sitting with them at the kitchen table. The samovar was boiling, the vodka gleamed in a carafe, plates had been set out with pickled mushrooms and sauerkraut. Artamon drank the vodka and the tea as greedily as a calf guzzles milk, ate a great deal, munched in a disgusting way, grunted and sniffled; the carpenter, for his part, deftly speared with his fork the smallest and finest of the slippery mushrooms, picked up his glass of vodka with two fingers, held it to the light and scrutinized the vodka with narrowed eyes, and, gulping it down, wrinkled his face.

"H-ha!" he exclaimed.

One could not help noticing that he did all this in his own peculiar manner, very easily and deftly. He was a disagreeable but interesting man. He was hardly mad. No, he was cunning.

"I can give a man every sort of pleasure I like," Kallistrat proclaimed, holding his glass between two fingers, while he delicately poised the other three. "However, let me tell you straight: I dislike people—they're stupid."

"O-oo, the devil," Artamon growled, leaning back against the wall and expanding his broad, superhuman chest.

"I'm clever, I am, and capable. I can do everything, anything at all; but I've no interest in simple matters. . . ."

Mironov, having drunk two glasses of what seemed to him revolting vodka, felt his head clouding. Through a mist he listened to the carpenter's usual boastful speeches, and experienced nothing but tedium sucking at his heart. He felt extremely put out when Artamon, who had drowsed off, suddenly emitted a loud snore and, waking at once, glanced with apprehension and guilt at the carpenter, who, twirling his golden mustaches with the fingers of both hands, commanded the carter: "Well, go off home now; you've eaten and drunk enough, you camel. . . ."

Artamon obediently went off. The carpenter then announced his wish to inspect the rest of the house. Mironov, as obedient as Artamon, conducted Kallistrat to his bedroom, a bright room with one window giving on the garden and another on the street. The carpenter, insolently punching the bed with his fist, declared: "You sleep soft."

Then, examining a shelf with books, he asked, "Have you read them?"

"I've read them."

"All?"

"All."

Mironov seemed to detect a note of mockery in the questions asked by his unwelcome guest, whose conduct grew less and less formal. After a minute's silence, during which he solidly established himself in the small sitting-room with a multitude of flowers on the window sills of three windows and on two sculpted ladders that his father had cleverly contrived, the carpenter declared: "You should get married."

All the objects in the room seemed to protest against this barefoot guest with a leather strap around his head: the boards creaked dryly; the lamp on the table tinkled; and the best china in the cupboard, the gifts of friends and Father's presents to Mother, jingled. Mironov felt offended by the carpenter because he, surprised at nothing, praising nothing, regarded everything there as familiar and commonplace.

"Of course—he's envious, but pretends to be indifferent, the devil...."

The glassware inside the cupboard jingled more loudly —because the carpenter began drumming on the cupboard door.

"A globe?" he asked.

"Yes."

"I know the thing. An approximate image of the earth. But why is it made of copper?"

"It plays music."

"Such a thing doesn't exist," the carpenter said with a negative shake of his head, and demanded: "Show me!"

Mironov opened the cupboard, placed the globe on the table, and began to spin it around: some of the pins had fallen out, others had been rubbed off; the steel comb had some teeth missing. But it was still possible to make

out the weary tinkling of the terrestrial globe as it turned
around on its axis:

Siskin, siskin, where have you been?

The carpenter started back from the table, listening,
and then he demanded:

" 'Siskin'?"

"Yes," Mironov replied with a mournful smile for his
memories, still turning the globe. Then the carpenter
stopped Mironov's hand and himself touched the continents, the oceans, flicking the copper with his fingernail;
he sat down on a chair and pondered, "Where did you
get it?"

"Father made it."

"And why does it play 'Siskin'?"

"It's a children's song. I was a small boy then. . . ."

"So," the carpenter said and, sticking the end of his
beard into his mouth, began to ruminate and chew at it
with his lips. He then blew his beard out of his mouth
like a spurt of fire and, flicking the Arctic Ocean with a
finger, laughed.

"It's an amusing thing. Only, perhaps, 'Siskin' is not
in keeping with the instrument. People study from it, and
here you get 'Siskin.' It's just nonsense! And your father
—was he a clever man?"

"Yes. Very. He was a cheerful . . ."

"Eccentrics, that's what they are!" the carpenter exclaimed, still scrutinizing the globe. And sighing, he
stroked the copper with a finger stained with polish, and
commented with dry irony, "A simple thing, yet how
clever! A drop of water, a few lumps of earth, and they
teach you that this hangs in the air. Remarkable. And it
is supposed that millions of people live on this little
globe, eh? A smart conclusion. Do you believe it, you
orphan?"

"But of course. Why, both you and I live here,"
Mironov dully replied.

The carpenter rose, held out his hand. "Well, thanks.
Till I see you."

He stopped in the kitchen and, grasping his beard,
said with a laugh: "It all depends on the size of your

head, but in the meantime—ah? Very remarkable! All the same 'Siskin' isn't suitable! That, you orphan, is just a lot of mischief aimed at astonishing. It's like whistling in church. It isn't 'Siskin' you need here, but 'Lord Have Mercy on Us,' for example. Something either ecclesiastical or military—a military march: ta-ra ta-ra-bum. . . ."

Thus, humming a march, the carpenter left.

"Go to the devil!" Mironov shouted after him in his thoughts.

Returning to the room, he wanted to replace the globe in the china cupboard but noticed that a portion of South America, having cracked and become unglued, was bent over to the south.

"He must have torn it off with his fingernail, the blockhead!"

Wetting his finger, he put the continent in order and spun the globe around on its axis. A gentle tinkling could now be heard, like that of a children's song faint with time. Mironov sighed, thinking: "Maybe he was right. It might be better to have another tune. But which?"

He recalled some other inappropriate songs:

> Along a rather dirty street
> Our friend Ivan came staggering,
> A little the worse for drink. . . .

He recalled his father's favorite ditty:

> Seven sous,
> Seven sous,
> What shall we do with seven sous?

What other songs were there?

> I'd like to tell you, tell you, tell you . . .

A portion of South America became unstuck again. It was strange to watch the light-blue piece of paper stir and furl itself.

"I'll glue it down tomorrow. Why did the carpenter say

it should play 'Lord Have Mercy on Us'? He doesn't, of course, believe in God either. . . ."

Leaning against the table, his forehead almost touching the globe, Mironov surrendered himself to a slow torrent of confused, unaccustomed thoughts.

The boys had splattered with dirt the sky-blue façade of the house and the window frames, had scratched the paint with crocks, and had scribbled obscenities on it; on the upper bar of the gate, someone, a grownup evidently, had written with great application the following statement in pencil:

"This house lives upside down in it, a fool."

Mironov was angered when he first read this dictum, but, noticing the ignorantly misplaced comma, he calmed down.

"You're a fool yourself!" he remarked.

The street demonstrated in every way its antagonism to the sky-blue house. But it was not this that disturbed and irritated Mironov: he lived oppressed by something else more weighty and serious. The carpenter and the carter stuck to him like two shadows. Artamon appeared almost every evening, swept the yard, chopped the wood, and worked, growling, in the garden; the carpenter, feeling himself manifestly the master of the house, busied himself with the repair of various household services and instructed the old, taciturn cook Pavlovna in her domestic duties. Listening to his strict, ringing words, Pavlovna would guiltily hang her head, but cross herself quickly and unobtrusively as soon as he walked away. Mironov had seen this happen more than once, and it caused him both to smile at the stupidity of the old woman and to take an even stronger dislike to the carpenter.

He sensed that the carpenter had cast a shadow over his dreams of a thoughtless, sky-blue life, raising before him an almost tangible barrier of vague fears and pushing him aside into a corner. One day he had the courage to protest: "This is all so trivial. . . ."

"And you just try living without these trivial things," the carpenter had admonished.

Mironov began to think of the man almost with fear.

The carpenter's dexterity of movement baffled him—he seemed to move with too great an ease about the earth. How smoothly, like a bird, had he dropped through the air from the fence into the garden that day! A disquieting premonition of something out of the ordinary lodged in Mironov's mind and weighed on him. Whenever he thought of Kallistrat, his ears caught the creak of boards and the gentle tinkling of glass. How was it that nothing stirred in the sitting-room when he himself entered, but everything creaked and tinkled when the carpenter came in? Mironov did not believe in sorcerers, but he had read and heard about men possessed of a special, mysterious power, and it seemed to him that very soon, the very next day perhaps, the carpenter would reveal all his power—reveal it in a terrifying manner.

Unexpectedly that day came to pass. One Sunday evening the carpenter arrived with a young woman. Stout and short-legged, she dazzled Mironov with her purple silk blouse and the greedy glitter of a multitude of fine teeth set in a small mouth rather like that of a perch. A purple blush flamed on her puffed-out cheeks, and a small pink stone gleamed on a finger of her left hand. To Mironov her eyes also looked pink, like those of a white mouse. . . .

"She's called Serafima," the carpenter announced, pushing her toward Mironov. "She's an excellent maiden!"

Serafima smiled, exhaling an irritating smell. When she sat down on a chair her white skirt, tightly stretched around the huge semispheres of her thighs, crept up, revealing a pair of stout, restless legs; she at once began to shuffle her feet over the floor, drumming with her heels. Her dark hair, smoothly brushed, braided and arranged in a bun at the back, was fixed with a large yellow comb. This made Mironov think of a hen.

"Och! How terribly hot!" she exclaimed, fanning her red-hot face with a white handkerchief.

The carpenter had dressed himself up in a gray canvas jacket and a blue Russian shirt with an embroidered chest, and his loose, baggy, cotton pants were tucked into a pair of high, brightly polished boots; he had evidently cleaned his copper-hued beard, and his curly hair writhed on his head like tongues of flame. His parched, hawklike face looked harsher and more restless than usual, while his greenish eyes glittered venomously, seeing everything, understanding everything.

"She's not spoiled, she knows how to run a house. And, as you can see for yourself, she understands the things of the body," the carpenter said, watching the "excellent maiden" pour the tea into glasses. As she did so, she asked Mironov in a sweet, throaty voice, "How do you like it—strong?"

Mironov sat opposite her, bending over the table; he felt his eyes quiver, his lips twist, and he had an irrepressible desire to stick out his tongue and lick his lips in the same way as the "excellent maiden" was licking the jam off the spoon. He smiled deliberately to allow this hen to see his ugly teeth.

Her lips were extremely red and thick, and somehow double-storied in appearance; they sucked the cherry-stones clean. Lips like these could suck all the blood out of a man.

The carpenter's words, "understands the things of the body," and her question, "How do you like it—strong?" made him blush, making him remember the indecent behavior of dogs and bitches. With his spoon he deliberately caught the edge of his glass, upset it, spilling the cooling tea on his knees, jumped up and ran outside on the porch. The rain was lazily sprinkling the hot earth; the foliage on the trees rustled gently; the bluish-gray clouds, contracting the space, condensed the sultry air.

"He wants to marry me off to this girl," Mironov thought, catching the large, rare drops of rain in the palm of his hand and spreading them with his fingers; in the air he sensed the irritating tang of the girl's perspiration. This tang stimulated in him both a feeling of repugnance and another sensation, quite as oppressive but also magnetic.

"Did you scald yourself?" the carpenter asked, walking out on the porch.

"Listen," Mironov said, addressing him in a soft, hurried voice, his palms pressed to his chest. "I don't want to marry, please—I don't need it!"

He remembered his mother's words and felt happy to repeat them with his clenched fist raised: "What sort of a husband would I make? A husband should be—like this! Take her away! I'd rather give her twenty-five rubles, and fifty for you, if you like. . . . I mean it!"

His legs felt like giving way under him. He was ready to fall on his knees before the carpenter, but the latter, gripping his beard and standing a step above him on the porch, laughed with irony as he delivered this irresistible homily:

"You've turned into quite a savage, Mironov, you son of boredom! No, you must marry—absolutely! You've got stuck here with your books, you orphan. You've been daydreaming, the blood's going to your head. Just look at yourself—you're turning blue! And your lips are trembling—why? Because of that very thing. It's time for you to live in a legal way! You'll get yourself a wife and have children. . . ."

"I can't, I don't want to . . ."

"Enough of that, and don't try to astonish people. You haven't got anything to astonish them with! They'll swindle you very soon. . . ."

Mironov lowered his head while the carpenter took his hand and raised it toward himself; then, brushing the raindrops from him, he began:

"I know people well! They'll make you think you're remarkable, pretend they're interested in you, and then rob and deceive you. That's just the usual . . ."

Shutting his eyes, Mironov pictured a drove of boys running along a street throwing mud at sky-blue houses; they were all his own children, and, sitting at the window, the "excellent maiden" was chewing soaked apples and fish pies. He could bear neither soaked apples nor fish pies.

Then he found himself sitting opposite Serafima again. She looked even more bloated; the balls of her breasts rose and fell heavily, stirring the stiffly creaking purple silk of her dress; her small round mouth wearily opened; in her sausagelike fingers she held the white lump of a handkerchief, with which she frequently wiped her perspiring temples; her pink eyes had melted in a smile. Mironov reflected that her perspiration was as thick as acle, and as sticky, and that most probably neither mosquitoes nor fleas would venture to sting her rubbery body.

And the carpenter, pouring the cherry vodka into his tea, drank the hot, dark liquid; it imparted a brownish tint to his parched face, made his eyes gleam more brightly, and strengthened the irresistible impact of his words. Boastfully, he went on speaking:

"What I enjoy above all is arranging weddings. I love noise, I love commotion. I'm pleased with every sort of confusion and people walking on their heads. When young people fall in love, it's great fun watching them. . . ."

But he did not laugh as he said this. There was not even a smile on his face. Observing him sideways, Mironov noticed that his face was twitching—and a terrifying face it was! A good thing the carpenter had not fastened his black leather strap around his block of a head.

"You, Mironov, you must learn to live merrily, you orphan. You must move about freely. If you sin, no harm's done. You don't have to account to anyone. You've got no master—do you understand? Who is your master, tell me that?"

"I . . . don't know . . ." Mironov stammered, for some reason frightened by this question.

"So-so! If Serafima were not here, I'd tell you whom you ought to serve at your age; but I can't say it in her presence, though she knows it, of course, the rogue! Don't you, Fimka?"

"I know nothing," the "excellent maiden" drowsily replied, and Mironov at once felt his foot being touched and then squeezed tightly between the boots of his female visitor. This touch, frightening away some vague but important and alarming notion, terrified Mironov; tearing away his foot, he leapt up and shouted, "What are you doing?"

A deep blush flooded the "excellent maiden's" chin, cheeks, and forehead, and the carpenter, slapping Mironov on the ribs, roared with laughter as he shouted: "She knows, the rogue, she knows!"

Mironov could not clearly remember what happened

afterward when the carpenter, laughing, left the room, and the girl approached him, smiling:

"Ah, what a man you are! You embarrassed me in front of my uncle. . . ."

She now sat beside him, asking him if he was fond of goose-giblet soup. Mironov informed her that in Paris goose giblets were thrown out to the dogs, that people there did not like trash or soaked apples, that only noble people lived there, and that none of them forced his way uninvited into a home. . . .

Then some unconscious power lifted him to his feet and spun him about in the thick hot darkness, which swallowed this "excellent maiden." But then the carpenter immediately materialized and seized him by the arms. As though from afar he asked: "What are you pushing the girl about for? How can you do that? She's my niece, and not your wife yet. And you've smashed the plates too . . . What's the meaning of this?"

Mironov listened, amazed. The carpenter stood close before him, while his voice seemed to issue from somewhere under the floor, from under his feet. There was a crunch of broken crockery underfoot, and everything floated and swayed in a peculiar way.

"If you can't drink, keep off it!" the carpenter admonished, holding out a glass of bluish water under his nose. Mironov glanced into the carpenter's eyes and firmly shut his own.

When he awakened early next morning, Mironov thought that the "excellent maiden" had been merely a dream like the fox. He had seen a large, reddish fox scurrying through the sky, licking off the stars and in this way creating a darkness so stifling and oppressive that the earth seemed cast down into a bottomless well, leaving only a semispherical portion of the as yet bright sky somewhere far on the horizon; but then Boris, the lavender-robed priest, was rubbing out the stars from that portion of sky and writing with incense from his censer the following sentence: "A room to let for a lone person."

Mironov remembered that, frightened by this dream, he awoke and went into the kitchen for a drink of water, but, stepping on something sticky, went back to bed again and, tormented by thirst, could not fall asleep for a long time. Sitting on the bed now, he noticed that both his foot and the bedsheet were smeared with cherry jam, and the damp floor, only recently washed, finally convinced him of the reality of what had happened the previous day. With a deep sigh he decided:

"The day after tomorrow I'll sell the house and everything else, and travel to Paris, and rent a room for a lone person. I must learn French. . . ." At once he took down a French grammar from the shelf and read out the following austere question: *"Que savez-vous sur Bernardin de St. Pierre?"*

Between the pages of the book he found a small, gray, flattened moth. Inspecting it, Mironov withdrew into dreary reflection: arriving in Paris, Parisians would question him about Saint Bernardin, but he knew nothing about that saint. . . .

Mironov, having closed the book, thrust it under his pillow and laughed, rejoicing at the unexpected kindling of a very simple, true notion: how amazingly good and convenient to know only the most essential words and ignore the remainder. This would give one the right not to understand people, not to have to worry about what they were saying. This would completely ensure the possibility of a serene life!

"That's so! That's so!" he muttered, nodding his head and watching the pendulum of the clock crawl to and fro on the wall and attempt without success to cut off two of the bouquets of sky-blue flowers on the wallpaper.

"Why sell the house the day after tomorrow? I'll sell it this very day. And they won't allow the carpenter into Paris. . . ."

He laughed straight into old Pavlovna's face when she suddenly appeared. Then he made a round of the rooms, inspecting and evaluating the furniture and the plants, and calculated rapidly that he should sell all this for four hundred plus seven hundred rubles.

"That's not the way to count," he corrected himself aloud. "The total comes to eleven hundred rubles."

But it would give him greater pleasure, he felt, to

deal with two figures—four hundred and seven hundred. These two figures gave him twice the number of noughts than when he counted eleven hundred. There was such a consoling simplicity about noughts.

"Noughts—noughts—noughts," he chanted.

Pavlovna, who followed him around, enjoined him severely to come and drink his morning tea.

Having drunk a glass of tea, which, for some reason, tasted very bitter, he decided to go out into the fields beyond the river, stretch out there on the sand among the juniper bushes, pass the whole day there, and then, when it grew dark, wend his way back to town and spend the night in a hotel.

"Try and find me then!" he thought.

But he changed his mind; picking up his fishing rods he set out to the river. As he emerged from the gate, he caught sight of Lisa in one of the windows of the Rozanov house; she was cleaning the windowpanes; he ran up to her and said in a soft, hurried voice, "It's absolutely essential to discuss Paris with you. Please come to the cemetery this evening. . . ."

Lisa started back and vanished without a word, but this did not trouble him; he was convinced the girl would turn up. He did no fishing and spent the whole day stretched out under the bushes on the riverbank, gazing at the sky—a pure sky that provoked no anxiety or brooding. He drowsed, woke up, and drowsed again until the hour when the sun, grown bloated and red as usual, almost brushed the roof of the main building of the psychiatric clinic.

Returning home, he ate his supper and donned his best suit. "The carpenter will come and ask me where I'm going. I'd better go into the garden," he thought.

But emerging on the porch, he sat down on a step. "The carpenter will see me in the garden. I'm very clever, very perceptive . . . That's because I dislike thinking. . . ."

Out of the soil in the yard, which Artamon had scythed and swept clean, the short hollow stems of severed burdocks stuck out like pipes, and a mouse peeped into one of these stems. Mironov fancied he heard these pipes gently whistling the familiar, soothing

dy of a children's song; they whistled so gently
d tenderly that even the mouse was not afraid of the
interplay of sounds. He pictured before him a slender
girl in a sky-blue dress and heard her speak. She was
unusually pleasing in her speech; he did not grasp the
sense of her words, but they sounded all the more tender.
He ruminated that he would sell his house to old
Rozanov, her father; sell it cheaply and in return her
father would allow him to take his daughter Lisa to
Paris, where they would lodge in the "room for a lone
person."

For a long time Mironov sat in a state of semi-
oblivion, coming to himself only when awakened by boys
shouting and running. The boys were chasing someone,
and their piercing howls rudely rent the evening quiet
of the deserted street.

"That way, catch him . . ." they yelled.

Mironov stood up; the small wall clock in the kitchen
warningly struck eight.

"It's time," Mironov exclaimed, "it's time!"

He walked through the gate and, swinging his cane,
strode along the street toward the sand mounds. The
whitewashed, brick quadrangle of the cemetery wall un-
dulated over the gray humps, and the tin cross on the
tower glowed dully. The cemetery was a new one, not
yet densely sown with graves. Between the graves rose
stunted reddish pines and birches, withering in soil that
had been insufficiently manured by corpses. Gray blades
of grass, piercing through the sand, stretched orphanlike
to the sky, and dusty green tufts of grass lurked in the
shadows by the edge of the graves.

Mironov walked slowly on a path strewn with rubble;
ants were dragging a stick of dry conifer; aiming his
cane at an ant, he lunged and missed.

"Well, all right, you can live!" he exclaimed, with a
laugh.

Over the cemetery wall he could see a strip of road,
which Lisa Rozanov must ascend on her way to the
cemetery. There, below, two torrents of houses and gardens flowed down toward the leaden river; toylike figures
appeared and disappeared among them now and then.
Mironov raised his cane threateningly in their direction,

exclaiming: "You should all be here, in the cemetery, but I'm off to Paris! Ough, I'm fed up with you. . . ."

Beyond the river a factory chimney belched dirty smoke, soiling the sky, which was still red on the horizon. From one side, a dark cloud with what looked like a tail was moving upon that reddish patch. Mironov then recalled the carpenter's favorite expression:

"Boredom."

At that very instant he perceived *him*: his beard gripped in his fist, his other hand thrust under the apron about his chest, the carpenter strode with a slow, measured step, as though measuring the ground along the side of the road. He was ascending toward the sand mounds.

Mironov froze to the spot, holding his breath.

"He's spying on me. I just thought of him, and here he is!" he thought.

The carpenter walked forty-five steps, and turned abruptly into a field away from the road in the direction of a couple of old pines, leading himself all the time by the beard.

"You're lying, but you won't deceive me," Mironov said softly and sat down by the cemetery wall, watching the carpenter through a square opening in the brick wall. His legs trembled, and somewhere in his body, in his chest, savage fear quivered. Mironov rose to his knees, pressed his chest against the warm bricks, and, flinging out his arms as though crucifying himself, thrust his fists through the apertures in the wall in a gesture of defiance.

"You're lying, you're lying . . ." he muttered.

The carpenter, down below, approached the road again, stopped, and began to do something with his hands. Mironov at once understood—the carpenter wished to convince him that he was counting on his fingers. The carpenter stood with his back to him staring at the street from which Lisa was to emerge, and when she emerged . . . Mironov could not imagine what would happen then, but it would be, of course, something terrible. Mironov wanted to shout. But Lisa did not appear. The carpenter removed the black strap from his head, shook his hair in a menacing way, put the strap again, and walked down the slope without haste.

"He'll hide somewhere and then catch either her or me. . . ."

Mironov now clearly realized that he could not hide from the carpenter. The carpenter would find him anywhere, force him to marry the "excellent maiden," compel him to do everything he, the carpenter, wished, and make an obedient dog of him as he had already done with strong man Artamon.

Pressing his forehead hard against the rough brick wall, Mironov suddenly remembered the carpenter's question, "Who's your master?" The carpenter had smiled so revoltingly when asking that question.

"He knows I have no one to protect me. He knows it. . . ."

Down below, from behind the edge of the earth, where the carpenter was lurking, clouds rose like a mountain, like the smoke of a huge fire—rose so dense that one could very likely walk upon them.

Shuddering with fear, he recalled the carpenter's talk, exploring its deeper sense.

"You've got nothing to astonish people with." To astonish people meant to live in a different way from other people, but the main thing was to think of nothing except banalities. To live without any interference. But evidently this was impossible with the carpenter about: he, the cunning fellow, had grasped that here was a man without a master, that this man was an orphan, and so he did as he wished with him.

"Of course—that's it, of course," Mironov almost shouted. "They all talk of God, of God, but it's the carpenter who manages things. . . . As he manages dogs. Like a hunter. . . ."

These exasperated, bitter surmises crushed Mironov. At the same time, he realized their futility and uselessness. It was the carpenter who had forced these thoughts upon him—he'd never entertained such thoughts before meeting him.

Gray crumpled tatters of cloud crept above the churchyard, smearing the sky with dirty stains. It reminded him of his mother staggering half-drunk about the house, wiping with a filthy rag the windowpanes, the glass of the cupboards and the mirrors, and blotchi.. their brightness with greasy smears.

The air felt humid as the last glimmer of light vanished beyond the sandy mounds of graves. Mironov got up and stared in the direction of the road, which the earth seemed to have swallowed. Then he set off home with rapid strides, trying not to make too much noise as he crossed the gravel path. As he came into the street, he noticed that the windows at the Rozanovs' were still alight. He ran up to a window and rapped on it with his cane. When Klavdia Strepetova thrust her round face out of the window, he addressed her in a low voice: "Tell her to be careful of the carpenter."

"What?" the girl whispered back in alarm.

"Yes, yes. He's spying. . . ."

Klavdia shut the window. It looked like a large bird folding its wings. Mironov thought he heard a cry of fear behind that window, followed by a laugh. Glancing around him, he crossed the street and walked into his yard. A small dark shape rose on the porch and, without touching him, pushed him from afar on the chest. He started back.

"Who's there? Who?" he demanded.

"Why, it's me. Who else?" Pavlovna replied.

Mironov stared more closely. It was, indeed, Pavlovna.

"The carpenter's been asking after you," she said.

"I'm not at home," Mironov declared in a firm but quiet voice. "I'm never at home."

Entering his bedroom, he undressed noiselessly without putting on the light, and got into bed. He could not sleep. Mosquitoes kept stinging, anxiety kept pinching. He seemed to sense the carpenter nearby, in the garden perhaps, squatting under the window or sitting on the roof near the chimney, tugging at his beard and plotting what to do with Mironov in the morning. Throwing off his quilt, Mironov sat up on his bed, let his feet drop to the cool floor, and listened. But he could hear nothing but the raindrops falling lazily on the roof. A dense warm darkness filled the room; a single stray mosquito whined. Mironov picked up a pillow and, placing it on his knees, waited.

kill that mosquito!" he thought.

...yed with weariness, rolled over on his side,
...d off without letting go of his pillow, and, awakened again by some inner shock, sat up on the bed; listened; watched the grayish dust of dawn slowly fill the room through the dark, motionless leaves of the potted flowers on the window sill; examined the bustling, disconnected confusion of memories, and waited obediently for the moment when all this would be interrupted and vanish. Such a moment did come: of a sudden everything was squeezed into a solid lump, and Mironov was pushed headlong into a black void, into a state of speechless immobility.

The moment arrived when the sun had risen, drenching the windowpanes with a flow of melted pearl. Mironov, stunned, collapsed on the bed and fell asleep, but was awakened almost immediately, it seemed to him, by a sort of strange creaking noise.

A man in yellow entered the room. Without ceremony he settled down on the bed, which creaked sharply; took Mironov's hand in his own moist, stubby hand; pulled out a black watch from a pocket and, staring at it, inquired like an old friend in a high-pitched voice: "Well, and how do we feel?"

"We-do-not-feel anything," Mironov angrily replied.

"What pains you then?"

"Panesyou—what's that?" Mironov asked with cutting sarcasm.

"And how did you sleep?"

"Lying down."

Mironov burst out laughing in admiration of the liveliness and wit of his own replies. He felt well and even cheerful. And he liked this man even though he smelled of boot polish; short and massive, he reminded him comically of a wooden Humpty Dumpty. His face was blue and swollen, and upon this blue background swam a pair of extraordinary yellow eyes that resembled rayless stars—the sort of stars one sees on a moist night. Mironov glanced at the window—a bluish cloud reminiscent of something unpleasant the day before floated rapidly across the sky. . . .

Snapping his jaws, the man rubbed his blue chin and said:

"You know me, don't you? I'm Isaakov, the medical assistant, Isaakov . . ."

Mironov was slightly taken aback and, wishing to conceal this, asked: "What time is it?"

"Twelve-thirty."

"Aha! I want to eat."

"That's very good," Isaakov approved, putting his black watch back into his waistcoat pocket.

It grew light in the room; words drifted in the sunlight like soap bubbles; watching their flight, Mironov said: "I wish it were always like this!"

"What?"

"All."

Within, he felt light, joyous, buoyant. Barefoot, in his underclothes, he went to wash himself in the kitchen, but stopped in the doorway on perceiving a fair head of hair with a band around it bent over the table: it was the carpenter, stooped, jotting something down in pencil in a soiled, ragged notebook. Mironov turned back without making a sound and sat down on his bed. All his cheerful radiance had been dimmed.

"What's the matter?" Isaakov inquired in a singsong voice, feeling Mironov's temples with his sticky fingers. Mironov pushed away his hand, shook his head, and asked in a whisper: "Was it he brought you here?"

"He did! What about it?"

"Where did he sleep?"

"How should I know? Normally people sleep at home."

"He's not normal."

"Why?"

Mironov did not answer either this or several other questions; with his hand propped against the edge of the bed, he rocked to and fro, biting his lips and straining to think. How could he get rid of the carpenter?

The soles of his boots creaking, Isaakov went off to the kitchen. Mironov at once ran to the window and began to throw the flowerpots from the window sill into the garden. He already had one leg on the window sill when a pair of iron hands gripped him under the armpits from behind. Without seeing, he knew whose hands were and, offering no resistance, yielded to their strength and in silence allowed himself to be led back to bed and to be laid out there on his back. Shutting his eyes firmly, he heard two voices whisper; and in the darkness he tried to see the gray hooks of words and watch them link and form meaningless sounds. Here was Isaakov whispering: "Anyouyes, inopun . . ."

Like gray, rough shadows, these words flew right through him, disturbing and alarming him. He opened his eyes.

"What's the matter with you, orphan boy? Fallen sick?"

The green beams of the carpenter's eyes awoke in Mironov a vague remembrance: he had previously seen these two beams, this sharp, hawklike face. He had seen them a long time ago when still a child.

"Well, what are you staring at? Don't you recognize me?"

"He's reminding me of it himself," Mironov thought and then replied, "I seem to have seen you . . ."

"Yes, yes."

"We must give him some bromide."

"Kind—I'm kind," Mironov thought. "They'll give me poison, I think. . . ."

He edged his way to the wall; sat up with his feet under him, the back of his head pressed against the wall, his eyes fixed now on a corner, now on the ceiling; and shuddered, his body grown chill. Projected on the ceiling he could see clearly the green square of the familiar painting, *The Death of a Sinner*. In the picture a sharp-faced devil with a goat's beard stood to one side, laughing silently. At once everything was clear and defined. He now understood why the carpenter had spoiled the sky-blue house, and why he slipped so easily through the air. That explained why he loved creating confusion and disorder.

"Who's your master?" he asked, triumphant in his knowledge: Konstantin Mironov did not believe in an ordinary God, in ordinary people. It was all clear to him now. But what was he to do? It was very terrifying, and hot, too. Without disentangling his legs or unclenching the hands round his knees, Mironov fell over to one side.

"I want to sleep."